Death on the Ocean

Martha Fischer

To Ingrid – with love

Martha Fischer is the pen name of a well-known author of historical novels.

Contents

Prologue

I looked in the mirror. A familiar image greeted me.

Some people say that I'm quite attractive – I don't know if this is true. I'm probably biased. I have straight brown hair, and whenever the sun plays with it, my hair turns a rich chestnut, a faint reminder of my Irish ancestors. My nose is a bit too short, and my eyes – although shortsighted – are probably my best feature, large and emerald green, although my grandmother would always insist that they're blue: "Always remember, only cats and witches have green eyes, my darling!"

But I love my green eyes. I think they make me special. To be honest, I could quite fancy being a witch, from time to time at least. Always being a good girl and someone's best friend can get a bit boring. The worst thing about all this is that being boring seemed to have become my fate – at least until recently.

I examined my reflection more closely. I found it strange that my face looked so normal and composed; somehow I thought it should look different, after everything that had happened…

The answer was simple. I had seen a murder today. And I was the only witness. No wonder my world had been turned upside down. And yet my surroundings hadn't changed: polished hardwood, genuine mahogany, the luxurious, mellow glint of brass polished to perfection, gleaming mirrors and crystal lamps, and a bed with striped satin cushions that could have landed right from a Hollywood movie set into my cabin, luxury and decadence everywhere!

I should apologize; I've forgotten to introduce myself: I'm Amanda, a teacher of English and history in her mid-thirties, endowed with no fortune and only a modest income, but I had made it onto the *Belgravia*, the most luxurious cruise ship you could imagine. Let me tell you how it all started, and how it was that I had managed to go on a cruise that was turning out to be as luxurious as it was murderous.

There could be no doubt that among my fellow passengers we had a killer on board.

And that I might become the next victim.

1

My Lovely Colleague

"Amanda, my dear!" shouted my friend Claudia across the school yard.

Officially Claudia and I pretend to be best friends. We embrace and exchange air kisses whenever we meet. The truth is that I detest her – and I'm quite certain that she feels the same about me. I must confess that I've hated Claudia from the first day I set eyes on her. I still remember the day we first met: Claudia walked into the staffroom, taking long strides in her flat, sensible shoes, as sure of herself as if she owned the world. She smiled broadly at me – but I knew immediately that it was all fake.

Claudia dyes her hair various shades of flaming red and as if this weren't hard enough to stomach, she loves to wear a top in shocking shades of purple or orange. It's impossible to miss an entrance by Claudia. When she gets excited – and she often does – her piercing voice can easily compete with that of a trumpeting elephant. Last but not least, let me add that Claudia is a fervent warrior in some obscure ecological grassroots movement, ever ready to save the planet and make sure that we don't stray from the path of ecological righteousness.

I wouldn't mind the latter so much, but I soon saw our hallowed coffee break abolished, to be replaced by "zen" sessions with green tea, handpicked from ecological plantations of course. Then I saw my favourite chocolate cookies being replaced by healthy wholemeal biscuits (at least for those colleagues who dared to risk their dentures). Although my surname is Lipton (a heritage from my English father), that's where any affinity with tea stops – I hate tea. I'm a coffee addict. I don't care what the doctors tell me, coffee is my vice. I also love my chocolate chip cookies. So do most of my colleagues, and this is why I had to hide them.

I still don't know how she managed to do it, but soon Claudia took over, and *she* manages the school nowadays. Of course we have a principal, but even he never seemed to have understood what kind of political manoeuvring inside the administration had catapulted him to the top position in one of the biggest and most chaotic schools in Hamburg, my home town. I guess he was just lucky, he's one of the countless and unmemorable compromise candidates that litter our administration and parliament these days. A timid person by nature, he has been putty in Claudia's strong hands ever since. In essence he handed the steering wheel to Claudia who was ever eager to spread her gospel. Our principal likes to spend his time confined to his office where he keeps his stamp collection.

***

2

As Claudia had spotted me already, what else could I do but greet her with the false enthusiasm I had so quickly learned to emulate?

"Claudia!" I chirped. "How absolutely *wonderful* to see you!"

"Amanda!" she chirped back, mimicking my tone. "I have the *most wonderful* idea for you!"

My heart sank; none of her wonderful ideas had worked out for me so far.

"I often think that you're by far one of the most intelligent members of staff... Oh come on, don't blush! I had a look at your CV, you finished university with an honours degree, you even have a PhD! Mind you, anybody can get a PhD nowadays! Nonetheless, you should be very proud of yourself!"

I looked doubtfully at Claudia. A compliment never comes without a catch, where she's concerned. I'm aware that I may be naïve, but I'm not that hopeless.

"Claudia, that's more than a decade ago!" I protested. I hated myself, as I had blushed like one of my sixteen-year old pupils. No, I'm wrong, they don't blush anymore nowadays, it must be the ten-year-old girls. But Claudia went on without taking any real notice of me, continuing her speech, so smooth and fluent that I'm sure that she must have rehearsed it beforehand.

"Amanda, my dear, our school urgently needs publicity. People must get to know us better, they must discover how much we care about our pupils and how highly qualified our staff is!"

I started to feel ill at ease, knowing that our school had figured only recently in the headlines of the local newspapers, labelled as a "breeding ground for a new illiterate generation, doomed for the dole queue." I didn't see quite how to change our reputation rapidly, especially as I shared a certain sympathy for the newspapers' conclusions. I betray no secrets when I say that most of my pupils have problems reading properly, let alone writing. And when it comes to history, all they're able to memorise seems to be the last text messages they've received on their smartphones, those awful devices that are constantly to hand, regardless of any sanctions we try to impose...

"Claudia, darling, whatever you want, I'm with you!" I smiled – Claudia was now in charge of the class schedules and the class allocation, and I needed to keep her sweet as I had just succeeded in getting rid of the worst class I had ever faced in my life – and believe me, I've seen a few!

"Oh darling," she trumpeted, "I knew that I could always count on you, you're always dedicated to our cause. I've taken the liberty of sending your application to Independent Media, you know, those people who run that silly show, "Who Wants to Be a Millionaire!" You go on the show, just be your brilliant self and tell the audience how committed we all are to our school and of course to our dear children. If you manage to win a bit of money it should go to the school, of course. You know the school is falling apart; we could do with some extra funds, the heating is a disgrace, not eco-friendly at all, and we urgently need solar panels. I'm counting on your generosity."

I swallowed hard. I'm a teacher. I'm used to standing in front of an audience – but to face a TV camera with millions of people watching me? I started to perspire.

"Now you're speechless!" Claudia couldn't hide her satisfaction.

"I am, indeed," I croaked, then I regained hope. "But the chance of them choosing me is almost zero, I'm too boring, too ordinary, just look at me!"

Claudia dismissed my concerns with a regal wave. "Don't be a goose, my dear. Of course you're rather timid and very bourgeois, but they like to put these kinds of people on the show from time to time, it makes the other contestants look so much more colourful. Just hide your English accent when it comes to questions on foreign countries."

"I got that from my father and it seems to have been all right so far," I protested.

"That's what I'm saying," Claudia insisted. "It sounds too foreign. In Germany you must speak English with a German accent, so everybody can understand you! But let's get back to the point: the guy who selects the contestants is a member of the Forest Warriors movement, I've known him for ages. He'll make sure that that you're in the final selection."

She smiled at me and as usual I wasn't sure if her broad business-like smile had just become a habit, a permanent part of her school outfit, or maybe she was just mocking me. To be frank, I was almost sure that she was mocking me.

"Claudia, that's very kind, but I couldn't do it!" Was there a note of despair in my voice?

Claudia shot me a foul look and her voice suddenly took on a steely note. "It's your decision, darling, of course. Not in my wildest dreams would I force you

4

to do something you didn't want to do. Aren't we all one big happy family here? I might consider asking Dr. Wagner to help out. But I'm pretty sure that he'll need lots of free time to prepare himself, you know him – he's nowhere near as brilliant as you are!"

In that moment I knew that I had been beaten. Dr. Wagner was a real lamb, always ready for the slaughter; he never objected to anything, he had even taken over my worst classes. Those classes he would gladly be handing back over to me once Claudia granted him time off. Staffroom bets were that Dr. Wagner was only months away from going loopy – probably destined for some mental institution. He was no match for those budding male sharks who pretended to be our pupils. I breathed deeply and replied, "All right, I'll accept the challenge! After all, it's for the wellbeing of our school…"

"Darling, I'm so proud! I knew that I could count on you! Your show will be on in six weeks, it's all settled! My friend understands that we need some positive news for our school as fast as possible."

"In six weeks! Claudia, you must be kidding, I'll have no time to prepare anything, I haven't a clue what to do!" I almost yelped.

But Claudia's pasted-on smile didn't waver for a second. "I've been thinking about that and came up with a brilliant idea of how to prepare for your appearance." With a dramatic gesture she presented me with a linen bag (no plastic bags were allowed in Claudia's vicinity) containing a heavy parcel. As if in a trance I looked into the bag and discovered a heavy box.

"Trivial Pursuit?" I breathed more than I spoke.

"It's the ideal preparation, my friend told me, there's nothing better!" Claudia beamed at me. "I bought it in English, so you can use it for your classes later. Wasn't that clever?"

"Nobody in my class would understand any of those questions – don't even think of them coming up with the answer in English," I replied, and then quickly regretted this unruly slip of the tongue.

"Don't be so negative, darling, our pupils deserve our very best efforts, I cannot tolerate them not being taken seriously!" she frowned. Joan of Arc must have looked a bit like this, mustering her pitiful troops, I imagine.

"I was just kidding," I answered feebly. "It will be fun to test it in class."

"That's the right attitude." Claudia was all smiles again. "Isn't it great, darling, how we always manage to agree? Now you owe me fifty euros for the game – but you can pay me back later. I'm ready to give credit to a future millionaire." She made a hoarse snickering sound and grabbed my arm. "Let's have a nice cup of tea together now, I have another surprise. I brought some fresh biscuits, the last ones disappeared in no time! Why are you laughing?" She looked at me suspiciously.

I quickly controlled my expression. I had just remembered how I had tried to feed the remaining biscuits to my neighbour's dog, a beagle. That dog is amazing, he gobbles any kind of food. But on being presented with Claudia's biscuits, the dog gave me a long and very reproachful look and refused to pay me any further attention...

Who Wants to be a Millionaire? I Do!

The next weeks flew by as if in a dream – or rather should I call it a sort of nightmare? I didn't know where to start or what to do, so finally I decided to test Claudia's game of Trivial Pursuit with my best friend – she's English – and quickly discovered that it was quite good fun. We ended up playing for hours! I checked all the information I could find on the internet – and by doing so my spirits sank more and more. Some opening questions were so easy that they were almost a joke, but many, far too many, just seemed hopeless, and especially when it came to sports or geography I quickly started to drown. Claudia had given me a mission impossible.

"I'll never even make it to the second round, it's hopeless and so embarrassing! When did Uruguay become soccer world champions – did they ever? " I complained, digging deep into the box of chocolates that had become my constant companion and only consolation – next to the steaming mug of coffee, that was.

"Haven't you been eating a bit too much chocolate lately?" My friend Susan frowned at me.

"The newspapers say that eating chocolate is healthy and enhances the neurological processes of the brain!" I defended myself. "I know that it's the right thing to do!"

"Not if you intend to wear that gorgeous blue dress you showed me last week; it was quite tight, actually…" Susan sent me a long and very thoughtful look.

Who needs enemies with friends like that? With a sigh I closed the lid of the chocolate box. "I had forgotten about the dress. "What about joining me for a salad for dinner, I might even throw in a spoonful of olive oil?"

"That sounds much better!" Susan beamed at me while she moved the chocolate out of my reach.

That's what true friends are for!

Perhaps I should explain at this point that I'm one of those modern, successful single women, leading a life dedicated to work and their community. My father would say I'm in danger of becoming an old spinster. My Mr. Right just hasn't turned up yet – or maybe I simply overlooked him. They say that you have to kiss a lot of frogs before you finally meet your prince, a statement that has turned out to be very true in my case.

7

***

The great day came soon, far too soon. I was put in the hands of a young make-up artist who applied his skills with a suffering face that said it all: who had dared to dump this country bumpkin on him? I was quite offended. I do happen to apply lipstick – at least, from time to time! After he had covered my face with a layer of make-up that would have done a good job of plastering my living room, he drenched my hair with hair spray. "Stop it! I can't breathe!" I cried, tears welling up in my eyes.

"Will you stop crying – you'll ruin the mascara!" he snarled at me furiously, but the can of hairspray disappeared. Small wonder, it must be empty by now.

We had been briefed before in the studio on where to enter, how many steps to walk, when to wave and to smile and I knew that illuminated signs would tell the audience when to clap and when to cheer. So much for the spontaneous reactions of the public – but I was excited as never before in my life.

Luckily the presenter's assistant took my arm and led me towards the exit, her warm voice soothing my taut nerves. "Don't worry, my dear, they've all survived this ordeal. Once you're out there just concentrate on the presenter, he'll guide you, he's a nice man!" she whispered and gave me a quick hug before I walked onto the stage.

Deafening music engulfed me like a tsunami, and resembling a drugged robot from a science fiction B-movie I staggered forward, following the thin white line on the floor the assistant had shown me beforehand. To my great surprise I reached the chair and the small desk with the monitor that had been set up for the contestants without creating any major havoc. Somehow I had been convinced that I'd never even be able to reach the chair, as not only had my hair had been covered with hair spray, my contact lenses had received a good dose as well. I sighed with satisfaction as I sat down, forgetting that the microphone was live already. My satisfied grunt echoed through the studio and immediately I turned a flaming red.

"I can tell that you're already feeling comfortable!" I heard the presenter teasing me. "Are you ready for the million?"

"Who wouldn't be?" I retorted. "And yes, thanks for your concern, the chair is most comfortable. I just hope you won't be pushing the eject button too soon."

Apparently I had hit the right tone. The audience howled with laughter, and the show could begin.

8

The strange thing is that you feel almost alone out there. The spotlights were blinding me, I couldn't see a single member of the audience – and yet they were very much present as I could hear them cheering, clapping their hands and often enough commenting on my answers. I made it quickly to the second level, as the first question had been a mere joke to warm me up, the usual procedure.

'Next, the 'clap and cheer' sign will go on', I thought automatically. I was proved right, and seconds later the cheering was followed by enthusiastic applause, partly coming from the audience behind the glaring spotlights, partly from the loudspeakers.

The show passed like a dream. Some people have even said I was very witty – I haven't a clue, my memory is almost blank. I seem to have expressed some warm words about my school and the children and how dedicated I feel – small wonder, Claudia had drilled me over and over.

As the dreaded sports question came I was prepared for it and didn't even try to come up with an answer of my own. I used my lifeline, the phone-a-friend. If there's one real expert in the world on sport, then it's my sixteen-year-old nephew. His reply came within seconds – don't ask me what the question was! – and he was correct, so I moved on to the €125,000 level.

As the figures on the board became more and more impressive I felt like I was in a trance, detached from real life. The situation was simply surreal; I was floating in a bubble, almost sure I would wake up in my bed soon enough, having had this wonderful and yet utterly crazy dream. But it all felt genuine enough, the heat emanating from the spotlights making me perspire, my parched throat, the voice of the presenter, the cheering of the audience, the vibrations of the floor whenever they stamped their feet.

When the last question came all my tension just fell away – it was a historical question, France, seventeenth century. I heard the voice of the presenter: "Which prime minister served under Queen Anne d'Autriche?" and he slowly listed the names of Metternich, Colbert, Richelieu, Mazarin. I must have smiled. It's my favourite period in French history and he would not mislead me by calling the queen by her maiden Hapsburg name. The presenter tried his best to plant some doubt in my mind. "Are you sure? Don't forget that the name of the queen is hinting towards a country further east…", but I wouldn't let him lead me down the wrong path.

"The right answer is clearly Cardinal Mazarin. Colbert came to office much later and he was no prime minister, whereas Richelieu served under her husband and Metternich wasn't even born!" I heard myself answering firmly. I'm afraid that I was showing off a bit – once a teacher, always a teacher.

9

The presenter still dragged out the seconds, pretending to hesitate before he suddenly jumped up and congratulated me. This was the sign the TV studio had been waiting for. The audience went berserk, I had done it, I had won the million! This was a figure beyond all imagination! How many pairs of shoes can you buy for a million? I'm not good at figures, but I guess it's far more than I could ever store in my entire bedroom!

The presenter came forward to hug me, and then after the show we spent a wonderful night with the whole crew and partied until I dropped, slightly tipsy, into my bed where I simply couldn't get to sleep – I had become a millionaire!

Still lying in bed I decided to give a nice chunk of the money to my nephew, and happy to have come to this gratifying conclusion, I must have dozed off.

The next day I returned to school, red-eyed and utterly exhausted, but still feeling elated, ready to embrace the world and thrilled by my unlikely success. I had been prepared to be admired – if not loved – but in any case, was sure of becoming a sort of a local hero. The local tabloids were lauding our school, and I had accomplished my mission.

But soon, very soon, I was to discover that I had committed the ultimate sin: I had won the money everybody else could only dream of. No more carefree small talk, conversations tended to end with a reproachful hint, such as "Well, for you it's probably meaningless, you don't really need to worry any more." The next day a young colleague approached me for a loan: "Amanda, it's just a pittance for you – and to us it would make all the difference ..." Incidentally this was the same colleague who had never taken the trouble to even talk to me before I had become rich. I turned her down and could see the disdain in her eyes.

It was not enough that I had become a sort of outcast at our school – my dear friend Claudia was on my back constantly to hand over the prize money to the school – my money! "Darling, we had a clear agreement that you'd pay for the solar panels, now we can even afford to put in new windows. I can get a discount if I order both. You'll love my idea, I'm even planning to organize an inauguration with the school choir in your honour!"

"I'll tell you what, you go and win it yourself, Claudia, if you're so smart. I'm not going to squander my money on a school where my colleagues either ignore me or ask me to open my wallet whenever they set eyes on me," I snapped back, upset by the constant harassment of the past few days. Claudia put on her 'I'm-going-to-save-the-rainforest' face and immediately started one of her usual sermons. But today I had no patience with her. I stormed out of the staffroom and slammed the door shut, leaving a hopping mad Claudia behind.

10

'Amanda, you're behaving like a spoilt child,' I chided myself, but I knew that I had to do something or would end up in a special institution – worse, I might end up murdering someone. All of a sudden I realized that the old life of Amanda Lipton was finished here and now, and I had become a stranger in my own school. I simply couldn't take it any longer.

Hadn't I just won a fortune, wasn't this some sort of sign that I should try new things? Deep in my thoughts I walked through the building – and found myself in front of the principal's office. I took a deep breath before knocking at his secretary's door. We happen to get on well – from time to time we exchange baking recipes, as she loves cakes. Her cakes are not only delicious, they'd qualify as true works of art. I'll never reach that stage of culinary sophistication.

"Can I disturb your boss?" I asked her.

She smiled back at me. Her plump face showed attractive dimples which made her even more likable. I imagine she's one of the few members of the staff who is held in esteem by everybody.

"I'm not sure, Amanda, is it urgent? Actually to be honest, I'm quite sure that he doesn't want to be disturbed, in fact, he never wants to be disturbed..." She smiled again and her dimples showed even more. "By the way, I saw you on TV, you were brilliant. I also loved your new hairstyle, you looked great!"

"Oh dear, they put me in the hands of the grumpiest stylist you could imagine and I inhaled more hairspray that evening than ever before in my life. I still don't know how I survived the ordeal." I shuddered. "But to come back to your boss, I just need to talk to him for five minutes, whether he likes it or not."

"If it's to ask for a sabbatical, better forget it, he's in a foul mood. This week we've had two colleagues announce they're pregnant and the new gym teacher's broken her leg; it's been an upsetting week. He'll need all teachers on board when the autumn term starts." She looked at me. She had immediately understood why I had come; she's by no means a fool.

"You can read minds! You shouldn't be sitting here, you should go and work as a fortune-teller – you'd make much more money!"

My friend giggled. "Great idea! I'll wind a scarf around my head, speak in a dodgy accent and call myself 'Maria the Psychic'. But to come back to your request, it's not difficult to guess the purpose of your visit. Since dear Claudia has taken over managing the timetables, most teachers who come into my office in a frenzy want to apply for a sabbatical." She finished her sentence with a telling glance. "Let me see what I can do for you."

Minutes later I was ushered into the principal's inner sanctum. He didn't look very pleased at being interrupted. Well, he had my full sympathy! A single stamp, from the German Democratic Republic commemorating the Moscow Olympic Games in 1980, was still on his desk. I guessed the rest of the stamps had found their way quickly into a drawer.

"Miss Lipton, what can I do for you?" He opened the conversation in a formal tone, not really implying that he would be keen or ready to do anything. I decided to attack like the Prussian army. There was no time for polite detours or the usual small talk.

"Marcus, since I won this silly TV game show, my colleagues have become unbearable. It will be so much better if we all have some time to calm down." I had learnt to be straightforward with him, as his attention span was limited. "Either I leave the school completely, or you grant me sabbatical leave, but I can't see myself continuing like this, there's too much tension, it's not good for me... or the school."

"There's no way I can accept your demand, Miss Lipton, I'm sorry. I have to deal with the problem of several colleagues being absent during the next term, you know the usual issues, some are pregnant, a nervous breakdown, a broken leg..." I could hear that he felt personally offended. A school was meant to teach children, but how dare his teachers produce any offspring themselves or disturb his peaceful life? He had also avoided addressing me by my first name, which was a bad sign.

"I'm close to meltdown..." This was spiteful of me, but I really couldn't envisage putting up with Claudia's bitchiness day after day.

Marcus gave me a vile look, every inch the annoyed principal. "Then you'll have to undergo an examination by the department of occupational medicine. I insist!" he retorted.

I was surprised by his harsh reaction. I hadn't thought he'd got the balls for it. An uneasy silence ensued and I examined his desk, as I didn't want to look him in the eye. At this moment I received some divine inspiration. I decided to change my tactics. "That's a nice stamp, Marcus, it's quite a rarity," I remarked casually, dropping my hostile attitude.

His face lit up. "Yes it is, those stamps came in a complete set, dedicated to each sport. As the games were boycotted by the Western countries, bizarrely this only added to their value. There was even a special commemoration postmark... very rare nowadays."

"I know, I have one at home, my father is a keen stamp collector, he gave them to me for a birthday when I was a kid."

"You have this stamp with a commemorative Olympic Games postmark?" Marcus became excited, his moist eyes glinting behind his glasses.

"Not only that, my father got hold of the complete sheet with the special Olympic Games postmark – he was very proud of it."

"Would you consider selling it to me?" he breathed.

"With pleasure, but only if my mind is at ease. If I'm at all stressed, I'm afraid that I won't be very motivated..."

"Amanda, you know that this is blackmail!" He sent me an evil look – but he had at least remembered my first name. My chances were increasing, we were making progress.

"Marcus, let me propose a deal. I insist it'll be better for the school if I stay away for a year. You have to understand that Claudia is furious with me because I won't give her any money for her cherished solar panels, and she wants us to be named ecological school of the year. It'll be daily war between the two of us."

"Oh yes, she would be mad, very much so. I never met a person with such a lot of energy, she does tend to wear me down..." He spoke more to himself than to me. "I suppose you're right, if there's a rift between Claudia and you, it's not going to help." Marcus paused and closed his eyes. He was trying to concentrate, and I crossed my fingers behind my back.

"All right, I agree to a sabbatical, but for one term only, not a full year. And that's final!"

"Thank you, Marcus!" I could have hugged him.

"Don't forget the stamps though – are you sure it's the complete sheet?" Marcus's eyes were as big as saucers behind his glasses now.

"Sure – and in the best condition, my father saw to that!"

So that is the story of how I obtained my sabbatical. Not in the most ethical way, one might observe, but I'm still convinced that leaving school was the best solution – for me and for the school.

Spring term was ending and we were quickly heading towards the summer holidays. Hamburg is not known for its warm weather but we enjoyed a rare spell of continuous sunshine that reflected my sunny mood – I had no foreboding whatsoever regarding events that were to come. Maybe I should have remained at home – but how could I have known that then?

Invariably the end of term is accompanied by weeks of exams and meetings. I had no option but to drag myself through these routines, looking forward to my sabbatical. I heard from my friend, the secretary with the dimples, that Claudia had staged a memorable scene when she discovered that I had been granted my sabbatical leave. Marcus reported in sick for two days.

Claudia and I still pretended to be friends though, and were exceedingly polite to each other, but I knew that my classes and timetables would be the worst imaginable once I came back – if I came back at all. Funny, how you can walk out of building that has been your place of work – actually your entire life for a decade – and feel nothing but relief. I was touched though to discover that some of my pupils seemed to be sad about my impending departure, a pleasant surprise I hadn't expected at all.

"We'll miss you!" wailed a group of girls with colourful tattoos on their arms. I could almost detect tears hiding in their mascara-laden eyelashes.

"How can you miss me if you're always late to class and complain that I'm too tough?" I replied. I was amazed, I hadn't anticipated this reaction at all.

"Because we like it when a teacher is tough. You make us work, but that's ok, you're quite cool actually…"

This was the nicest compliment I had heard in a decade, I must admit. Maybe my life as a teacher hadn't been a complete failure after all.

Adventure, Here I Come!

"What am I going to do now?" I complained to Susan. Normally I have my routines. During the school holidays I used to leave Hamburg for a trip to the mountains where I tended to end up in the sad companionship of other single teachers. Strange, how we always find each other.

But this year I wanted something different, I felt adventurous. I was even facing a new and very strange problem, as I had no classes to prepare. I was starting to get bored. For years and years I had complained that my precious holidays were eaten up by odious preparation for the next term, and for once I didn't have to do it – I didn't know what to do!

"Go shopping? I might join you, I need new shoes," Susan proposed. She tends to be down to earth and to ignore my bouts of self-pity.

"Everybody will say that I'm frittering my money away," I protested. "It's unbelievable, they all seem to have watched this horrid show. Just imagine, yesterday a journalist from that ghastly *Watch* tabloid wanted to interview me about 'my new life'. I simply hate it." I was sulking by now.

But Susan had no compassion. "Stop crying on my shoulder, you're being paranoid. Go abroad, travel, fritter your money away. Everybody thinks you're doing it anyhow. Or do you want to keep it for your dear friend Claudia?"

I love Susan, she's so practically minded. "Where should I go? I hate these excursions they sell to unhappy singles like me. 'Explore the heritage of ancient Greece – travel in the companionship of like-minded sophisticated guests'. They always promise you that you'll meet the man of your dreams, but the buses are full of single teachers – mostly middle-aged female dragons with good reason as to why they're still single. I don't want this. And just imagine staying in a family hotel, you can't even talk to a man there because his wife will stab you in the back the moment you say hello to her husband."

"You have a point, the only way to get to know interesting people and avoid other teachers is to travel in luxury. Don't make faces, I'll take over now, you'll be spending money on a good cause! Listen to Susan!" Susan was thrilled, her fingers tapping away on her tablet. "Look what I found here on the internet: 'The *Belgravia* is the luxurious flagship of Astra Lines, the most magnificent cruise liner ever built. She offers all the amenities of a large cruise ship while offering a club atmosphere for her discerning guests. The *Belgravia* offers unrivalled culinary experiences, suites of outstanding elegance and a service that has become the benchmark of the industry'."

Susan's fingers kept tapping at her tablet. I shut my eyes – would I really be standing on a steamship like beautiful Kate in the arms of her Leonardo?

"Stop dreaming!" Susan's voice woke me up. "There's a suite available for an Atlantic crossing, a voyage that can be extended to include a trip to Canada in about three weeks' time. That's plenty of time to spruce up your wardrobe and get ready!"

I opened my eyes and shut them again in panic. Susan's manicured finger was pointing to the price, a figure that equalled half of my last year's salary! "That's impossible, who would spend so much money for only fourteen days? Susan, forget it, it's simply obscene!"

"No, darling, it's a bargain, see, they're offering you a huge discount. It's a unique opportunity, I insist, my friend, you need it and you deserve it!" Susan had taken over now; she spoke firmly with the voice of authority and I must confess, I was a consenting and easy prey, ever so ready to stray from the path of virtue.

"Will you join me?" I stuttered, intimidated by my friend's enthusiasm. "I'll pay!"

"No, my dear, forget it. Weren't you just complaining about buses full of single females? There's nothing worse than two single women travelling together, it's a guarantee never to meet anybody interesting. I'm fine and I'll stay here, thanks for the generous offer, it's very much appreciated but I won't spoil your holiday." She kept hammering away on the virtual keyboard of her tablet until I heard a satisfied grunt.

"Here we go, that's done, you'll receive a booking confirmation and an invoice – I'm afraid your credit card allowance will never cover the amount they're asking for just to start the reservation procedure. Susan studied the screen once again and cried out: "Wow, look at this! Here it says 'Your mini bar will be stocked daily with the Champagne of your choice', now that's what I call service! 'Caviar and Foie Gras Canapés will be served with mouth-watering French patisseries at tea-time in your suite if you desire'. Amanda, better buy some loose-fitting dresses, this sounds fabulous!"

I looked at the pictures. Mouth-watering was an understatement. I was hooked.

The next weeks passed as if in a dream, the most wonderful dream I've ever experienced. Several extensive (and very expensive) shopping sprees filled my brand new suitcases until they were almost bursting. "Don't you think that we're overdoing things?" I voiced my concern while I flopped into my comfortable armchair. I was totally exhausted and with a sigh of satisfaction I kicked my shoes into the corner – they must have shrunk during the past few hours! Who invented high heels? He or she must have hated women!

"These are the basic necessities!" Susan replied with the voice of authority. She still had an excited twinkle in her eye; she simply loves shopping, she's a born bargain hunter. And she had been the smart one; nothing beats flat shoes when it comes to a shopping marathon. All the same, don't get me wrong: it would be difficult to find a more consenting victim to Susan's shopping mania than me.

Day 1 – On Board

The great day had arrived, and my adventure was to start today. My heart was beating like a drum as I experienced a mix of joyful, almost ebullient anticipation combined with a loathsome chicken-hearted trepidation. As I was about to trespass into a new world, would I discover that the *Belgravia* was the favourite holiday hotspot of a bunch of snobs who wouldn't even talk to me?

Susan had insisted on driving me to the ship's berth where she hugged and kissed me good-bye but refused steadfastly to join me on board. "I might regret my decision to let you travel alone. Actually, I'm regretting it already." She winked at me. "Just pretend you're a grown-up girl and go on your own now. Have a great time!"

I'm a bit sentimental. For those who know me well it would have come as no surprise that tears were welling up in my eyes as I watched Susan's reassuring figure disappear into the crowd. But I had no time to wallow in any kind of self-pity, as a capable stewardess dressed in a dazzling white uniform was approaching me and took immediate charge of me. Feeling like a true VIP I was led to a reception desk where a welcome drink was waiting for me. The stewardess addressed me by my name. I was for once a member of the chosen few who can afford to spend thousands of dollars or pounds on mere pleasure. As soon as the registration procedure was finished, I was led along plush galleries into a lift which whisked us noiselessly to one of the upper decks. Now I understood why it was called the penthouse suite – the ship was as huge as a skyscraper. The lift was built like a glass box; it was amazing how fast we zoomed upwards dwarfing those passengers who had remained on the lower decks.

My capable guide led me down a long corridor while gentle music wafted through the passage. Here we walked on carpets so soft that they swallowed any noise of our steps until we reached the door of my cabin. The electronic key activated the lock and I was allowed to enter the luxurious dwelling that would be my home for the coming fortnight. I was not to be disappointed; it was beautiful!

From the elegant furniture that included a cushioned sofa and an inviting-looking armchair to the tasteful wallpaper, the mellow lights and the huge bed, I couldn't have imagined anything nicer or more luxurious! A large window equipped with a sliding door led to a private balcony, shielded from the wind by large glass panels. It was simply wonderful! I sent a quick prayer of thanks in my mind to Susan. Without her resolve, I'd be probably sitting in my usual bus, heading to some boring mountain resort with a bunch of even more boring fellow teachers.

Soon it was time to dress up, as I was to dine in the Westminster Grill. Curious to know what would be waiting for me, I had studied the photos of the *Belgravia* again and again on the internet. Therefore I already knew that the Westminster Grill would certainly match the refinement of my cabin.

Astra Lines still stick to the old proven ways of segregating the classes, meaning we, the chosen few, were allowed to eat in this restaurant at the time of our choosing. This was the first time that I was part of the 'we' – usually I'm 'them' – a brand new experience for me. I should have been disgusted at this elitist attitude and I had to smile as I tried to imagine Claudia with her dyed hair and her clogs in this setting – she'd be a fish out of water.

The French Revolution might have identified the key values of mankind as being liberté, égalité, and fraternité, but apparently the ripples of the French Revolution had never reached this ship, as only a notion of liberty applied to the *Belgravia*; a ship is a universe all its own.

So here I was on this wonderful cruise ship, feeling like Cinderella. A pity there'd be no prince desperate enough to look for my slipper (although I had brought plenty of those – just in case). But did I really care if a prince turned up or not? I felt wonderful and adventurous as rarely before in my life. I shrugged at my reflection in the mirror. A woman with bright eyes looked back at me. I suddenly remembered how I had looked after I had passed through the capable hands of the young and arrogant make-up artist at Independent Media – quite attractive, really. I took some kind of consolation from the fact that no model ever looks like a model without make-up. In hindsight I should have invited the young man from Independent Media to join me on the cruise, as apparently he had performed a miracle with my looks. But would I really like to see him looking down his arrogant nose at me day after day? I grinned at my reflection. The champagne had made me feel carefree and I was ready to embrace the world. That first night I had no idea at all what kind of adventures fate had in store for me – you only ever find out when it's too late.

Studying my image in the mirror once again, I decided that I looked attractive and elegant, and that the money for my new clothes had been well spent. Following a sudden impulse, I went back to the bathroom – a bit of make-up wouldn't do any harm, after all. Minutes later a transformed Amanda looked at me. I liked the new Amanda and in the best of moods I left my cabin, ready to conquer the world.

Earlier, the capable lady at the reception desk had indicated that most guests preferred to partake of dinner around 8 pm, and so the canapés and champagne that were waiting for me in my suite certainly helped to bridge the gap, as I felt exceedingly hungry by now. Waking up that morning I had been a bundle of nerves and couldn't stomach a proper breakfast; a cup of coffee had been all I could manage. My lunch had been a hurried affair, but now – as all tension had been replaced by a wonderful feeling of elation and excitement – I felt as hungry as a wolf. Carefully I poured a second glass of champagne and walked to the large glass window leading to the balcony, *my* balcony, that is. I had to walk with care, as my new shoes were extremely slippery on the soft carpet.

Sipping happily from my glass I looked through the large window; the era of tiny portholes had long since been forgotten. My eyes scanned the grey mass of water while the engines of the *Belgravia* hummed like good-humoured bumble bees. Slowly I could see the silhouette of the German coast disappearing in the evening sun.

I was sea-borne and toasted my reflection in the window: "Cheers, Amanda – and here's to adventure, I'm coming!" I had no idea how true this would prove to be.

Around a quarter to eight I left my luxurious cabin in search of the Westminster Grill. I felt decidedly nervous, not only as I have the unfortunate habit of getting lost on unknown territory, but in my mind there lingered a feeling of unease at trespassing in a world that wasn't really mine. I felt like an imposter, pretending to move among the rich and beautiful – and I was neither. Would the other guests ignore me, would they look down on me? What a stupid idea, ever to have booked this cruise at all!

In this state of nervous tension I entered the Westminster Grill where the headwaiter greeted me by name. How did he recognize me? He led me to a large round table with a beautiful view on the sea. Thank God I was not the first one. Richard Gere was waiting for me – well, sort of. The man sitting at the table could have been his brother. Politely he rose from his chair to greet me and I, stupid, clumsy Amanda, I sailed directly into his arms as my treacherous new shoes slipped on the thick carpet. Luckily he caught me before I hit the table, grasping me in his firm, strong arms.

He looked down on me with mocking eyes and drawled: "Good evening, I see I've been greatly misinformed. My friends had warned me that on a cruise ship I'd be surrounded by senile passengers well into their eighties. I must say I'm positively delighted, not only are you young and attractive, your very personal style of entrance has a very spirited zest to it…"

"I'm awfully sorry, I promise I won't repeat this every evening!" I smiled back. Had I really heard him saying that I was young and attractive? Could he repeat this, please? I could get used to this! "Although – after careful consideration, I might be tempted to do so!" I answered a bit brashly. Was it really me, speaking like this?

He laughed and this did nothing to lessen his attraction. I must be on my guard, I decided, but as usual this kind of consideration came far too late.

"May I introduce myself? I'm Daniel. And you are?"

"I'm Amanda. Please don't say it's a charming name, I know it isn't, but my parents fell for it."

"Amanda is a very nice name. Let's sit down and occupy the best seats before our fellow passengers turn up. To be early on the first night is a very strategic move!" He looked critically at the table and chose a chair that had a beautiful view out to sea, unimpeded by the other passengers who had started to flock to their tables.

"I'd suggest this chair for you," he offered gallantly, totally ignoring the waiter who had moved forward, eager to be of service. I accepted Daniel's offer with a shy smile, and not waiting for any further invitation he placed himself next to me.

In no time I found myself engaged in relaxed small talk as if I had never done anything else but sit with a smart-looking stranger at a table decked with beautiful linen, candles and flowers, laden with the finest porcelain, glasses of all sorts polished to perfection and gleaming silver cutlery of a never seen variety. We were still chatting when the next passengers arrived.

I gasped, as I knew one of them; well, both of them actually.

It's time to come clean: I'm a fan of breakfast TV, at least on those days when I don't have to teach listless and bleary-eyed teenagers. I like to delve into the colourful world of travel, dream about royalty, participate in the chit chat about society and pretend that I'm an expert on the latest fashion trends. One of the icons of today's fashion design is Charles Peltier, top designer of the label icon-U, the absolute must for any young woman in society. I know this much from my diligent study of the tabloid press. Nobody has ever been able to discover Peltier's true origins, and like his age they remain a secret, which in itself is an achievement in our age of Facebook, Twitter and total internet transparency. I had watched several interviews and fashion shows on TV featuring Charles Peltier. Doubtless he was a man of great charisma, at ease in several languages, a truly remarkable personality. As usual his grey hair was bound into a ponytail, and tonight he was dressed in a sober black silk suit with a white collarless shirt. His only concession to colour was his right cufflink, black enamel with a large dot of striking yellow – corresponding exactly to the yellow and black varnish he had applied on a single nail on his left hand. I was thrilled; this was the real thing, so much better than sitting in front of a TV!

The young man (he introduced himself as Frank) who accompanied Charles Peltier was none other than the handsome young make-up artist who had done his best to make me presentable for the TV show. Both of them greeted us, but Frank just granted me a short nod of recognition. I guess that I hadn't really been of any importance to him, and probably never would be, as I was not part of his glittering world. After having greeted me politely, they forgot about my existence and focused all attention on my neighbour as they engaged Daniel in animated conversation. From the topics they covered I could deduce that they seemed to be loosely acquainted with him – maybe they had met during the boarding procedure.

I must admit that I felt a bit jealous. I had enjoyed talking to Daniel very much. But the fact that I was not actively involved in their conversation granted me the opportunity to study Daniel's face more closely. He was a handsome man, but (as I noted with a tinge of relief) far from being the perfect model type. His nose sat slightly askew (had he been a boxer?) and although I liked his square jaw it wasn't perfectly proportioned. My glance went to his brown eyes; they were nice, but did not have the brilliance of a Latin lover, the kind of eyes that promise to drown you in a sea of passion. And yet Daniel was a very attractive man. I would need to be careful.

From time to time Daniel tried his best to include me in their conversation, but my remarks were mostly ignored and I preferred to listen. Soon I overheard that the three of them were planning to disembark in New York. Charles Peltier confessed that he felt claustrophobic in airplanes. With an apologetic smile (including me for the first time!) he declared, "I can survive a short flight of an hour or so – but only in a private aircraft and I cling to my bottle of vodka, but can you imagine in what state of body and mind I'd arrive in New York after a seven-hour flight? For me there's no alternative to the sophistication of travelling by sea – and isn't it so much more relaxing to tune your body to the time difference by adjusting daily just for an hour?" We all agreed with his statement, as all experienced travellers surely would, and then turned our attention to the agreeable task of choosing our appetizers, as a waiter had appeared and was waiting for our orders.

"Has Peltier ever tried the pleasures of flying Ryanair?" I muttered under my breath to Daniel.

"I don't think so," Daniel grinned at me. "I guess he'd arrive in a coffin; his bottle of vodka wouldn't have helped him much!"

"Ryanair wouldn't really mind, they'd have charged him of course – for being oversize," I commented drily. Daniel exploded with laughter.

"Can we share the joke?" Charles Peltier asked curiously.

"Sorry, it's a private joke!" Daniel gasped and hid behind the menu.

We were still studying the menu and trying to make up our minds when the next passengers arrived. It didn't take me long to pick up that they were Americans.

"Honey, which seat would you prefer? "

"Darling, I really don't mind, but I suggest you choose this chair, you'll have a beautiful view!"

She smiled at her husband. "You're ever so considerate, honey!"

Before they sat down though, they went through the elaborate motions of greeting us. It was not just a casual 'Hi, how are you?', but hands were being squeezed, I received a kiss from honey and darling and she became ecstatic about my dress. I started to like darling.

It didn't take us long to discover that they were New Yorkers and wanted to disembark in the Big Apple as well, as their journey on the *Belgravia* was the crowning finale to an extensive trip to Europe. I therefore was the only one – so far – intending to travel on to Canada.

"Oh, travelling through Europe is simply wonderful," darling sighed, close to ecstasy. "I need this experience from time to time, I couldn't live without travelling to Paris once or twice a year!" I concluded from her simple statement that money and time did not put any constraints on her considerations. They seemed to be simply at her disposal.

"You Europeans, you have such sophistication, so much culture, the food is so authentic, whereas America is always so crude…"

"I always thought that New York was brimming with culture!" I couldn't help saying. "You have wonderful museums, opera houses, a vivid art scene, nothing in Hamburg can compare!"

She smiled. "Oh yes, New York is different, but it's not really America, my dear. Most Americans think that New York is the reincarnation of Sodom and Gomorrah. I have friends in Minneapolis who wouldn't dare to put a foot in New York, they call it Sin City."

She smiled indulgently. "Call me Marge, by the way, my real name is Margareta, but I hate it. What's your name? I can hear you're British, how come you're living in Hamburg?"

"My name is Amanda and I'm German actually, but my father was British, we used to talk English together, so I guess I'm bilingual."

"How exciting!" Marge's husband suddenly dropped in. "I'm John, by the way. I wish I could speak French as well!"

"She said she's German, John!" Marge hissed. I discovered that Marge could show a very different side when she wasn't pleased.

"I was just joking!" John answered, his face blushing. I concluded that Marge had a habit of correcting him, a habit he didn't seem to appreciate.

We were interrupted as a waiter appeared with the cocktails. I had opted for iced orange juice as I wasn't sure if the ship was swaying or if it was the effect of the champagne I had savoured in my cabin before. "Would you know if the remaining passengers joined us in Hamburg?" Marge interrogated the waiter.

"No, madam, they'll be joining in London. May I take your orders now?"

I had noticed already that four places had remained empty and I was a bit disappointed, as I'd have to wait another day to discover the identity of the passengers with whom I'd be sharing a table over the coming days. I was burning with curiosity – would another celebrity turn up? On the *Belgravia*, I was sure by now, anything could happen! But I would only know later how true this statement turned out to be.

What is it that makes choosing from a menu so difficult? I never know if I should try something new and exotic, or rather opt for a safe choice, knowing that it will please me. I'm always lost in front of a menu, it doesn't matter if it's a fast food or a starred restaurant. I choose, I consider, I doubt, and the moment the waiter has left the table with my order, I regret it and would love to change it. Having finished this strenuous exercise (opting for a light tomato mousse as a starter, as regretfully I had been too vain to follow Susan's suggestion to buy loose-fitting clothes), I was able to concentrate again on my fellow passengers.

24

Daniel was engaged in small talk with Marge. I could hear him praising her pearl necklace: "It's very rare nowadays to find a necklace with natural pearls of this size and almost pink lustre. Most pearls are cultured pearls; you must be very proud to own such a wonderful rarity."

Marge blushed with pride. "Oh, I didn't realize that my pearls were so exceptional! You must be an expert in this field. To me, the pearls were always special as my father gave them to me on my twenty-first birthday. I'll never forget that day, my parents organized a wonderful party for me. Now you mention it, my father did say something about this necklace being unique – he had acquired it on a business trip to Japan and had all sorts of problems getting it out of the country and through customs!"

"And you looked stunning that day, honey, I still remember your pink dress… as beautiful as a spring flower."

Marge looked at him acidly, torn between the pleasure of having received a compliment from John and the obvious fact that he had forgotten what she must have been wearing. "It was a white dress, honey, but it doesn't matter, I remember that you were quite cross that day – you wouldn't even look at me in the beginning." She turned towards me and continued in a gossipy tone. "John was a great quarterback at that time in college. All the girls adored him, he looked simply great, such a wonderful leader on the field. But the day before my birthday party took place, his team had lost an important match, and it took a bottle of champagne to make him forget and finally make the effort to look at me."

John grinned a bit sheepishly as she blew him a kiss over the table.

"I've never looked at any other girl since that day," John stated simply.

Regrettably he used this reminiscence as an excuse to start boring me with every detail of this long forgotten match. I have never been a very sporty type of person; American football is a complete riddle to me. All I understand is that overly padded guys are constantly losing their strangely shaped ball while they keep banging their heads together. Remembering my good manners, I continued to look at John with a (hopefully) attentive expression and exclaimed 'oh my god', and 'wow' at regular intervals. I must have been very successful with this strategy as John was glowing with enthusiasm.

"Darling, you're boring Amanda to death!"

"Oh, not at all, Marge, it's fascinating!" I protested. Regretfully John took my comment at face value and didn't listen to his wife. Content to have found a sympathetic ear, he continued to describe the match in the tiniest detail until the waiter interrupted us with the starters. I could only hope that football would not remain our major topic over the days to come. I'd need to Google the basic rules, as sooner or later I'd give myself away and say something ridiculous.

Quickly I seized the opportunity to start a conversation with Daniel. I was almost sure I saw a sympathetic wink in his eye. He seemed to be smiling at me, 'Let me save you from this bore'.

"You clearly know a lot about jewellery?" I opened the conversation.

"O yes, I do, it's a hobby of mine. I can spend hours in a jeweller's shop, drive them to distraction – and then leave without even buying anything!" he laughed. Daniel seemed to be quite the expert in this field, a subject I find fascinating as well, even if my ownership of necklaces and rings seems to be limited mostly to mere costume jewellery. But you can adore a Picasso even if you don't have one hanging in your living room.

Charles Peltier and Frank sat opposite me and I couldn't help noticing that a kind of unease, even visible tension was hovering between the two of them. Frank ate listlessly, but he drank a lot, guzzling the exquisite, honey-coloured Chablis like water. There was no doubt about it, he was sulking like a child. And then there were honey and darling, they were a riddle to me. Marge seemed to be so open and communicative, but wasn't it all just an elaborate façade she had set up? John apparently worshipped his wife, but was it genuine dedication? If you happen to teach in a school, you either end up becoming a subject for a psychiatrist yourself, or you become an expert on human nature.

I had seen many girls like Marge in my classes, fragile flowers on the outside, a core of steel and determination inside. Marge might be a wilted flower by now, but she maintained her aura of beauty and fragility to perfection. I had also met a lot of Johns – nice men, not brilliant, the perfect material for reliable future husbands. But John seemed to be on his guard all the time. Maybe my imagination was running wild, but from time to time he seemed to send her a thoughtful look – was he worried? Why? About what?

Hours later, leaning back in the soft pillows of my Hollywood-style bed, I couldn't get to sleep. It had been a most amazing day. I still couldn't believe that it was really me – lying here in this sumptuous bed! My thoughts wandered to the people who had shared my table tonight. Highly interesting, and what a difference from a bus full of dull fellow teachers. A pity that Susan hadn't joined me, as it would have been great fun to discuss with her every fellow passenger in detail.

Maybe I'd have skipped discussing Daniel though. Handsome Daniel, with his attractive smile…

'Amanda, stop thinking about Daniel!' I chided myself. I was under no illusions; in no time hordes of unmarried females would be chasing him here on the boat. Rich widows or divorcees, skilled at hunting down their next husband. I didn't stand a chance! 'Maybe you can impress him, you talk several languages, you can be witty…' an irrepressible voice inside me suggested. I sighed. I knew that realistically I had no chance whatsoever of making a man like Daniel interested in a teacher from Hamburg, travelling on the cruise of her lifetime. 'You have beautiful green eyes' the stupid voice could be heard again, but deep in my heart I knew that those eyes wouldn't help either. I'd better forget about Daniel.

I must confess that it was a bit difficult to tear my thoughts away from the subject of Daniel, but finally Charles Peltier and his companion occupied my musings. Peltier had run the show later at the table, naturally so – can there be a more fascinating subject than fashion? A topic that has all the thrilling ingredients of money, power, glamour – even drama. And then there was Frank, how should I best qualify him – Peltier's assistant, boy-friend, muse or lover? He hadn't talked a lot. Looking at him without the stress of having to appear on a TV stage, I could see that Frank had the Scandinavian-type of fair and boyish good looks that must have appealed to a designer like Charles Peltier. Frank was a slender young man with broad shoulders but small hips who would show off any designer's creation to its full advantage. Why was he on this cruise? Certainly there was no love or passion between them, I hadn't picked up any such signs from Frank's side! Nor had Charles Peltier been doting on him. Was it just money, the hunger for fame, or was Frank just looking for a new career in the fashion business? I would find out, I was sure. I was curious.

Still sleep wouldn't come and my thoughts raced on to Marge and John, darling and honey. A harmonious couple at first glance, maybe too good to be true. But I was sure that I had sensed some dangerous undercurrents beneath the surface. I suddenly remembered a colleague in school, a man like John, an elderly teacher, devoted to his wife, the heart and soul of his soccer club. Until the day, that was, they discovered that he had embezzled a huge amount from his club's funds in order to pay for the favours of a girl, and to make things even worse, a pupil in his class. Actually she was quite mature, in many aspects, if you ignored her academic achievements. Our principal had managed to hush up the scandal, teacher and pupil were quickly and noiselessly removed from school, the former being pensioned off early and left to the purgatory of married life, the latter (as we learnt later) to a career in escort services which was probably a better match to her undeniable talents than anything else we at school could have taught her. Of course, it's always dangerous to jump to conclusions, but I sniffed a rift, and it would be interesting to continue watching them.

My thoughts went back to Daniel, although they shouldn't. I had no clue as to what kind of person he was. Handsome, a bit too polished in some respects. Why was he still a bachelor at his age? A widower? No, I concluded, nothing sad about him, more likely divorced. Daniel appeared to be keen on jewellery, that much was certain. Unusual for a bachelor – and clearly it was a great passion and not part of his job, he had been quite clear about that point. I suddenly felt a frisson of excitement, remembering the movie *To Catch a Thief* with Cary Grant. Grant had played a cat burglar, who specialized in robbing the most exquisite jewellery from the obscenely rich on the Cote d'Azur. What better opportunity than to sail on a cruise ship like the *Belgravia* – I had seen the most expensive jewellery glittering at every table tonight. Daniel, a gentleman burglar? My wild fantasies were running wild. Somehow I couldn't believe it, but how could I be sure?

I forced myself to drop the fascinating but disturbing subject of Daniel and tried to imagine what the next passengers would be like, and who they might be – wouldn't it be nice if a movie star were among them? Or a retired internet mogul (didn't they retire young nowadays?). But most probably it would be someone much more mundane. No doubt I would find out soon enough.

Day 2 – Southampton and London

I awoke the next morning as bright daylight was filtering into my cabin. That didn't tell me much about the time, as in Northern Europe the sun rises early in summer, and in Scandinavia night doesn't even fall. The steward had reminded us to set back the clocks by one hour and reluctantly I opened my eyes to have a look at the digital clock that was placed next to my bed. It was still early, seven something – but although I tried to go back to sleep, I was too excited: this would be the first full day of my cruise, my big adventure!

I decided to try something that I hadn't done for ages: I'd have breakfast in bed. As I couldn't really decide what to choose (nothing new there, then…), I opted for the full breakfast with all the bells and whistles. About fifteen minutes later the door bell rang (in soothing tones, nothing brash would be allowed on the *Belgravia*) and my steward pushed a large trolley inside, loaded with food. I wondered if unknowingly I had invited someone for breakfast.

"I'll never be able to eat even a quarter of this!" I exclaimed.

The steward smiled at me. He was a pleasant young man with oriental features, probably Chinese. His uniform fitted to perfection and he held himself erect like a soldier. "May I introduce myself, I'm Kenneth. I'm your personal steward on this cruise. If madam has any requests, I'm here to make your stay as comfortable as possible."

"Thank you so much, Kenneth!" I smiled back. What a nice change from my life at school where most people apparently focused on making my life as miserable as possible. I glanced at the dishes. "Those look lovely, but it's far too much!"

"Our American and Russian guests appreciate a full breakfast," he replied, allowing himself a quick smile. "May I serve the eggs Benedict? They're so much better if they're warm and the Hollandaise sauce is still fresh and creamy." He withdrew the silver dome which had covered the delicacy and as the wonderful aroma of fresh Hollandaise, crisp Canadian bacon and eggs filled my cabin, I suddenly felt hungry. While Kenneth poured a cup of steaming hot coffee from a silver jug I discovered that the *Belgravia* had allowed a concession to modern times in the form of a silver-plated thermos flask. I was happy. I like my coffee hot and steamy – and not just the first cup. Kenneth poured the fresh orange juice, arranged the flowers on the trolley and served the toast before he withdrew. I sighed. I could get used to this!

As I sampled my way through the different delicacies that I had ordered at random, I decided not to make my day miserable by counting any calories. I would take a day off. Fired by this bold decision I ate far too much, but the food was so good! A last Danish pastry was fighting for my attention, but I had to surrender, I had already eaten far too much. As I poured a fresh cup of coffee, I was becoming aware that an important decision was now awaiting me. The *Belgravia* would be moored not far from London for a full day; should I disembark and play the London tourist or should I stay on board – and just do nothing? Doing nothing sounded tempting, but I'd have plenty of time to discover the *Belgravia* in the days to come on the Atlantic where there wouldn't be any stops, so London it would be. For once the decision had been an easy one.

Clad in comfortable jeans and a marine-style striped T-shirt I passed the reception desk where I ran into Marge and John, obviously about to embark on the London tourist excursion as well. Marge was wearing a pair of jeans and a bright pink summer blouse. Her outfit was complemented by a large pink straw hat matching the colour of her blouse. She was hiding her eyes behind Gucci sunglasses with lenses the size of saucers. If it hadn't been for John, I might not have even recognized her. John couldn't be overlooked though; his Hawaiian shirt stood out from the crowd, to say the least.

"Gee, who's that?" Marge exclaimed. "Amanda, my dear. Where are you going?"

To be honest, I hadn't made up my mind. Deciding on excursions is as tricky as choosing something from a menu. I never know what to choose: culture is nice, but a stroll through Hyde Park, maybe a quick glance at Buckingham Palace would be tempting as well, you never know if some royals might be driving along the Mall. Susan would die from envy if I could tell her that I had happened to see the Duchess of Cornwall with one of her big hats – or maybe even the Queen. Add to all that the crown jewels, flea markets, Covent Garden and so on, and the list of interesting activities is simply endless. But I couldn't say that, I needed to sound like I knew what I was doing!

"I was actually planning to go to the British Museum," I answered in a brisk tone. "It's been ages since I was there." You're stupid, my inner voice chided me, shopping and lunch in Covent Garden would have been much more fun.

"The British Museum!" Marge exclaimed in a voice full of awe. "May we join you, if you don't mind, my dear? I must confess I never know what to do in London, this city always overwhelms me, I never can decide what to choose. I know it may not be very bright of me, but that's stupid little me." She looked at John who took this rightfully as his clue. "Not stupid, my love, it's normal to feel overwhelmed, it's really quite confusing, this city!"

Marge flashed him a quick gratifying smile and continued: "But the British Museum sounds wonderful, everybody's been talking about it since it was renovated by Sir Norman." I made the appropriate noises, although in reality I had no idea that the British Museum had been renovated lately at all. I guess she meant Sir Norman Foster, the globally renowned architect in demand almost everywhere.

The comfortable bus hired by the *Belgravia* stopped close to Piccadilly Circus. We climbed out of the bus and feeling almost like locals we took the Tube and dived into the usual dirt, stench and chaos of the London traffic. I think I can close my eyes and identify the Tube just by its penetrating smell, a peculiar mix of engines, grime, people, age and certain unsavoury ingredients.

Since we had boarded the bus, Marge hadn't kept quiet for a single minute. I could only pity John. He must have had the patience of an angel. Her topics ranged from fashion to gossip, and unwillingly I became her confidante regarding all kinds of illnesses that had befallen her over the past years. Her stream of conversation continued uninterrupted well into the British Museum. Not really knowing what we wanted to see, we navigated to the section that is close to the entrance and ended up in Ancient Egypt.

It's a big collection and it took us more than an hour to cross only half of it. As a history teacher I am familiar with the VIP pharaohs like the great Ramses, the infamous Hatshepsut and the ambitious Ikhnaton – but don't ask me about the endless list of pharaohs that ruled the Nile delta over thousands of years; they'd challenge the memory of a specialist. I'm always awed by the idea that this civilisation was in existence millennia before the first city in Europe was ever built; to the Egyptians we must look like mere parvenus.

Even Marge's stream of uninterrupted gossip died down as we walked along the endless row of gruesome statues that stared down at us in contempt. They would have regarded us as part of the faceless mass of commoners disturbing the eternal peace of ancient deities, now downgraded to the status of mere tourist attractions. I felt some sympathy for them; they had deserved better.

John, who hadn't talked much so far (not that he or I didn't really have any opportunity to do so), suddenly opened his mouth. "These mummies and statues leave me feeling parched, darling, I think I'm going to have a quick beer outside. I saw a stand selling drinks just in front of the entrance. You can find me there when you're finished with Egypt. I have no idea what's keeping you here, I never saw such a depressing bunch of statues, if I'm honest."

31

Darling opened her mouth as if she wanted to utter some protest, but John had turned his back and was already gone. "Men," she sighed, "aren't they dreadful, but it's so difficult to do without them!"

"I seem to manage," I remarked drily.

"But you're different," Marge said, looking at me with admiration. "You're so strong and independent. I'm afraid that I need a strong shoulder to lean on. I wish I could be a teacher like you or something else, something useful. You know, I never had a proper job in my life, I was just a daughter – and then a wife." I was just about to utter the usual non-committal reply when I realized that she was crying.

"Excuse me," she sobbed. "I once had a daughter, we lost her years ago, but we never recovered from the loss. I still remember that terrible day. The sun was shining, it was such a beautiful day when the police called me. I will never forget. Sometimes I ask myself, why, how can life be so cruel?"

I was at a loss as to what to answer. The usual platitudes wouldn't do. My glance went up to the impassive deities. Yes, Marge was right, they looked cruel. Thousands of years ago, Egyptian mothers must have thrown themselves at their feet, crying over the children or husbands they must have lost. And I was sure that there had been no answer then, either.

"I'm sorry, Amanda, I didn't mean to spoil your day. But since that day John has been drinking too much. I'd better tell you truth right now, you'll notice anyhow, you have a sharp eye."

"It's ok, Marge, I understand. But I don't know what to say, everything that comes to mind just sounds so inadequate. I wish I could comfort you. Sometimes I also wished for children of my own. I still envy my colleagues whenever they announce with pride in the staffroom that they're expecting a baby. I have nothing, not even a husband to care for. But life is like uncharted waters, my father used to say."

Marge smiled and murmured, "Then we're like sisters, I'm really glad that I met you. But not a word to John, please. You have to promise me!"

"Promise! But now let's walk out of this depressing section. I'm afraid John was right. Let's move on to something more cheerful. There are rooms dedicated to the 16th and 17th centuries, my speciality actually. I'll try not to bore you too much, but I can tell you many stories, some quite juicy ones, actually. The ladies may look prudish and aloof, but I can assure you, they were not! "

"You mean they had lovers?" Marge giggled. She liked the idea.

"Loads of them!" I smiled back. "In fact, marriage among noble families was nothing but a political agreement or a kind of contract to increase their wealth. The first child had to be born in wedlock but as for the others, nobody seemed to care too much as long as appearances were kept up."

We decided not to drag John along and spent quite an amusing time in this section, no longer under the cold stares of frustrated deities but looking at jewellery, costumes and pictures of long-gone gentlemen and former society beauties.

"How would they ever have been able to undress in order to go the bathroom, their dresses must have weighed tons. See, this one was loaded with pearls! Look at this Spanish princess, she looks like a doll to me, I guess she could barely move in her dress," Marge exclaimed, while she pointed to the picture of a royal Infanta of Spain, painted in all her regal splendour.

"You're right, her dress weighed tons. It was often interwoven with golden and silver threads as the splendour of her dress was meant to stress the superiority of her royal blood. But to come back to your question: they didn't use bathrooms, there weren't any."

"They didn't use a toilet?"

"Not in our sense, the high nobles had toilet stools, but even the highest born princesses would not wear any underwear at all. Undressing and getting dressed would have been simply too time-consuming."

Marge looked at me. "You must be joking!"

"I swear, Marge, by all we know, that's the truth."

Marge was shocked – how could they!

An hour later we had seen enough of the museum and were hankering after a nice lunch. We picked up John who was sitting outside on a sunny bench with a bottle of beer – he didn't seem to be missing us at all. Together we decided to take the Tube to Covent Garden, as three hours of the British Museum had been enough exposure to ancient culture for one day. In Covent Garden we sat outside on the terrace of a cosy restaurant with a nice view onto the old buildings and the colourful shops while we listened to street singers who tried (but didn't always succeed) their best to cope with the vocal complications of the latest chart-topping songs. We endured the music in a forgiving mood, maybe because we had ordered a bottle of rosé to go with our late lunch and were feeling a bit tired and tipsy from the excellent wine. It was a lovely summer afternoon, almost too hot, as London can become stifling during summer.

"Oh, my God, did you see the time?" Marge suddenly shrieked.

I hadn't but I realized that our bus must be waiting already. Quickly we paid the bill and returned to Piccadilly where our bus was already waiting for us. We were the last passengers and our entrance was welcomed with loud cheers. Once settled in his seat, John started to snore as soon as the bus was set in motion which made us laugh, but I must have fallen deeply asleep as well, as I opened my eyes only when we stopped in Southampton, ready to embark once again onto the *Belgravia*.

Back in my cabin Kenneth appeared with the evening treat of canapés and champagne, but I didn't feel like having anything. "Thank you Kenneth, but we had a late lunch in the city. I really love London, what an exciting city!"

"I hope to study one day in London," Kenneth replied to my surprise. "I'm working on the *Belgravia* to save enough money, as I don't want my parents to pay for my studies;they work hard enough without this extra burden."

"That's great, Kenneth, my best wishes for your future studies. What subject have you chosen?"

"It will be related to economics, but I don't know yet which specialization. At high school I was the best in my class in mathematics. I might become an investment banker – they can make a fortune in no time."

While he was preparing my room for the night we continued discussing the different universities London has to offer (there are plenty, but most of them are outrageously expensive for foreigners) until it was time for me to change into more formal clothes, as dinner time was looming. I didn't feel particularly hungry, but I was curious to meet the new passengers who'd be joining us here in Southampton. Until now, I had enjoyed every minute of my trip. Susan had been right: I didn't regret a cent of the money I had spent so far.

When it was time to leave my cabin, I navigated my way down the long corridor, proud to find my way with only one small detour (why did all the decks look alike on this boat?). Therefore I arrived just after eight at the table where Marge and John were already waiting, occupying their seats of yesterday evening. Marge was sitting in front of a fancy cocktail with a pinkish liquid (called a lychee dream) while John had chosen a classic dry martini. Frank was sitting opposite, his sulking airs of yesterday gone, as he was in animated conversation with a young man I hadn't seen before; he must have been one of the new passengers. They were a striking pair; they could almost have been brothers. The young man rose from the table to greet me. I guessed that he must not be much older than twenty or so.

"May I introduce myself?" he bowed formally.

I was pleased; none of my pupils had ever bowed to me.

"I'm Thomas Olstrom, from Canada, but please call me Tom!"

"I'm Amanda Lipton, but please call me Amanda. Miss Lipton makes me sound so old."

We continued to exchange the usual small talk about the *Belgravia*, the weather and so forth when his eager expression suddenly became clouded, almost petulant, a reminder of how Frank had looked the day before. Stiffly he added, "May I introduce my father, Walter, and his wife, Veronique."

Tom was pointing to a couple who were approaching our table. Walter, actually Sir Walter Olstrom, as I was to learn later, must have been in his early fifties, but looked younger as he had retained his full head of hair. He was fair like his son, with only some light grey streaks showing at his temples. Sir Walter was quite stout though, of a totally different build compared to his slender and tall son. He reminded me of a retired rugby player, all muscle and ready to strike, which reflected his powerful personality. His wife Veronique must have been a good twenty years younger; no wonder that his son was not amused – she could have been his sister.

Veronique was a stunning Asian beauty, slender and graceful, her long black hair glowing in the light of the candles. She walked elegantly on shoes that I couldn't even imagine wearing for 15 seconds, shoes with polished silver high heels of a height that might make them a lethal weapon. Did she need a special licence to wear them? With her looks, she could have taken a modelling job, although she was perhaps a little too short for that. Maybe it's a bit mean of me, but I was happy that I had found at least one shortcoming in her! I always find it depressing to be presented with human perfection. A quick glance in Daniel's direction told me that he had no problems looking at human perfection – why do men always go for a beautiful façade? I felt a pang of jealousy which only reinforced my initial dislike of Veronique. Later I was to learn that the couple had met and married in Hong Kong; it had been a fairytale story of love at first sight – at least on Sir Walter's side.

Veronique was the kind of female that brings out the worst in me, a refined Gucci version of the cruder Claudia. Self-assured, she expected her husband to dance to her attention all the time – and soon I discovered that she expected the same of us – whenever she condescended to take note of us, that is. What annoyed me most this evening was the fact that she continually teased her stepson without mercy, making him appear awkward in the extreme. I could have boxed Tom's father's ears, as he seemed totally blind to the spiteful game his wife was playing. He probably thought Veronique was just being funny. 'There's no fool like an old fool,' the saying goes. Rarely have I heard a statement that's closer to the truth.

Marge was tugging at my sleeve. We were best friends now, I concluded. "It's 'the' Olstroms," she whispered, or at least she thought that she was whispering. I was sure that every single word could be heard across our table.

"Who are 'the' Olstroms?" I whispered back, knowing that I was being impolite, but she had awoken my curiosity, a bad thing to do.

"Sir Walter Olstrom, the Canadian multi-billionaire. Oil, timber, shale gas, he owns it all. He married her last year in December, a surprise marriage, the US papers all covered the story. She's quite brilliant, she's even got a PhD in management." Luckily the waiter had started taking orders and cheers from the neighbouring table drowned most of her comments. I'm not generally one of those superficial women, who goes for money or fame. But who wouldn't be impressed at dining with a real celebrity, a billionaire? The closest I had ever come to a billionaire was Scrooge McDuck from the Disney comics. But I could have done without Veronique; she spoilt the evening.

It so happened that Charles Peltier then entered the room. "Sorry if I'm late, I had a quick drink in the bar, it's the only place where you're still allowed to smoke. I simply can't live without my Cuban cigarillos," he added with an apologetic smile. As Charles Peltier saw the other guests I saw a shadow of dismay flicker across his face as he realized how well Frank and Tom were getting on with each other. Interesting, I thought. He was jealous, I was sure. So Frank must be more than an assistant. No real surprise there. Quickly changing back to his normal jovial self, Charles Peltier introduced himself to the newly arrived guests. I was amazed to see Veronique's reaction though.

"You're 'the' Charles Peltier," she cried, while rummaging in her Louis Vuitton bag until she found her iPhone. She tore it out of its diamond studded case and hastily opened a folder with photos in it. Proudly she put it under the nose of a surprised Charles Peltier. "You see, I wore one of your creations for my engagement party last year!" She was breathless and her face was flushed with pride.

I was amazed. I had never expected to discover that Veronique might be capable of showing real passion beyond dealing with her bank account, but apparently she was a fashion addict.

"This is a very special dress!" Charles Peltier seemed genuinely pleased and looked more closely at the photo. "You see the embroidery on the left shoulder? I had it made in Persia, only in Persia do they still have the skills to embroider the subtle patterns I had designed as I took my inspiration from ancient oriental court dresses. But then all my effort seemed in vain, and our trader couldn't obtain the licence to get through customs. There was no alternative but to have it smuggled out of the country, as nobody in Paris could supply me the intricate stitching that I needed for the golden threads. It cost me a fortune to arrange, but I wanted this special embroidery; without it your dress would have been meaningless, just one of many. I may have broken the law, but we artists are perfectionists, I simply couldn't envisage putting my collection on stage with anything but the best. You have an excellent eye, madam; it's certainly one of the most valuable pieces of last year's collection."

Veronique soaked up his words as a starving bee would soak up nectar. I concluded that Charles Peltier was an excellent salesman, who had sized up Veronique and given her exactly the story she craved.

"I sure paid a fortune for it," Sir Walter interjected. He wasn't used to being ignored. "By the way, nice to meet you, I'm Walter Olstrom, Veronique's husband. She loves your stuff, I think we must have a wardrobe full of Peltier dresses, coats, shoes – she's a great fan of your designs."

Peltier made a small bow towards Veronique. "I'm honoured – and let me add that it's the dream of any designer to work for a customer like you, a woman who knows how to wear fashion. How often we have to deal with customers who shouldn't really be wearing haute couture at all... a nightmare."

Veronique sat at the table, eyes glued to Peltier as if he were a pop star, while Peltier savoured her adoration. Like any artist he loved to be worshipped. Well, who wouldn't?

I had noticed that our table had been laid for one more additional person. It was unlikely that the waiter should have made an error, not on the *Belgravia*. I hadn't even finished my train of thought when the missing passenger appeared. Looking insecure, he was lean and tall, a man in his late forties. In truth he looked as if he had landed from a different planet and was trying unsuccessfully to figure out how and why he had arrived here. His evening attire was of undefined age and ill fitting, he wore large glasses and his head was crowned with a mop of untidy fair hair. His blue polka-dot bow-tie sat slightly askew. His appearance was a clear sign that our new fellow passenger must be a colleague from the academic world, most probably British. His astonished baby-blue eyes examined us as if he was having problems remembering why he was standing here at all. Luckily I knew how to deal with this type of person. I had met plenty of those forlorn intellectual fellow teachers in school and at university.

As he was standing there, lost for words and unsure what to do, I rose from my chair and greeted him with a welcoming smile. "Hello, you must be the missing link on our table tonight! Let me introduce myself: I'm Amanda, this is Marge and her husband John, welcome to our table!"

He smiled at me, thankful that I had saved him from being awkward. His smile transformed his face, making him look younger, almost boyish, quite handsome. I blushed as I saw his eyes appraising me. He looked at me like a professor would look at a promising student. "May I introduce myself? I'm Neil Hopkins."

"Do you teach at a university, by any chance?" I couldn't help asking.

He laughed. "I can't deny it, but is it so obvious? What gives me away? The bow-tie?"

"Not only that!" I smiled back. "I'm a school teacher myself. I guess I can catch the scent of fellow teachers when they're still miles away."

"What's your subject? Let me guess: it must be something like arts or... languages maybe?"

"English and history, you're right, how did you guess?"

"By the way you dress." He winked at me. "I've never seen a colleague from the science department dressed elegantly. They're like me, we start dressing and half way through we remember some interesting question or a problem and get carried away. I'm sure I've forgotten something this evening..."

I laughed. I was starting to like my new fellow passenger. "A comb?" I suggested.

His hand went want up to his head as if discovering for the first time that he possessed any hair at all. Then he smiled at me ruefully. "A comb, you're right, I must look a mess!"

"An intelligent mess." I tried to cheer him up.

38

Neil Hopkins turned to Daniel in order to introduce himself, but Daniel looked at him and immediately cried out, "Professor Hopkins, now that's what I call a celebrity at our table!"

Neil Hopkins blushed like a trapped schoolboy. "Not at all, not at all!"

Daniel looked at me, ignoring Neil's attempts to hush him up. "Professor Hopkins was awarded the Nobel Prize for medicine last year."

Now it was time for me to blush. Wasn't that just typical of me? I have a genuine Nobel Prize winner in front of me and what do I do? I tell him that he forgot to comb his hair! I'm a hopeless case.

In the meantime the other guests realized that we had a celebrity among us. Walter Olstrom was especially intrigued, his wife less so, as I'm sure that she didn't like sharing the limelight. Apparently Sir Walter had just bought a start-up company using Professor Hopkins's research to optimise oil output. How this was linked, I have no idea.

"What is his field of research?" I asked Daniel, hoping not to sound too stupid.

"His specialty is rare toxins that might be used in the war against resistant bacteria, which has led to new insights into the structures of the DNA of bacteria."

Marge answered instead, "A fascinating field of research. He's a great man, a brilliant mind!"

I was stunned. I'd never have guessed that Marge could be interested in Nobel Prize winners and knowledgeable about their field of research.

This evening proved to be even more entertaining than the last. I bathed in the attention of two men, and even John became talkative when he discovered that Neil was a fan of American football (not a fake one like me). And yet, in hindsight, there were a lot of undercurrents. I should have been prepared for trouble to come.

The two young men at our table soon discovered a common enthusiasm for some obscure computer games. I always pride myself on speaking English fluently, but I must confess, I barely understood a word of their conversation full of abbreviations and strange names. Yet I understood enough to notice that their 'games' must culminate in some sort of extensive – hopefully virtual – butchery yielding the possibility of gaining zillions of points which apparently were in high demand in the gaming community. I also noticed that Veronique intervened from time to time; she obviously hated to be ignored. Her comments were supposed to be funny – and Walter probably took them at their face value – but with the subtle viciousness women can use as a weapon, she did everything to make Tom look like a stupid boy, not like the promising young man he actually was.

"I always marvel," she could be heard saying, "how people can obtain hundreds of thousands of points in these games, but manage to ruin the gearbox of my Porsche…"

"Tom!" Walter could be heard shouting. "You ruined her Porsche? It's a collector's item, a unique piece. I had it specially fitted for Veronique – are you mad? What happened?"

"Don't get worked up, darling!" Veronique soothed him but her false motherly tone must have given Tom the creeps. "He's just a boy after all, and boys do make stupid mistakes. It's nothing, I've had it fixed already!" she shrugged.

Tom's face turned scarlet, rather negating his stuttered assertions that he hadn't done anything wrong but had found the Porsche already with a problem. The point is, I had seen in my life many Veroniques and many Toms. I admit that I was biased but I was inclined to believe Tom. I could swear that his stepmother had set him up. As Sir Walter kept pouring scorn on poor Tom I noticed a quick satisfied smile flashing over Veronique's face, as she sat there like a purring cat.

I couldn't follow the rest of their quarrel though as Daniel was interrupting my thoughts with an important question. "Amanda, I've got no clue what kind of dessert I should choose, they all look so tempting. Any bright ideas?"

Of course I had to reply to his plea and give the matter my full attention. After long and careful deliberation we settled for a mousse au chocolat with fresh raspberries served in an almond tulip, a good choice as we were to discover. I adore mousse au chocolat, but rarely do the chefs get it right; they add too much cream, too much sugar and do not use the right chocolate – it must be Belgian chocolate with its strong flavour and distinctive taste of vanilla, nothing else will do. Tonight the dessert was perfect, the creamy chocolate mousse melted in my mouth, the crispy tulip was freshly baked, and added the intense aroma of roasted almonds while the fresh raspberries added a subtle fruity kick. I closed my eyes and felt like I was in heaven.

Coming back to reality I remarked that relations between Charles Peltier and Frank seemed to be complicated as well, to put it politely. Frank had been quite rude, talking with Tom most of the time and had steadfastly ignored most of Peltier's attempts to speak with him. But now Charles Peltier started a new topic of discussion, the forthcoming fashion show in New York.

"Frank, I'm looking for a hair style to match the theme of my new collection, something fresh and unusual, out of the ordinary. I am envisaging a hint, but just a hint, of gothic. That would be great, but it must be subtle, just a sombre note, if you understand what I mean. Marc Antoine had a vampire theme last autumn and it looked awful, like a B-rated Hollywood movie," he shuddered.

Frank responded with interest. He called the waiter to bring him a pen and paper and sketched some ideas onto it. I was surprised to discover that Frank was a very talented artist. Only a few dotted lines, but immediately I could catch the essence. It dawned on me that Charles Peltier might not only be interested in Frank's boyish good looks after all.

"Fantastic, Frank, brilliant!" Peltier showered praise on his protégé.

But it didn't last long and Frank lapsed back into his previous sulky mood and silence. I wondered, wasn't it a fantastic opportunity for an unknown youngster from a provincial TV studio to visit the New York fashion show as the protégé of one of its stars? Being in the limelight with Charles Peltier – he should be out of his mind with joy, so why was Frank so subdued, so quiet? My curiosity was awoken, never a good thing.

Suddenly Tom stood up and left the table with a face like thunder, but I didn't pay too much attention as every family has a bit of drama from time to time. As long as there are people, there will be love, tension and quarrels. 'Happy ever after' is reserved for trashy novels and TV commercials. But nothing that happened at table or that I overheard during that night's dinner prepared me for the events that I was to witness soon. Even looking back, I couldn't have foreseen it. People usually speak about premonitions; well, I had none. I just enjoyed my dinner in the company of fascinating fellow passengers – and two charming neighbours who did their best to entertain me.

As Tom left the table, Frank decided to accompany him. They seemed to be getting on really well together. Weird how similar they looked, like brothers, a handsome pair. Charles Peltier didn't look pleased but he didn't comment on Frank's sudden departure. We all pretended not to have noticed this rift and concentrated on sampling our excellent desserts while our conversation continued at a lively pace.

Neil Hopkins had left his academic ivory tower and became quite talkative during the evening. He thrilled us with terrifying stories about his expeditions. In fact, Neil had spent several months in the Amazon Basin where he had been collecting rare plants, insects of all kinds, then chasing after rare coloured frogs in the quest for rare toxins. He showed us pictures of evil-looking species on his mobile phone and I concluded that I wouldn't fancy having one of those near me any time soon.

Once Neil had overcome his natural shyness, he transformed into a fascinating storyteller. I almost choked on my brandy when he told us how he had woken up one night in Brazil. Drowsy from sleep he had touched the knob of his bedside table-lamp, wondering vaguely why the switch suddenly felt strangely soft and hairy. As the light went on, he discovered a tarantula that had left her hiding place on a night-time hunting foray. Luckily – probably panicking as much as he was – the tarantula retreated fast into a dark corner and didn't consider him serious prey.

Daniel tried his best to top this story by telling a hair-raising tale of his climbing exploits in the Highlands, but to no avail – we all agreed that he couldn't beat the story of the tarantula.

Marge was still shuddering when we left the table. "I hate spiders of all sorts, Amanda, I'd have dropped dead right on the spot, frightened to death. Just imagine, this horrid spider ran off into a dark corner – how could Professor Hopkins even close an eye afterwards? I'll have John check our cabin tonight thoroughly, and if I set eyes on even the smallest spider, I'll have a fit!"

Dinner finished and our group dispersed into different directions. Daniel, Neil and Charles Peltier voiced their intention to take a drink in the bar where Charles could savour an after-dinner cigarillo. Marge, John and I decided to fetch our coats and stroll along the deck before joining the gentlemen later in the bar.

As we left the Westminster Grill, I could hear Veronique's vitriolic voice hissing, "Are you proud that your precious son has left with that fag? It's no secret why this nobody, Frank, has joined Peltier. Peltier may be a genius but he's as gay as they come. I'm getting used to the idea that Tom's a total failure but I always thought that at least he was straight!"

"Hush, Veronique." Walter tried to calm his irate wife. "Everybody will hear you. Tom's still very young…"

"If you don't take care, your son will be in the tabloids: 'New lover boy for the heir to the biggest fortune in Canada' – do you want that?" I couldn't hear Sir Walter's answer as he had quickly dragged Veronique away from the crowd but I saw them gesticulating as they strode in the direction of the lifts, Veronique no longer walking like the fragile catwalk doll she usually pretended to be, but marching with long strides, like the Chinese People's Army on manoeuvres.

As soon as I had fetched my coat I met my new friends at the exit to the middle deck. I was glad to have brought a coat along, as the fresh air was wonderful but chilly. We walked alongside the railing while we listened to the reassuring humming noise of the ship's engine and the gurgling of the foaming water below the *Belgravia*'s bow. I closed my eyes and let my tongue taste the hint of salt on my lips, a taste so typical of the North Sea, a sea I've loved since I was a child. Put me on a boat and I'm happy.

Marge suddenly discovered that she had torn her tights. "Oh look, Amanda, how stupid of me. But I can't really join you folks in the bar like this, I look terrible." I tried to convince Marge that nobody would even notice her mishap in the dim light of the bar, but she insisted on making a quick detour to her cabin and changing them. There was no way of making her change her mind, and to be honest, I'd have done the same. Marge therefore hurried back to her cabin while I remained alone with John. There was a moment of silence, a nice change after Marge's incessant talking. While we watched the star-studded firmament I couldn't suppress the thought that it could have been a very romantic rendezvous if Daniel had been standing close to me and not John… or maybe even Neil…

Some minutes later, we broke the silence and started the usual small talk about the wonderful cruise, the weather and so on. Suddenly John cleared his throat. "Amanda, may I ask you a question regarding Marge?"

"Why not, she's your wife, why shouldn't you be allowed to ask me something about her?"

John didn't answer directly. I could see that he was fighting with himself, and suddenly his face looked grim. "Did Marge make any private confessions to you?" he asked bluntly.

I was taken aback. I hate such direct questions, I prefer a more subtle approach. "Well, I'm sorry, I'm mean, yes, she did actually. But don't worry, she explained to me why and I can fully understand, that under such circumstances, I mean, it's been a terrible blow…" I was lost in my own words and hated myself for being so awkward.

"She told you that we lost our son?" he asked, not willing to beat around the bush.

"Yes, I mean no, she mentioned your daughter, an accident, I understand…" I hated every second of this painful conversation.

"So it's a daughter this time. Well, you see, Amanda, we never had any children, it wasn't meant to be. I'm afraid that Marge never came to terms with this, but I'm really worried, as it's not the first time she's invented things. It frightens me. Her mother died peacefully, but they'd had to put her away, I don't know what to do. Whenever I propose that Marge go and see a specialist, she accuses me of wanting to put her away as well. This is why we travel all the time. 'At home they'll see through me,' she used to say. I'm sorry to share my troubles with you, but I'd better tell you the truth. I love my wife, whatever she says, and I'll take care of her. But I thought you'd better know. Promise me though, not a word to Marge!"

"I promise!" I said, but I must admit, I was rather confused. Marge didn't give the impression of being imbalanced, or needing a psychiatrist. After Marge's disclosure that morning that John might be a heavy drinker I had watched him discreetly during dinner. Although the waiter had filled our glasses with the most magnificent wines, John had never emptied his glass. In fact I must have been drinking more than John (and I'm not a heavy drinker) – either John had remarkable self-control in public, or Marge had made the story up. But why? Now, as John was talking to me, he seemed sober enough. Luckily I was spared further confidences as Marge appeared, a bit breathless as she must have been hurrying to catch up with us.

"Sharing confidences?" she joked.

"Oh yes, but we won't tell you which ones!" I answered in a light tone. Having enjoyed enough of the fresh air we decided to join the other passengers in the bar.

There we had a hilarious night. First Daniel convinced me to try a cocktail called 'Sex on the Beach' – quite good actually, then persuaded me to sing a song with him, as a sort of improvised karaoke. I'm not good at singing at all, but at least nobody left the bar howling in protest. It was long after midnight when we said good night and split up in order to return to our cabins.

I had just reached my cabin door when I realized that I must have lost one of my earrings in the bar. Nothing serious, as I only wear costume jewellery – and for good reason, as I always seem to manage to lose something. But it was still annoying as the earrings matched my necklace and I decided to give it a try; maybe someone had found my earring and had handed it to the bartender for safekeeping. I walked back to the bar and found it less crowded now. Only the old faithfuls would stay on until the early morning; I guess some people live their life on a bar stool.

The bartender recognized me immediately. "Can I serve you one more 'Sex on the Beach'?"

I laughed. "Thanks, that was enough sex for one evening!"

"We could crown it with a 'Screaming Orgasm'," and he winked at me. He was a handsome guy and he knew it.

I declined his invitation politely. "Actually I came back as I lost my earring. Has anyone found it, by any chance?"

He frowned. "I don't think so, but let me have a look. Was it valuable?" He looked concerned. I guess most guests had jewellery worth thousands of pounds.

"Don't worry too much, it's just costume jewellery, but I like it very much and it matches my necklace. It would be great if you could find it!"

"Sure, don't worry. I'll have look right now, you can join me if you want to!"

Quickly the bartender searched the corner where I had been sitting, but although he moved the furniture, we couldn't find anything. "What else did you do tonight, madam, did you sit anywhere else?"

"I massacred Celine Dion's 'My Heart Will Go On', you must remember me, I was terrible."

He flashed me a quick smile and walked to the microphone, where indeed he spotted my missing earring lying on the piano. I could have hugged him but I gave him a fat tip instead. I'm pretty sure he'd have preferred this option.

Happy to have found my missing earring, I walked straight back to my cabin with all the best intentions of getting undressed and going to bed like a good girl should. But after this incident I wasn't feeling tired any more. It had been a fascinating day, I had met the most interesting people – and best of all, I hadn't seen any fellow teachers! Instead I had bathed in the attention of two charming men. What more could I ask?

Yielding to temptation I opened the bottle of champagne that was waiting for me in a silver ice bucket. I sipped a glass of champagne, but still no fatigue would set in; I was still ready to conquer the world. I flicked through the TV channels but there was nothing that grabbed my attention. What else could I do but sneak out of my cabin and stroll around the *Belgravia* until I felt tired? I took a last sip of my champagne, savouring the bubbles that tickled my tongue, then I grabbed my coat and left my cabin.

Until early into the night all decks were lit with glaring floodlights, as there were plenty of passengers moving around, some of them playing tennis or squash until the late hours or doing their daily jogging – weather permitting. But after midnight the lighting was toned down and to my dismay there were plenty of dark shadows. I didn't feel insecure – who'd want to have a go at someone who must probably be the poorest passenger on board – but I must admit, I didn't feel completely at ease either. I left the deck and opened a door that led to a corridor, thinking it might be more comfortable to walk inside. Soon I discovered that I had ended up in the part where the most expensive suites were located. During dinner I had overheard that Frank and Charles Peltier were staying in the Princess Royal Suite, the King's Suite and Queen's Suite having been booked already by other passengers. I guessed that Sir Walter Olstrom and his wife must be residing in one of those.

Feeling like an intruder I almost tiptoed further on, but as I progressed further it was impossible to ignore the sound of angry voices echoing through the corridor. I know that any well-behaved person should have left immediately, but although I pride myself on being well-educated, my curiosity was stronger and I was irresistibly drawn closer to the argument that was unfolding close to me. As I reached the door of the Princess Royal Suite I understood why I could hear their quarrelling so clearly, as the door had been left slightly ajar.

"You're nothing but a spoilt brat and an ingrate!" Charles Peltier was shouting at the top of his voice. I could almost see his face in my mind's eye – he must have been frothing with rage. "I offer you the world, I pay a fortune to get you on a luxury trip anyone else could only dream about – and what do you do? You leave the restaurant together with this boy from Canada – you were probably banging him round the next corner!"

"You're sick!" Frank's voice was almost cracking under the strain. "You make me laugh – the great Charles Peltier is offering me the cruise of a lifetime. You're so generous, I'm stunned! I played on the playstation with Tom, you filthy pig, nothing else. And there will be nothing else going on between you and me either, I'm not going to become yet another of your toy boys you play with for a month or two. You and I know the truth, you need me! You were desperate, burnt out – the great Charles Peltier had no idea what to present for his next collection. Then you saw my sketches, the winter theme – shades of white, combined with woven Russian folklore motives but I had given them a new life, modern, no kitsch – and you knew that this would save you. I saw the pictures of your new collection, you added a bit of glamour, silver embroidery, you gave it more warmth, but basically you stole all of my ideas – and now I'm being fed a morsel of luxury, Frankie-boy is allowed to go to New York, to share a bit of the limelight of the great fashion designer! But not with me, 'mit mir nicht'!" Frank was so angry that he had lapsed into German.

46

"You filthy nothing! What sketches? I don't know what you're talking about."

"You know very well, you took photos of them, but you didn't realize that my webcam was recording you – I have proof, the great Charles Peltier is nothing but a thief of ideas – a marketing machine at best."

I heard steps, heavy breathing, the noise of a body falling heavily on a chair or sofa, and after a minute's silence, Frank's cold voice. "Stop this cheap soap-opera act, you and I, we know the truth. The world doesn't need to know, but I have my terms…"

The rest was silenced as Frank must have discovered the open door and pushed it shut with one angry move. I felt let down. Having heard their argument from the beginning, I was burning with curiosity as to what kind of reward Frank would claim. His last words had had the foul taste of blackmail. If Frank was so upset, so morally injured, why had he ever agreed to join the cruise? He must have just been waiting for the right occasion to present his demands. There had been a boy in my class, he had known for weeks that a fellow pupil had stolen his mobile phone, but he had waited patiently before making it known, to be sure that he could steal the other boy's girlfriend. How offended he had seemed, how cleverly he had prepared his case…

I walked on, deep in thought, and took the lift. I don't even remember which button I must have pushed, but somehow – after trial and error – I ended up on one of the upper decks that would lead to my cabin. Having enjoyed enough drama tonight, I suddenly felt dead tired. I undressed, quaffed a glass of water (no more champagne, enough is enough) and fell into my Hollywood-style bed. I was starting to get used to the luxury of my stately bed, which presented a potentially tricky development; at home only a frugal bed from Ikea, assembled with more enthusiasm than skill, would be waiting for me.

Day 3 – On the Atlantic

It didn't come as a surprise that I had slept late – again. Therefore I decided to wallow once more in the luxury of having breakfast in my cabin. This had been a fabulous treat and demanded a rerun! Twenty minutes after I had given my order over the phone, Kenneth appeared with the silver trolley. Today I had opted for a choice of oven-warm waffles and scrambled eggs, but as soon as I put the phone down I was tempted to change my order to fried eggs. When will I ever be able to decide on something and stick to it?

Kenneth looked almost smug, radiating satisfaction. As he arranged the fine china with the crest of the *Belgravia* and the silver cutlery on my table, I couldn't help asking: "You look happy today, no annoying guests at this time of the day?"

He smiled. "On the contrary, I received some good tips yesterday and this morning, I really cannot complain. If my luck continues, I'll be able to afford to go to the LSE after serving a year or two on the *Belgravia* ."

"Wow, the London School of Economics, that sounds expensive," I remarked. I'm not a specialist but even I was aware that he'd need a substantial wallet to study there.

"It is, but it's one of the top-ranked universities," Kenneth answered, and added after a short pause, "I want the best."

"Who were the generous guests then?" I couldn't help asking.

"Yesterday evening I helped out in the King's Suite as the senior steward was not available. The guest staying there is one of the richest tycoons in Hong Kong, maybe you've heard of him – Richard Wu. When he discovered that I was born in Hong Kong we soon found out that our ancestors come from the same village in Guangdong province, which means, according to Chinese tradition, we're considered relatives. He encouraged me to aim to study at the LSE and gave me a most generous tip." Kenneth's voice was full of awe.

"Richard Wu, no idea, should I know him?"

Kenneth quickly listed some well known brands and Russian petrol companies of which he was the major stakeholder. I was impressed.

"But that's not all, lately he acquired a large stake in a Canadian gas field, you know the new thing – shale gas."

I did know. Claudia had asked us to sign a petition to stop the extraction of shale gas, and for once I had some sympathy with her. I didn't like the idea of pumping millions of tons of chemicals into the ground to release the gas, somehow it felt weird. "And then, who else was so generous if I may ask?"

"This morning there was a bit of a drama in the Queen's Suite. The Canadian billionaire, Olstrom, is staying there with his young wife. She's Chinese as well. When I entered to serve the breakfast I heard her shouting, first in English, that her precious diamond ring had disappeared, then later she switched to Cantonese, cursing her worthless stepson who she thought must have stolen it. She was really worked up. I managed to calm her down and started to search. Ten minutes later I found the ring. She had left it hanging on the soap dispenser."

"That was clever of you, Kenneth!" I was impressed.

"Not that clever, it happens more often than you imagine. But her husband was so relieved that he pressed five hundred pounds into my hand. I was so stunned, I almost forgot to thank him."

"That's really a lot of money. I'm afraid I won't be able to come up with that kind of a tip!"

"Oh, we know – and that's ok with us, madam. We all know that you won this trip, in a TV show or something like that. We wouldn't expect you to be so generous, don't worry."

I thanked him as he left the cabin but his last remark had the effect of sobering me somewhat. Having dined and partied with my fellow passengers, I had forgotten that I was the Cinderella on this cruise ship, but Kenneth had opened my eyes to the fact that all the others certainly wouldn't forget it.

As I looked out of the window of my cabin, I could see that the weather had changed and the sky was shrouded in grey. Spending my morning on the deck in a lounge chair didn't seem so inviting now. I decided therefore to pursue my exploration of the *Belgravia*. There was so much to see and to discover! I scanned my wardrobe to find something smart but comfortable enough, then suddenly I stopped and had a closer look: my clothes had been rearranged and neatly folded. Either this was a special service offered by the *Belgravia* – or Kenneth was a bit too curious for my liking.

Next I looked at my shoes – elegant versus comfortable. I chose the comfortable sneaker option; there was a chance that I might end up in the ship's gym, not a very likely one, but at least I'd be prepared. Having had a full breakfast, a bit of exercise would be the right thing to do, so I tried to motivate myself.

But the gym never got to see me as unluckily (or maybe luckily) I discovered the *Belgravia*'s library, my last stop after a good two hours strolling around the ship. I had spent a good portion of my time in the sprawling shopping mall although I was just browsing the shops for fun. My clothes were brand new, so I didn't really need anything. I was quite proud of myself – usually I yield to temptation. And so, exhausted from my virtual shopping spree I was happy to have discovered the safe haven of the ship's library, a cosy universe tucked away in a quiet part of the ship. The library offered a large choice of new hair-raising best sellers, but also a solid selection of historical fiction and British crime stories, my favourite books when it comes to passing the time and relaxing. As I sank into one of the broad, comfortable leather armchairs with a book that had aroused my curiosity, time stood still and my mind travelled far back to the seventeenth century.

The next time I looked at my watch, I saw that it was already half past one, time to go to lunch. But I didn't feel hungry; my hearty breakfast of scrambled eggs followed by Danish pastries had had the effect of making me feel like an overfed python. I preferred to continue reading and would look for a nice cup of coffee later on, maybe two. One hour later, my fascination for the adventures of my heroes was starting to dwindle as I was craving a cup of coffee by now. I would keep the book and continue reading it later in my cabin, but now it was definitely time to start my quest for a cup of coffee.

Early afternoon is a very quiet time on a cruise ship, I was soon to discover. This holds some logic, as most passengers retreat to the shelter of their cabins for an extensive nap or siesta after lunch. Although, of course, the numerous honeymoon couples may have different priorities on their minds when they return to the intimacy of their cabins. A ship has her own rhythm and you're lulled into this routine. It's part of the charm of going on a cruise that the usual breathtaking speed of life seems to slow down, and time flows gently by like the ocean that surrounds you.

I suddenly remembered that I had discovered a nice place for a coffee break the day before. The Buckingham, a small and relaxed place, a kind of coffee shop, nestling beneath a huge glass veranda, was an ideal place to take a cup of coffee while watching the ocean and the occasional seagulls without being disturbed by a chilly breeze. The only inconvenience was that the Buckingham was located on the opposite side of the cruise ship, which meant at least a good twenty minutes' walk from my library. For a good minute I hesitated, thinking of returning to my cabin and ringing for Kenneth to serve me a cup of coffee but the better part of me took this as a good opportunity to get some exercise and so I opted for the coffee shop.

Once I had made up my mind, I shoved my book into my Mary Poppins handbag and left the library. I'm not endowed with a keen sense of direction and soon I was lost in those endless, silent corridors that house a good two thousand or more passengers. Thick carpets muffled the noise of my steps as I walked. I could have been part of an old silent movie, lost in time and space. I didn't feel especially at ease. You know of course, that on a ship like the *Belgravia* nothing untoward can happen, but on the other hand, walking alone through endless and deserted corridors left me with a creepy feeling. I could have been the only living human being around, and apart from the reassuring humming noise of the engines an eerie silence engulfed the ship.

As I arrived at a hallway that connected to one of the outer decks I saw a figure hurrying through one of the doors. I felt relieved that I didn't seem to be only human being around. For a fleeting second I saw Daniel's face, or at least I was almost sure that it must be him. What was Daniel doing here at this time of day? But before I had the chance to greet him and make him aware that I was here, Daniel had already disappeared as fast and noiselessly as he had appeared before.

On my own once again, I opened the door to the deck (I have forgotten which one, maybe deck twelve or thirteen) where a fresh breeze and – to my great surprise – the sun greeted me. The drab, sulking sky that had confined me to the library that morning was forgotten. A harmless flock of scattered clouds were dotting the blue sky like lazy sheep, giving the Atlantic an almost Mediterranean feeling. I was thrilled and sighed happily – this was exactly how a journey on the sea should be like! Sitting in a cosy library is nice of course, but breathing the wonderful fresh air while listening to the lulling sound of the foaming ocean beneath me was something entirely different, a wonderful and soothing experience.

I squinted and scanned the horizon, trying to figure out where the azure sea ended but my vision was blurred by the blinding light. The ocean was bathed in sunshine, a boundless carpet of molten blue. Miles and miles away the sea blended seamlessly into the sky, an amazing blue world without limits. I scanned the ocean but I couldn't spot any fellow ships. Only the clouds and the occasional seabird were our faithful companions while the *Belgravia* cut majestically through the foaming ocean.

I had stopped at the railing from where I could not only watch the ocean, but also had a good view onto some of the other decks, lying quiet and deserted like the rest of the ship at this time of day. The sun was really nice and warm; why not stop here for a break? The cup of coffee could wait. I found a spot, nice and sunny, hidden from troublesome draughts by a large protective windbreak where I settled comfortably in a lounge chair that, by a stroke of luck, must have been reserved especially for me. I must have dozed off for some minutes until a gust of chilly wind woke me up and reminded me that I was after all on the Atlantic Ocean and not cruising along the shores of the sun-baked Mediterranean.

As my eyes tried to adjust to the glaring light, I noticed the shadow of a fellow passenger, or to be precise, two of them passing by, one following the other. I'm quite sure that they must both have overlooked me. As they disappeared towards the bow of the ship, I wondered if this could have been Tom, maybe followed by Frank – didn't they look surprisingly similar? How could anybody tell them apart, especially from a distance and just seeing their silhouette from behind? Fashion dictates that boys today all wear the same style of shapeless hooded sweatshirts, with jeans slung so low that you can see their underpants (if not something even more unsavoury), and to make it even more confusing in this case, Tom and Frank looked almost like twin brothers.

Basking in the sunshine, I had nothing else to do or worry about, so my mind continued to dwell on this question, trying to figure out if it could have been Tom and Frank, or possibly both, whom I had seen passing by. Compared to the taller figure in front, the second person seemed to be quite slender, almost delicate, at least – but maybe I was mistaken and I was misjudging their size from my perspective. From my sheltered position I could see both boys standing some distance apart at the railing. One of them, the slender one, pointed towards some point on the horizon. Immediately I tried to figure out what could have aroused his interest – maybe he had spotted another ship or perhaps a whale on the horizon.

I couldn't see anything special though, not even a small trawler, but as my eyesight is not my strongest point I wasn't astonished as such. I was a bit disappointed though, as I'd have loved to see a whale. The slender boy beckoned his companion over and waved excitedly at something. Almost automatically I stood up and tried to follow the direction of his arm but this made me look straight into the sun, a move I regretted instantly as the glaring sun hurt my eyes and I had to close them.

Seconds later I opened my eyes again and gasped: I saw Tom – or was it Frank? – leaning over the railing, looking at the sea, and then suddenly the other boy bent down, grabbed both of his legs and tipped him in a swift movement overboard. It looked so easy – over and done with in a second.

I remember crying out, "No! Stop!" – how stupid of me!

There are moments in your life you can never forget, however hard you try. They stay engraved in your memory forever. Heroes tend to know what to do and how to act, but I was to discover that I was not born to be a hero. I was just frightened, a bundle of nerves, paralyzed. Had I heard a scream? I don't think so. Had I been dreaming? For a second I hoped that all had been just an illusion. I closed my eyes, hoping to find myself somewhere else once I opened them again. But of course this was silly, I was still standing on the deck of the *Belgravia*, the sun was shining, and the only difference now was that the deck was totally deserted.

A peaceful silence, only interrupted by the random cries of the ever greedy seagulls, reigned while the ship glided through the ocean. The mere thought that I could have just witnessed a terrible accident, let alone a murder, seemed like *lèse majesté* to the *Belgravia*.

I must be mad. The deck was empty, all was calm, I must have been day-dreaming. I've heard about that, people can fantasize, apparently it happens to everybody. So why shouldn't it happen to me? It was a comforting thought, but deep in my heart I know that I've never been prone to fantasizing. I'm simply not good at inventing things.

But I needed to know, to be certain. I rushed forward to the railing, to the very spot where I had seen the two boys before. I felt very uneasy as I leant over – I think I expected a hand to appear from nowhere and push me over as well. But all I could see were crowns of white froth on the greyish sea and the ship's bow cutting majestically through it. No head or body bobbing on the waves; it all seemed so peaceful. I must have been dreaming.

I grabbed my coat and started running, fleeing from the deck, trying to escape from this nightmare, frightened to death. Instinctively I avoided the long and deserted corridors, as like a headless chicken I careered along the alleys of the shopping mall, collided with furious passengers out jogging, almost knocked down a little boy in search of his toy. All I wanted was to be back in the safety of my cabin. At least at that moment I was convinced that I'd be safe there.

'You coward,' a voice inside me was raging, 'you must raise the alarm, immediately! The poor boy may be fighting for his life, just imagine, drowning in those cold waters...' The voice of reason answered, 'That's impossible, it couldn't be. Just imagine making the captain stop the ship. It will cost a fortune, people will be mad at you – all for the fleeting impression of a second, you weren't even fully awake, you couldn't even swear that you saw anything at all! Stop being hysterical.'

I simply couldn't decide what to do. I was reduced to a bundle of nerves, the kind of reaction I usually scorn in others. Blinded by the tears I was trying so hard to suppress, I suddenly bumped into someone. I simply hadn't seen him approaching. My nerves were so on edge that I screamed. Even looking back today I'm still ashamed. I must have appeared quite melodramatic.

"That's no way to greet a friend!" Daniel greeted me good-humouredly. "At least, until now I was under the impression that I was a friend!" I was so stunned that I didn't know what to answer and an uneasy silence ensued. Daniel looked into my face and without a further word he seized my arm and pulled me firmly but gently inside the bar that was conveniently located in front of us.

I'm an independent woman and I can cope with most things that life throws my way. I don't need a man meddling with my affairs – or worse – telling me what to do or what not to do, and yet, I'm ashamed to admit, I was thankful to have a broad shoulder to lean on. Gently Daniel made me sit down before he left for the counter while I tried to regain my composure. Minutes later he came back with a steaming beverage in his hand, Irish coffee, the perfect brew for my nerves. I started to sip the hot coffee and while the fire of the whisky and the warmth of the coffee spread through me, Daniel opened the conversation: "Now, let me know if I can help you in any way. If it's something personal, it still might be good to talk, even if I'm a stranger. Sometimes, I find it's actually easier to talk to a stranger than to your own family or close friends."

He looked at me with his dark brown eyes. They seemed very kind, very understanding. I had to suppress an urgent impulse to throw myself into his arms, but even in my present state of mind I was lucid enough to know that this would not be a good idea.

"I must look completely stupid!" I croaked.

Daniel answered by making some soothing sounds, although he probably thought that I was completely stupid.

"Daniel, I simply don't know what to do! I'm almost sure that I saw a murder only minutes ago, but I keep telling myself that it's simply impossible, I must be mad. I really don't know what to do!" My hands were suddenly shaking and I splashed some Irish coffee on the table.

Daniel looked at me. I guess he wasn't sure himself what to do or what to say. In his defence, it's rather unusual that you go on a luxury cruise and are expected to discuss a case of murder with your fellow passenger who looks as if she's close to breaking point. Given these unusual circumstances, he rose admirably to the challenge.

54

"Tell me exactly what you saw, Amanda. I know enough about you to understand that you don't invent things. If it was Marge telling me this…"

I was flabbergasted. How come he knew that Marge had a loose grip on reality sometimes? Daniel insisted gently and I obliged. I told him every detail. First I gave a quick résumé of my visit to the deck, the sheltered lounge chair I had found, I even mentioned that I had dozed off for a short nap, then told him about the two people who had passed by me – and finally the scene where the taller boy went overboard – the emptiness – and my panic.

Daniel listened attentively, he made me repeat every step exactly. I guess he wanted to make sure I didn't contradict myself. But I didn't. This horrid scene would stay in my memory forever.

"That's no dream, Amanda! This sounds far too realistic to be just some fantasy or a bad dream." He rose and strode to the counter. "Get me the first officer, immediately!"

The bartender obeyed instantly. Daniel had spoken with the voice of authority. I heard him barking some sentences into the phone, then he returned to my seat and made me gently drink some more Irish coffee. I must admit, this worked wonders on my morale, and my hands became steadier. Only minutes later a young officer rushed into the bar in order to guide us to the captain's bridge.

My image of ships had been formed by films where the officers and their captain are invariably standing in gleaming white uniforms behind a huge mahogany ship's wheel, stroking their well-kept beards pensively while they keep looking out to sea with a reflective frown, hoping to spot a whale, or oil tanker, if not a dangerous iceberg. Alternatively they should be busy drawing mysterious symbols on ocean charts to avoid collisions with random islands or shallow reefs. But as the door opened, I arrived in a sort of business-like office with a 360° view onto the ocean, studded with computer screens and joysticks. The only part that matched my image was the white uniforms.

Daniel greeted the captain and explained in swift words the situation. I was fully prepared to be cross-examined and to dig in my heels and defend my position – thanks to the Irish coffee I was ready. But I was wrong again. I was just being questioned to describe exactly where I had been; luckily I could identify the deck and my exact location because I had seen the shuffleboard just below me, which gave the captain a clear indication of my position. I was now to discover that the *Belgravia* was equipped with a network of spy cameras. Daniel explained to me that all of the tiny glass domes we could see in the corridors and outside were in reality webcams. It took only two minutes and I could see on the monitor two figures approaching, they disappeared quickly but were then immediately picked up by a second camera, and worst of all, I had to witness the horrible scene once again: the killer grabbing the legs of Frank or Tom – and we all saw the victim disappearing into the sea.

I cried out, "No!" As if I could undo the crime! Then I covered my face and I started to cry. The cold proof was there: it hadn't been my imagination running wild, it was murder, beyond any doubt.

Daniel took me into his arms to comfort me and from the shelter of his embrace I saw that all hell was breaking loose on the bridge. The captain bellowed a command and ordered the engines to be stopped, or put into reverse. His officers called the coastguards of Ireland and France – whoever was closer – and all the ships in the vicinity were informed and requested to join the rescue operation. Helicopters were to search from the air with infrared cameras, probably the only chance of finding the victim. But the captain made no secret of the fact that the chances of survival in those cold waters were infinitely small, and only a miracle could save them. Even if I had reported the incident immediately, the chance of finding the person alive would have been practically zero, he told me, in an attempt to comfort me.

"The *Belgravia* is too large, it would push any small object or a person immediately below the surface; but all the same we have to launch a rescue operation, we owe it to the passenger. Do we have a chance of even retrieving the body? I don't think so." He paused. "Miss Lipton, we're obliged to you. Without your vigilance, murder would have been committed without anybody ever having noticed it. Normally our cam recordings are only be kept for 24 hours for reasons of guaranteeing the privacy of our passengers. I'm sorry to ask you this, but could you help us to identify the persons you saw on the screen?"

The first officer made some clicks with the mouse and the blurred picture on the screen was enlarged. But to no avail, the images were not clear enough and worse, they showed the figures only from behind.

"I'm not sure, the boy on the right side looks like Tom Olstrom or Frank Mueller, they look very similar, fair hair, quite tall and slender. The second person – I have no idea. I can only recognize a hood and a grey sweatshirt."

"I think it's Tom Olstrom," Daniel could be heard. "At least he wore this kind of sweatshirt when I met him at breakfast – but it's the fashion, it doesn't prove anything. He's staying on board with his parents. Frank Mueller is staying as a guest with Charles Peltier in his suite."

I noticed that the captain's brows moved ever so slightly upwards, but he refrained from any comment. He ordered his officer to check if both passengers could be found on the *Belgravia*. "Please page them, make it urgent!"

"What's worrying me," Daniel continued, turning towards the captain, "is the fact that the murderer avoided the cameras and made sure to keep his hood up. We're dealing with a crime that has been planned, it's no coincidence that he was wearing this outfit. The jeans are loose fitting, the sweatshirt is oversized, it's impossible to recognize anything in particular. This looks far too professional for my taste."

I looked closer at the sequence of images that were repeated again and again. Daniel was right, the murderer made sure never to turn his face, whereas I could see Tom – or was it Frank, turning around at least once, smiling. This completely undid me; how dreadful it was to see the boy walking into a deadly trap, smiling at his killer.

"This confirms the uncomfortable feeling that the murder must have been planned rather than a crime committed in the heat of the moment," I heard Daniel say.

Meanwhile I had come to a different conclusion. I, Amanda Lipton, was the only witness. I swallowed. I didn't like this train of thought. I had seen too many movies where the only witness became the next victim, chased by a ruthless killer. In the movie there was always the presence of a hero, mostly some grumpy kind of cop or detective who was ready to rescue the witness, but this was no movie. Daniel must have been reading my mind as he squeezed my hand quickly; it was kind and reassuring. I didn't even care that it held no romantic notion at all. My mind was on different things – where could I find a personal bodyguard?

We spent the next twenty minutes not really knowing what to do. The suspense in the air was palpable, almost unbearable. You could argue that there was no doubt that a murder had been committed – and yet – it felt strange and nerve-wracking to know that the loudspeakers of the *Belgravia* would be paging urgently for two passengers, one of them who most probably must be dead by now. When the news came that Tom Olstrom had reported his presence to the staff, although there was no hard proof, the fact that there was no answer from Frank Mueller made it a sad probability that it was Frank who had been pushed overboard.

"We'll search the ship to make sure," the captain decided. "Peter, you arrange to meet Mr. Peltier privately in his cabin and prepare him for the news that that there might have been a fatal accident. Don't mention the word 'murder'! This instruction is valid for all of you!" The captain sent a telling glance to his crew,

"Unless you want to become the next victim. There has been no murder; we have to deal with the sad case of a fatal accident. Is this clear?"

"Yes, sir!" the choir of voices answered instantly. I almost joined in.

Peter, the first officer, grimaced but left the bridge without further delay in search of Charles Peltier. I was content that it wasn't me who would be the bearer of this terrible news.

We were dismissed and Daniel was sweet to me, guiding me back to my cabin. He proposed to come back that evening and to take me for dinner to the restaurant. I should have been happy; this was almost like having been invited for a date, but I felt depressed. The first rush of adrenaline was gone and as I fell into a deep black hole, I had problems coming to grips with a peculiar mix of emotions: sadness, compassion, shock – and I'm loathe to confess – a deep irritation that my holiday of a lifetime had been tarnished by an event I could never forget.

Back in my cabin I tried to read, but there was no way of concentrating my mind on the plot of the story. The next exercise was to flick through the channels of the onboard TV, but once again nothing could hold my attention. I longed to call Susan, but when I looked up the charges for satellite phone calls, I dropped the phone like a hot potato – just five minutes would amount to my monthly phone bill in Hamburg. I guess men like Sir Walter don't bother about phone charges, but I do. Especially when I'm speaking with my best friend, when one hour can go by in a flash.

I must have dropped into an uneasy slumber when the door bell rang. No more careless shouting 'Come in'! Nervously I tiptoed to the door and glanced through the peephole. I'm sorry to sound pathetic but my heart was beating as if I were expecting to be electrocuted the second I touched the door knob.

But it was my faithful steward Kenneth who was standing there with the late afternoon trolley loaded with champagne and canapés. There might have been a murder, or an 'accident' as the captain might insist on labelling it, but such an incident was certainly not important enough to stop the well-oiled routine of the *Belgravia* from functioning.

Kenneth pushed the trolley inside and started his usual routine of preparing the cabin for the night. He was busy and efficient, as usual, and yet I could feel that he was bursting with news. "Did you hear about the accident, madam?"

"Not really, Kenneth, what happened?"

"Frank Mueller, the passenger staying with the famous fashion designer, Charles Peltier, he disappeared this afternoon. It seems that Mr. Peltier has been out of his mind since he heard the news. The doctor is with him right now – he needed a sedative!"

I swallowed. This seemed an understandable reaction, but while I had been alone in my cabin, my mind had gone feverishly through all the options – and I had only been able to find three potential suspects: Tom (out of jealousy, rejected love?); Veronique (to avoid a scandal?); and the obvious one, Charles Peltier. He had a lean figure and compared to Frank, Peltier was less tall, he might have been the murderer. Baggy jeans and a sweatshirt could be worn by anybody. Could it be that Charles Peltier was an excellent actor? I noticed that Kenneth was waiting for my reaction. I couldn't just stand there and say nothing.

"But that's terrible, Kenneth! Poor Frank!" I managed to say. "Do you have any idea what happened?"

"Not really, madam, it's all hush-hush. Maybe he'd been drinking too much. Of course the management doesn't like to admit it, but he wouldn't be the first one to go overboard after too much booze. You cannot imagine how crazy some passengers become once they get drunk."

Automatically my hand stopped – I had just been about to pick up the glass of champagne which he had poured for me. But it would do me good, I decided and took a large gulp. The champagne tickled on my tongue, a comforting sensation. Instantly I started to feel a bit better. Suddenly I realized how hungry I was as I hadn't eaten anything for lunch. I couldn't resist and a canapé followed the champagne. Smoked duck breast with fresh fig, not bad at all!

"Anything else I can do for you?" Kenneth asked me. He must have been convinced by now that I was a hard-boiled customer. While he was speaking about a fatal accident, there was I, helping myself to champagne and canapés. My only excuse was that this was an act of self-defence.

"You have no further information? Poor Frank, he never seemed very happy whenever we saw him at our table!"

Kenneth shrugged his shoulders. I couldn't detect much compassion for poor Frank.

"Yes, I'm sure, and I agree it's tragic. Should have been drinking less.... if you ask me, these fashion people lead crazy lives. Maybe it's not even booze but drugs, cocaine seems to be the fashion, who knows? But I have to leave now, Mr.

Olstrom's wife has ordered a noodle soup, Chinese style, for her afternoon snack and she'll not be happy if her soup arrives late or cold!" With these words, he hurried out of the room.

***

I had been convinced that I wouldn't be able to manage any dinner after this ordeal. It may seem unsympathetic of me, but by the time Daniel rang at my door to accompany me to the Westminster Grill, I was really hungry. My only excuse is that this must have been the effect of the champagne. I had consumed a glass more than usual, so I was slightly tipsy by the time Daniel was supposed to call for me and I didn't care anymore if it was the killer or Daniel who might be ringing at the door. It was Daniel, luckily enough.

Somehow it felt good not to be walking alone through the long and silent corridors. But suddenly I felt a cold chill as the image of Daniel hurrying through the deserted corridors flashed through my mind – hadn't I seen him just before the murder took place? What had he been doing there? For a second I contemplated asking him, but couldn't muster the courage.

Paying attention for the first time I suddenly noticed the numerous cameras that blended inconspicuously into the decor. I guessed that someone had been ordered to watch all of these recordings as of now, everything had changed, and our proud ship had become the home of a murderer. I had to suppress an urgent longing to wave at the cameras – it must be the effect of the champagne, I was becoming a bit silly.

We arrived at our table where the general mood – to no surprise – had all the exuberance of a wake. Marge must have been crying, as her eyes were still red. Veronique was absent, as was Charles Peltier. Walter and Tom Olstrom sat in brooding silence. I imagined that Walter had preferred to endure the depressed atmosphere at the table compared to the thunderstorm that must be brewing inside his cabin. Veronique would see the disappearance of Frank as a personal insult, a threat that might tarnish the reputation of the Olstrom name. I was sure that she wouldn't invest too much thought into the situation of her stepson though. Poor Tom, he must be feeling dreadful. He looked as pale as a corpse. I didn't think that Frank had been anything else but a friend with a shared interest in computer games, but losing a friend is terrible enough.

At the beginning of the evening everybody was on their guard, and we barely spoke. But after the first course and the first few glasses of wine, tongues loosened and soon speculation was spreading like wildfire. I guess this is just human nature.

"It must have been drugs," Marge whispered, but as she was rather deaf, her whisper reached the other end of the table and I noticed that Tom shot her an almost lethal glance.

"Why?" I asked her. "Doesn't that seem a bit far-fetched?"

"This is how they stimulate their creativity, I've heard." Marge didn't even try to whisper anymore. "These artists quickly burn out, but they have to keep delivering – cocaine is the stuff, you read it again and again. It's no secret that half of Hollywood is hooked. You see a beautiful face, all radiant smiles and a year later you read that they've disappeared into some kind of institution."

I had to admit, Marge had a point there. But I knew better, it hadn't been an accident, nor a suicide, as Marge was apparently thinking. It had been a planned, cold-blooded murder. I shivered.

Daniel, who knew the truth as well, sent me a reassuring smile, but he decided to pretend to follow Marge's ideas: "You think he took too many drugs then?"

"Yes, an overdose – or he couldn't get enough of this horrid stuff on board and got depressed. Poor soul, it's so sad." Marge suddenly started to cry.

I felt a bit guilty. I suppose I should have been crying as well but somehow Frank had remained very elusive to me. John tried to comfort his wife and quickly she dried her tears. "I apologize, I know I shouldn't behave like this. I'm a bit sentimental. Amanda, I admire you, you're so composed. "

"I don't think it's linked to drugs!" John could suddenly be heard. "When I trained my youngsters in football, I had enough contact with drugs, it's impossible to avoid it. But I'd always know when they started to do silly things, often enough I could intervene on time. Most don't want to take it; if you help them early enough, it's ok, they still have a chance. Frank didn't look to me like a drug addict at all, but he seemed to be very moody   or at least under a lot of stress. You'd be surprised – often it's love. Unbelievable how a bad relationship can ruin a career!"

I was amazed. I hadn't expected John to be such a keen observer. You should never underrate a person! I couldn't answer though, as Neil Hopkins nodded and intervened: "You're absolutely correct, John. I could tell you things about my most promising students. I totally agree with John, I haven't seen any signs of drug-taking either, Frank just seemed to be a very private character. I couldn't help but notice a lot of tension between Mr. Peltier and his protégé. If you think about it, isn't it a bit unusual to sit there sulking if you've accepted an invitation to go on a cruise – I mean normally you're grateful to the person who's invited you and is paying the bill!"

Who'd have thought that Neil was a keen observer of the human species as well. I had thought that his interest was limited to the smaller species – the toxic and the crawling ones. Neil must have been reading my thoughts as he suddenly grinned at me – which made him look much younger, quite attractive. I felt trapped and blushed as he continued, looking into my eyes, "I know that people expect scientists to spend their lives confined in laboratories and solving the great riddles of mankind, but wouldn't that be a bit boring, day and night?"

"Don't other people look or sound ridiculous to you sometimes?" I couldn't help asking.

'Not you!" he answered – and I was speechless.

Meanwhile Tom and his father had managed to bury the hatchet and were discussing some business matters in remote Canada. I could hear the critical phrases 'shale gas', 'land rights', and 'environmental groups' (not in Sir Walter's good books, although Tom seemed to be more open and more realistic as to how to deal with these issues).

Suddenly I caught a snippet of conversation with a name that I had heard before. "I've heard that Richard Wu, that rat, is also on this ship. If he dares to show his face, I'll strangle him. I'm absolutely positive that he was behind this hostile bid. He might be Chinese, but he's in league with the Russians!"

"Sure he is!" Tom laughed. "He invested a fortune in the Russian oil fields – he's got no option but to run with these dogs, and plenty of his money is tied up there!"

"I heard rumours that he urgently needs cash," Sir Walter stated.

"I'm sure that's not only rumours. Why otherwise would he sell his African mobile phone network, it's been producing profits, regular as clockwork. He didn't even launch an IPO, he sold it to a private equity group below value last week. If this doesn't smell bad…"

Walter looked at his son with pride. "You're right, I didn't realize that this could be linked. I'm amazed that you've been following our friend so closely…"

"No, you're convinced that I spend my time doing stupid things like demolishing Veronique's cars." Tom's voice was bitter and Sir Walter fell silent.

62

Nobody was surprised that Charles Peltier didn't show up. Our group dispersed quickly after dinner was finished, and nobody felt like having a drink or visiting the evening show in the Grand Theatre. Our strange dinner hadn't given me any further clue as to the murder. I just noticed by the end of the evening that Tom seemed to have taken a rather cool attitude towards it, which seemed a bit strange, as he had seemed quite close to Frank before.

Later that night I couldn't get to sleep. Even the comfort of my Hollywood bed didn't help. I kept going over the scenes from the afternoon and analysing the reactions of my fellow passengers. Somehow I was convinced that the key to the mystery must be among them, but it was a key that was well guarded and well hidden! And then there had been that casual remark by Neil – had this been an invitation to a bit of flirting?

'Amanda, you're being silly!' I chided myself, but I liked being silly. And, I must confess, I had started to like Neil Hopkins.

Day 4 – On the Atlantic

I must have fallen asleep after all and I'm almost ashamed to confess that no nightmare had marred my slumber. It was Kenneth who woke me up and as he brought a breakfast trolley with him, I couldn't really complain.

"I thought that you must be tired after yesterday's ordeal, madam, therefore I thought that a nice warm breakfast would be welcome. As I didn't know if you'd prefer eggs Benedict or scrambled, I brought both."

I could have hugged him. I'd have a bite of both, one decision less to take! "That's really thoughtful of you, thank you so much!"

"It's a pleasure! By the way, tonight the captain has organized the traditional pirate party, it's the absolute highlight of our cruise. As the weather will be good, we'll also have a barbecue near the pool. You can find all the details here in the *Belgravia News*."

Kenneth handed me the *Belgravia News* of the day. How I would miss Kenneth at home! I don't think that even my mother could ever match this level of service.

"The management will tone it down a bit in view of the accident that happened yesterday, but as they say, the show must go on. But they decided to scrap the part where the passengers are thrown into the pool; the captain said that this would be grossly inappropriate."

Kenneth left and I sat in the comfort of my bed, nibbling happily on a freshly baked croissant with marmalade. I skipped the British breakfast traditions by ignoring the salted butter that should go with it; somehow I had never come to terms with this sacred tradition. The *Belgravia News* consisted of four pages dedicated to world news (the usual disasters and wars on terrorism, ending with the latest woes of the world economy), but much more interesting and edifying were those pages dedicated to social gossip (Veronique Olstrom had been nominated among the ten best-dressed women of the year), the weather forecast (sunny) and the events of the day. A small notice at the bottom mentioned that a tragic accident had taken place. The notice had been skilfully hidden among advertisements for the mall's fashion, underwear and souvenir shops. Clearly it was intended to be overlooked and quickly forgotten.

All passengers were invited to dress up like pirates for the evening. I felt the adrenaline rushing through my veins – I simply love fancy dress parties, I've loved them since I was a child. This promised to be great fun! I made a mental check of the contents of my wardrobe. A striped T-shirt and a pair of jeans would do the trick. I'd add a scarf and some make-up and I'd look like a pirate crew member; more Disney-style than real, of course.

I must have been really tired as I dozed off again after my sumptuous breakfast, which meant that I missed lunch once again; would I ever make it on time? The weather being magnificent, I opted to do some exercise on the outer decks and to catch a bit of sun. I didn't want to admit it (even to myself), but I also wanted to see again the place where Frank had been pushed into the sea. I don't know what I expected from my foolish idea, but coming back to the spot where Frank had been standing with the murderer yielded absolutely no information whatsoever – it just gave me the creeps.

I fled from the spot and was relieved when I reached the section with the outdoor swimming pool. This was a favourite location for the younger passengers in holiday mood who loved to hang around the pool bar, having a great time. I settled in a striped lounge chair but after half an hour, the combination of screaming children, partying adults and the bright sun started to irritate me.

I suddenly remembered the cosy library, a haven of peace and quiet – and shelter from the sun that was roasting me alive. The decision was an easy one, so I grabbed my book and fled from the noisy swimming pool, just in time to escape from a boisterous drinking game that had been started by a gang of young students. As the doors of the library closed behind me, I breathed deeply – finally alone! But I was to discover soon enough that I had been too optimistic.

Minutes later the door opened and Charles Peltier walked in, or to be precise, he swayed rather than walked. He recognized me and looked startled, as if I was the last person on earth he'd want to meet. Not very flattering for me, on all accounts. Peltier was already halfway out of the door when he suddenly changed his mind. Like a sinking ship he swayed in my direction and plunged downwards to be rescued by an armchair next to me. Charles Peltier, the world famous designer, reeked of vodka. I guess this must have been his breakfast – I prefer eggs Benedict and a coffee.

"Frank is dead!" he whined, or at least this is what I made out of his slurred speech.

"It must be a terrible loss for you!" I answered lamely. What do you say to a man whose relationship with the victim is at best ambiguous, not to say that he was among my primary suspects?

"Frank was a genius," Peltier continued in a peculiar mix of whining and talking. "He'd have become a greater fashion designer than I am, he had the –" He glared at me, searching for the right word. "Frank had the gift!" he belched, which didn't induce any warmer feelings in me towards him.

"I don't understand, I thought that Frank was just a make-up artist?"

"He only took this job to make some quick money. Frank had just finished at the design school in Antwerp, there's no better place in Europe for young talent at the moment."

"What about Paris and Milan?" I objected.

"Yesterday's fashion, haute couture for the elderly!" Peltier moved his hand as if he were dumping Milan and Paris into a trash bin.

"Frank was the future, a genius!" And he started to cry, helplessly wiping the tears away with an angry gesture. I was starting to hate every second of this strange conversation. We paused awkwardly. I didn't know what to answer, and he had probably forgotten that I had ever existed. Automatically I opened my handbag and grabbed some tissues; I may not be able to boast an imposing personality, but I'm practically minded, which is generally of greater use in everyday life. I handed the tissues to Charles Peltier and he suddenly seemed to remember that I was still sitting there.

"I killed Frank!" he whined, tears gushing down his face.

I was surprised that he didn't fall on his knees.

"I'm guilty, how can I go on living with the knowledge that I killed a great talent?"

Now I was stunned. The case was closed. I was sitting here with Frank's murderer. Not a comfortable thought, being alone with a killer! As a teacher you face many bizarre situations in life, but how to conduct an interview with a killer has never been part of my remit. I needed to improvise – and most of all to calm him down. I cleared my throat: "I'm a bit confused, Mr. Peltier, I mean, it's a bit unusual that you should have killed Frank, I mean, you just said he was a rising star, why did you kill him then – and how did you do it?"

How stupid of me! Hadn't I just decided that I needed to calm him down? Why then did I start an interrogation? For a minute I worried that Charles Peltier might become furious at my insistent questions, but I was wrong. Charles Peltier seemed only too happy to come clean. Even his way of speaking became more fluent and more understandable.

"I admired Frank, he was a young man of such extraordinary talent. Fresh ideas, bold colour schemes, but not too extreme, he had an eye for the kind of design that could be suitable later for mass production. People always think we design for the lucky few, but if a designer label wants to make money, we must license our designs, that's where the real money is nowadays, haute couture hardly pays the bills. Frank was also handsome, the public goes for this, he had all the makings of a real star."

"Why did you kill him, were you jealous of his success?"

"I stole his designs. Amanda, I was desperate!" I was amazed, Peltier had even remembered my name. Maybe I had underrated my charisma.

"My last collection was a flop, the press started to write about it, to circle around me like hungry sharks, scenting blood: 'The great Charles Peltier – yesterday's man'. Can you imagine, I, Charles Peltier, a man of the past?" He shuddered, and his pony tail twitched on his back.

"I knew that they'd be waiting out there, ready for the kill, a pack of dogs, baying for blood. One more bad show and I'd be out – forever. Under this stress, I couldn't work, I was blocked, new ideas wouldn't come." I could see tears of self-pity welling in his eyes, he looked like a wreck.

"And then, I met Frank. Let me be honest, I was attracted at first by his looks, but when he showed me some of his designs, I knew that he was a fledgling genius. Those designs were fabulous, I should have created them. His ideas were bold, new, sensational. Secretly I took photos of his designs with my phone, changed them – I improved them, toned them down, added some ideas, made them more commercial. I have this gift, the eye that can translate a sketch into a dress, I know which fabrics to choose and how to make the designs come alive. Frank was still too young for that. When Frank saw my collection, he knew immediately that I had stolen his ideas and he contacted me. I was flattered in the beginning, he was so handsome – but then Frank started to blackmail me, in a subtle way – but there could be no doubt that the situation might turn nasty for me. I thought that it was all about money…" He broke down and started to sob. The great Charles Peltier had become a bundle of nerves.

"Then – how did you kill Frank?" I asked softly.

"I underestimated his pride! He committed suicide because of my vanity. I refused to make him my partner in the business. It's obvious, he couldn't live any longer with the knowledge that I had usurped his fame. I was selfish. Amanda, believe me: there was never an accident; Frank must have been drinking too much and in his despair he jumped into the ocean – and it's all because of me, I'm his true murderer! I shall accept my responsibility!"

I must have looked like a fish out of water. I opened and closed my mouth, but no words would come. Clearly Peltier had no idea how Frank had met his end. He might be guilty of stealing Frank's ideas, but clearly he was not his murderer.

I tried to console Peltier, saying that I didn't share his severe judgement; certainly copying Frank's designs was a grave issue, but murder is something entirely different. Strangely enough my words succeeded in calming him down.

"Amanda, you've just saved my life. I was ready to follow Frank and end it all. Now as you suggested, maybe I should dedicate my New York fashion show to him, I think he would have been proud of that!"

A relieved, almost happy man left the library – but he left me with my mind in turmoil. We were back to square one. My mind was racing. I needed a coffee, fast! I needed to think and put some order into the chaos of my brain, my little grey cells, as the famous Hercule Poirot would have said. Where was Poirot now? I needed him!

***

I was lucky, the Promenade Café was almost empty and I could dive into one of the comfortable rattan armchairs with a nice coffee and have a think in peace. As for the coffee, I'm a purist, usually no sugar, no milk, unless I'm tempted to have a Cappuccino or an Irish coffee. After some minutes savouring the coffee, the turmoil in my brain subsided and I came to a very sobering conclusion: there simply weren't many possibilities left. If one discarded wild ideas of Frank being followed by the Mafia or some other sinister secret group, I could only come up with two explanations that would make sense: either his relationship with Tom hadn't been a harmless one at all – or Veronique was involved. Either to eliminate a potential threat to the Olstrom reputation, or because she had fallen in love with Frank and he had rejected her. The famous 'crime passionnel' one is always reading about it. I must confess, I liked this version very much. As an avid reader of crime stories I know of course that it's important that you discard all personal feelings when you analyse a crime, but somehow I liked Tom – I didn't like the idea of Tom being the murderer. I had no problems though imagining Veronique as a killer, I rather liked this idea! I was sure that she could be very ruthless. I was also sure that her relationship with Sir Walter was based on money, rather than the power of love or attraction. Yes, Veronique might be the answer to the riddle, I'd need to watch her. Even better, start to befriend her.

Suddenly another chilling thought flashed through my mind. Hadn't I forgotten to take Daniel into account? I had seen him close to the deck only minutes before the murder had been committed. I swallowed hard. I didn't like this option, I didn't like it at all!

I was still deep in my thoughts when I heard a familiar voice teasing me: "Brooding over crime – or even worse, over your school?"

I sat up, startled, and looked into Daniel's smiling eyes. 'Dangerous', I thought. 'This man is no good for my inner calm. I should avoid him!'

"Would you like to be my pirate mate tonight?" Daniel asked me.

"With pleasure!" I heard myself answering – so much for avoiding Daniel. There must be a shortcut in my brain, avoiding all logical thought – a sure way to end up in trouble.

"I'll knock at your cabin to fetch you around eight tonight. I've heard they're preparing a barbeque and special pirate cocktails at the swimming pool because the weather forecast is brilliant – and members of the crew have prepared a surprise for us! We should be able to watch a fabulous sunset, with a cocktail in our hands. Not a bad way of starting the evening…" Again those unsettling eyes looked deeply into mine. I stared back like a rabbit transfixed by an attractive but highly dangerous snake.

"That sounds lovely!" I woke from my trance and smiled at Daniel. "I might even consider having 'Sex on the Beach'".

I had wanted to appear witty, but – dear God! – this sounded so crude, almost like an invitation.

He grinned back. "As long as it isn't 'Sex on the Boat' in public – mind you, I'm sure nobody would object!"

Daniel left me behind, totally confused, but upbeat. I had a date tonight. If only Susan were here; what a pity not to be able to discuss Daniel in detail with her.

'So what do you really know about Daniel?' my annoying inner voice suddenly asked me. I had to admit, I knew nothing! Apart from the fact that he had helped me in a very difficult situation. 'And what was Daniel doing when you saw him?' the voice kept asking me. 'Are you sure he's the white knight? He never speaks about his work or his family – isn't that a bit fishy?'

I hate my inner voice. It's always spoiling my best moments.

***

"Your cup is almost empty!" A voice suddenly interrupted my thoughts. "Let me fetch you a fresh one – you take it black, no sugar, no milk, right?" How would a Nobel Prize winner know my coffee habits? Maybe it's noting the tiny details that makes one a good scientist. Neil smiled timidly at me and I smiled back.

"That's it, Neil, no sugar, just black."

Minutes later Neil came back with two cups, his own topped with milk foam and some sugary syrup. "I like it sweet," he commented with a touch of guilt. His latte smelled tempting, but I still like my coffee black.

Sipping at my fresh cup I looked at Neil and couldn't suppress a wry smile. Today Neil had on an atrocious flaming-red sweater – a horrendous mismatch with his bright fuchsia polo shirt. I felt an urgent need to put my sunglasses on.

"Why shouldn't you like it sweet?" I answered, after I had recovered from the sudden shock of his colourful appearance. "Thank you so much, Neil! I do love my coffee hot, it's really nice of you to bring me a fresh cup! By the way, don't you think that it's a bit too hot today for a woollen sweater?"

Neil looked down as if he were noticing his sweater for the first time. "I was feeling a bit uncomfortable, but I didn't really pay attention, anyway, it doesn't really matter." He was stirring his cup and we started some small talk, British-style, about the weather.

I must admit, talking about the weather is always a good opener. Whereas Americans don't seem to have the slightest problem starting a discussion with a stranger on the topic of their pay slip, the mortgage on their home or by recommending the psychiatrist who helped their adolescent daughter through a difficult time, the British tend to be more discreet. Having discussed the weather in detail, I noticed that Neil hadn't even sipped at his latte, and was still stirring it.

"I don't think that the coffee will get any better if you keep stirring it," I couldn't help saying.

Neil looked at his cup as if he had long forgotten that he had ever intended to drink it. He cleared his throat and asked a bit sheepishly, "I was wondering if you'd fancy accompanying me tonight to the pirate party. I mean, I don't want to impose myself, if you've made any other arrangement already…"

Neil ended up looking a bit confused, like a schoolboy asking for his first ever date. How could I flatly decline such a kind invitation? I decided to wrap my refusal in a statement that would give it a decidedly positive note.

"That sounds lovely!" I managed to say, "but…"

Neil beamed with joy. He hadn't caught the importance of my 'but'. I should have known that beforehand – he was a man after all, and do men ever listen?

"Thanks a lot, Amanda, you know I was really nervous asking you, I felt like a young boy asking for his first date."

Neil was a changed man, he was radiating with joy – how could I now tell him the truth, that I already had a date with Daniel? I simply didn't have the heart. Then Neil frowned. "Exactly what kind of dress do they expect us to wear tonight?"

"It's a pirate party, which means that you're supposed to dress like a pirate!" I hated myself, I must have sounded like a governess, Mary Poppins at her worst.

"Oh!" he exclaimed. "I didn't really get that. I hate these complications. I have no idea what to wear." The frown returned and a short silence ensued, followed by a desperate plea.

"Please help me. Why don't you come to my cabin? You would probably find something suitable!"

It was not the most romantic invitation imaginable, but I understood that men like Neil, who could propel the world into a new era, were incapable of finding a matching shirt in their own wardrobe. We finished our coffee and left the café to walk to his cabin while I wracked my brains to find a way to deal with two dates at the same time.

'That's just typical of you, Amanda.' The hateful inner voice was back. 'You've got the chance of a lifetime for a romantic date with a man like Daniel and you screw it up! Great, really impressive! Have you any idea how to deal with this situation?' I didn't. As usual, my inner voice was right, and I had got myself into an impossible situation.

Neil had a slightly smaller cabin compared to mine. Clearly his Nobel Prize money hadn't been squandered on paying for this cruise. I suddenly felt a pang of guilt that I had been so extravagant myself. I had expected to find the cabin a bit untidy; from my experience most men tend to have a loose relationship with clearing their stuff and tidying things up. But Neil's cabin was meticulously neat and tidy, and only his small desk was littered with piles of papers.

I had certainly not expected to find a large sort of travelling cage, fitted with solid glass windows. A red lamp was glowing inside, reflected in the water of a small pool. My curiosity got the better of me, and I just had to get closer and look inside where I detected several small snakes, coiled up inside. I'm no lover of snakes, but those specimens held a strange sort of fascination.

"I'm so happy that you didn't scream or tell me that they're cute." Neil looked at me; I could see that he was truly delighted. "That is what people usually say. I know most people don't like snakes – and these are definitely not cute, they're very dangerous. These snakes – " Neil cited a Latin name, " – contain a potent neurotoxin and I can't even tell you how much paperwork I had to fill out to get them out of Brazil and into the UK – and now on board. I guess it'll be a nightmare getting them through US customs. But my colleagues at Harvard will need them to continue the tests that I started – tests that look really promising!"

One of the snakes had woken up. It shot me a vicious look, maybe because I had interrupted its slumber, before it slowly moved closer to the warm light. I counted five of them.

"They need warmth and humidity," Neil commented. "They wouldn't be able to survive in our British climate."

"Which is good news." I replied. "They look fascinating, but somehow scary with their red and black stripes. Do they have an English name, I mean, a name that I could actually remember?"

"They're called coral snakes; in Mexico they call them the '20 minute snake' – that's the time left to the victim to get the anti-venom or die! Never ever come close to them. Look, the cage is locked. Only I carry the key, I don't take any risks."

"Thus you're not too keen on touching a snake when you switch on the light," I joked, remembering his tarantula story.

"No, I wouldn't survive long enough to tell the tale!"

I had seen enough of the snakes and remembered that I had come here on a mission. Dutifully I started to search in his wardrobe. Neil had been right, not a lot of choice there. Finally I managed to dig out a pair of jeans, striped marine-blue socks – and a striped pyjama top with very vivid colours, to say the least. The rest of his disguise would need to be achieved with a bit of skilful make-up.

Neil looked sceptically at me. "You don't really expect me to walk around a party in my pyjamas, you're joking?"

"You told me yesterday that you never really notice what you're wearing," I protested. "You have to admit, there's not a lot of choice. And I'm afraid to say that a pirate in a suit with a bow-tie doesn't look credible at all!"

Neil sighed. "OK, you have a valid point there. It'll be the pyjamas then, but won't I look far too ridiculous?"

"We'll all look ridiculous, that's the point! Nobody goes to a fancy dress party in order to look serious, you're supposed to look a bit crazy; it's not an academic conference!"

Neil grinned. "You've no idea what our conferences look like! We're a strange bunch of people; I often think that my colleagues could belong in a theme park, you know, a haunted mansion theme."

I broke into laughter. "If ever they need more characters, I could offer to help out with some of my fellow teachers!"

I gave a last glance to the vicious snakes, but they ignored me. They were probably fully aware of their importance to the scientific world. I said good-bye and walked back to my cabin, still smiling. It hadn't been a romantic encounter at all, but I liked Neil's humour. And whenever he remembered to comb his hair, he didn't look too bad at all…

As I strode along the endless corridors, the carpets muffled the sound of my steps. Somehow I didn't feel at ease anymore in those forlorn parts of the ship. The dim lighting might be a result of the noble aim of saving energy, but it only added to my discomfort. Suddenly I picked up a noise, steps behind me, I was sure, even if I could barely hear them. I walked a bit faster, then the steps behind me became faster as well. My heart started to race. I didn't dare turn around and face my pursuer.

I started to run…

***

"Amanda, stop, why are you racing off? I need to talk to you!" I heard the breathless voice of Marge behind me. I suddenly felt very silly.

"Just getting a bit of exercise," I replied lamely, but clearly there have been better excuses.

Marge was out of breath as she reached me. "I wanted to talk to you, Amanda. Would you fancy an improvised 'get ready' party in our cabin? We could share a glass of champagne while you help me with my make-up and my disguise. I'm sure you've got some great ideas!"

Why does everybody think that I should be a genius when it comes to dressing up? But suddenly an idea popped up into my head. Marge could save me from my dilemma – this might turn out to be my saving grace!

I flashed a big smile at Marge. "Marge, what an absolutely brilliant idea! With pleasure, let's say half past seven! What about inviting Daniel and Neil to join us? John will be bored to death while we dress up and get ready, he'd probably love to have some male company."

"Fabulous idea, darling, we'll throw a proper party then!" Marge almost squealed with delight and we parted on the best of terms.

Half an hour later I rang Daniel to tell him that I had been compelled to help Marge out (female solidarity and all that…), but that I'd be delighted to meet him for a drink in Marge's cabin while I was busy helping Marge to put on suitable pirate make-up.

I'm almost sure that I heard a note of disappointment in Daniel's voice (I liked that), but being a true gentleman he pretended to be fine with whatever change of programme I had in mind. Then I rang Neil. He had problems at first understanding what I was talking about. I had a sneaking suspicion that he had already forgotten about our date, and he needed to be reminded about the evening's special event, the pirate party. I could imagine Neil sitting in front of his laptop, lost in his own world, maybe watching his snakes, but certainly not thinking about me.

***

I arrived and knocked five minutes early at Marge's cabin. She was residing in a luxury suite, even bigger than mine. Being on time is a bad habit I share with most of my fellow teachers, whereas our pupils tend to be more relaxed. Marge was a bit flustered to see me on her threshold so early.

"I'm sorry, Amanda, I seem to be running late, would you mind calling the steward and organizing some drinks and snacks for our guests. I guess they'll be here any minute as well?"

If my memory was correct, I had been invited as a guest. But Marge was already diving back into her bedroom, and before doing so she pushed the phone into my hand. What could I do but oblige? I thus dutifully dialled room service and ordered whatever drinks and food came into my mind for throwing a successful party.

I had somehow expected Kenneth to arrive with the trolley, but ten to fifteen minutes later two young, very attractive stewardesses arrived, pushing heavy trolleys loaded with drinks and all kinds of delicacies. Seeing the result of my ordering spree I felt ill at ease but Marge – who had chosen just this very moment to come out of her bedroom – was delighted.

"I knew that you'd get it right," she exclaimed.

I cleared my throat as the sound of the popping cork of the pink champagne echoed through the cabin. "I'm afraid I got carried away, this looks rather expensive." I looked doubtfully at the bottle of vintage champagne, fresh foie gras and crab cocktail with a topping of something that looked suspiciously like caviar, but Marge didn't seem to be bothered.

"Never worry about trivial matters like money, my dear, life's too short! Enjoy!"

My thoughts went to my last electricity bill; it hadn't looked at all trivial to me. But Marge was right, tonight was not a night to worry about stupid things like electricity bills. Like young college girls we started to giggle as we toasted each other and tasted the bubbly liquid. I let my imagination run wild and painted heavy eyebrows and a fat mole onto Marge's face, then we grabbed a very reluctant John and planted a black mole and a huge fake moustache onto his face. Poor John had tried hard to escape our attentions, but there was no way he could escape us in the confinement of the cabin.

As a consolation we offered John a glass of champagne. He claimed that he still preferred his ice-cold Budweiser, but graciously let us know that he could live with the pink stuff. I was to be the next victim of Marge's painting skills and soon my nose was covered with fake freckles. I looked in the mirror and was still laughing when Daniel rang at the door. Seeing me, he immediately claimed that he couldn't face the evening without some freckles as well and as soon as Neil arrived our little party was in full swing.

Marge had chosen a Dior blouse studded with shimmering sequins. "I somehow don't feel that a pirate would dress in Dior…" I remarked, looking at her doubtfully.

"Why not," Neil suddenly intervened. "I could imagine a real pirate going for anything that looks expensive and glittering. I mean, that's why he became a pirate after all." We looked at Neil with admiration; he had a point there.

"But no bow-tie," I couldn't help teasing him. "No bow-tie, I agree," he smiled back at me.

Neil looked funny in his striped pyjama top, like an exotic parrot. But I had to admit, he endured his strange disguise with grace. When the bottle of champagne was empty we took it as sign that it was about time to join the pirate party. Kenneth had told me that it would be taking place all over the ship. He was right – there was a party mood wherever we went. As we crossed the ship's theatre, I marvelled at the decorations. The ship looked like the film set of 'Pirates of the Caribbean', it was amazing! We walked on through the carefree dancing crowds until we reached the deck where the central swimming pool was the major attraction – and its bar, of course.

Kenneth had told me that the real action would be taking place there. And, no surprise, he was right. This was the central hub for all aspiring party-goers. Members of the crew were playing Caribbean tunes, forming an improvised steel band, and a sumptuous buffet was waiting for us. The (fake) palm trees surrounding the swimming pool had been decorated with black pirate flags and lighted swags, the bulbs shaped and painted like small skulls, a bit eerie – but nevertheless it looked brilliant!

A buxom mermaid, mysteriously glittering fish, even a fierce-looking pirate complete with a hook had been carved from solid blocks of ice and were illuminated in the most fantastic colours. Passengers were moving and dancing to popular tunes, joining in from time to time when they recognized a well-known song. Before I fully realized what was going on, I found myself sucked into this happy crowd as if into a black hole, dancing with Daniel among my fellow passengers. I simply loved the evening. I felt happy and carefree as rarely before in my life. I could have hugged not only the world but also the twinkling stars above us.

Neil, meanwhile, had been dragged onto the dance floor by a bulging female pirate. I couldn't suppress a feeling of satisfaction that he had fallen prey to a dancing partner who was a good deal older and not particularly attractive. Neil didn't look entirely happy either. My reaction was a bit mean, I fully admit it. But then my attention shifted back to Daniel who was an excellent dancer. As my eyes met his, I caught a telling glance that made me blush. I was sure now, Daniel had more things on his mind than just dancing. But what did I want? I didn't know.

The dance floor was open to the star-studded night sky, but well protected from the chilly winds. Word must have spread that the real action was taking place here at the pool and as time passed, the dance floor became unbelievably crowded. The music blaring from the loudspeakers was so loud that any form of conversation was impossible – this could not compare to those tame school staff parties where attendance had been less a pleasure than a duty.

All of a sudden a fellow passenger, virtually only a girl, with tight-fitting jeans and a thin blouse that left nothing to the imagination, started to make advances towards Daniel. I was not amused. But Daniel managed to escape her attentions and danced his way closer towards me. He smiled at me as he must have noticed my obvious displeasure. I cursed inwardly; I must take better care to conceal my feelings. 'People can read you like an open book,' my best friend Susan used to say, but then she usually added, 'That's one of the reasons I like you so much.'

As we moved and mixed with the boisterous crowd on the dance floor, Marge and John joined us. It all became increasingly chaotic, and somehow I ended up dancing with Neil. It was quite fun to teach him some dance steps; apparently dancing to the tunes of a Caribbean steel band isn't among the usual skills required to win a Nobel Prize.

A second later I spotted Tom among the crowd – not very difficult, as he hadn't chosen any particular disguise, but was just wearing a scarf and a black shirt with a printed white skull. It was a clever choice; the nice boy suddenly had a daring, sexy look. Tom ignored us as he was flirting outrageously with a girl of his own age, thus my theory of any kind of romantic involvement with Frank – unlikely as it had seemed from the start – didn't seem to hold true any more. I know that there are people who're open to all kinds of adventures but as I moved close, I could see in his eyes that he had truly fallen for the girl, and she wasn't just a random dance partner he had picked out from the crowd.

Suddenly I felt a pang of guilt. Here I was, dancing, having the time of my life and only yesterday Frank had disappeared into the sea, pushed overboard in cold blood by his murderer. Maybe it's the curse of being a history teacher but all of a sudden pictures of medieval paintings came to my mind: people dancing and feasting while the dark figure with his scythe passes among them leaving devastation in his wake. Weren't we all here behaving a bit like those people, shutting our eyes to all the bad and evil things we all wanted to ignore? The world can be a cruel place. I was rescued from further dark thoughts by Neil, who had stepped on my toe, effectively diverting my thoughts!

"Ouch!" I cried out. It had genuinely hurt.

Neil was inconsolable. "Amanda, I'm so sorry, now you know why I don't even come near a dance floor under normal circumstances. I'm a danger to mankind!"

I laughed. "It's nothing, don't worry, these things just happen!"

But Neil noticed immediately that I was still in pain. He made me sit down and offered to fetch me a cocktail, which I gladly accepted.

"Sex on the beach?" he teased me.

"No, thanks, I feel more like a 'Pirate's Mortal Revenge'," I smiled back, and off he went to fetch a drink. As my eyes followed Neil fighting his way to the bar, I suddenly noticed that Daniel was watching us. He looked a bit upset – did I even detect a hint of jealousy in his eyes? I suddenly felt wonderful, my hurting toe forgotten. I was relishing a situation I had never known before – two attractive men fighting for my attention. Helen of Troy must have felt the same when she had to choose among the rivals for her favour, not that her later fate was all that encouraging…

Suddenly the band stopped playing and with a great fanfare a limbo-dancing contest was announced.

"Any volunteers?" the lead singer shouted into the microphone. He must have been one of the ship's officers.

Neil was still struggling through the crowds, trying to organize the promised drink for me when he was spotted by the man at the microphone.

"Here we go, let's invite the pirate with the exciting orange and blue striped top!"

Poor Neil was dragged by a charming, yet merciless, young female crew member to the stage. I really pitied him as he stood there, next to the steel band, in front of the jeering crowds. A young dancer showed him how he was supposed to bend backwards and dance under the pole to the rhythm – he couldn't have looked more ridiculous. I felt guilty; if it hadn't been for me, Neil would never have been singled out for this stupid contest.

"Any more volunteers?" shouted the voice. "Come on, be pirates, not chickens! The winner will receive a voucher – free cocktails tomorrow, for the whole day! No need to empty your mate's wallet."

Not really thinking, I stepped forward, my painful toe completely forgotten by now. I simply had to rescue Neil from this humiliation in front of the cheering crowd. What better way than to deflect their attention by ridiculing myself beside him.

"I volunteer!" I croaked as I stumbled forward.

"Me too!" Daniel suddenly popped up beside me with a wide grin on his face.

"Have you ever done this before?" I whispered. "I'm scared to death that I won't even get under the first bar!"

"Sure I have!" Daniel grinned back. "Actually it's not that difficult, but most people tend to be too rigid, the secret is to stay relaxed! This will help you!"

Daniel pushed a cocktail into my hands. Heaven knows how he got it so fast. I sniffed suspiciously at the liquid, but all I could indentify was a strong note of vodka, a very strong note actually. My instincts warned me but Daniel insisted.

"Don't be a chicken, go on!"

I followed his advice and downed the glass. The stuff was so strong it made me cough. Minutes later I wasn't walking anymore, I was floating on my own private pink cloud, ready to bend my knees to the rhythm of the music and forget how ridiculous I must look to the public.

"I'll join you!" Marge's breathless voice could be heard from behind as the music started to play and the limbo contest started. The crowd was clamouring and cheering. I imagine the audiences in the ancient Coliseum in Rome must have sounded pretty similar when their favourite gladiators marched into the arena, ready to fight under the indolent eyes of their Emperor.

It seemed that our performance wasn't too bad after all. Marge surprised us all, beating Daniel, who had been decidedly more flexible than Neil or me. To put it bluntly, Neil and I had been total failures – but the crowd was merciful and clapped their hands when each of us received a bottle of champagne as a consolation prize. Only later, as we congratulated Marge on winning the voucher, did she confess that she still took regular ballet classes.

John was bursting with pride. "My girl did it, wasn't she great? You were brilliant, honey, just like a teenager," and he planted a big kiss on her cheek. Marge hugged her husband, blushing like a schoolgirl.

"Amanda was great too!" Neil praised me, but I couldn't blush, my face must still have been bright red from the strong cocktail and the ordeal of the limbo contest.

"Thank you, Amanda, for rescuing me!" he whispered. "You're adorable, I hope you know that!"

I didn't and I was speechless.

Day 5 – The Day After the Pirate Party

I slept until noon. Small wonder, as I hadn't crawled into bed until five o'clock in the morning. When was the last time that I had stayed up so late? I couldn't remember.

Having skipped breakfast, I should have felt hungry, but maybe it was still the mood of elation after such a great party or the simple fact that I had eaten too much from the wonderful buffet; all I wanted was a good cup of coffee. I was tempted to call Kenneth, but I changed my mind as I imagined how nice it would be to walk on deck, breathe the fresh air and drink a fresh cup of coffee while I looked out over the ocean. Decision taken, I took a quick shower, dressed quickly and spent a bit more time and care than usual on my make-up, first to remove the last traces from yesterday and second... well, you never know.

The weather was still pleasant, almost hot, and I found a lounge chair with a side table where I installed my book, a cup of coffee, and a chocolate chip muffin that I had added in a moment of weakness. Could life get any better? I breathed deeply and as the salty air of the Atlantic Ocean filled my lungs, I felt ready to conquer the world. Minutes later I had plunged into my book and had travelled hundreds of years back in time, totally forgetting my surroundings. Well almost, I might have travelled back in time, but not long enough to forget about my cup of coffee.

I must have been engrossed in my book as I didn't hear the footsteps behind me. Suddenly two hands covered my eyes from behind and I shrieked as if I was to be the next murder victim.

"You're a bit nervous, darling," I could hear Marge's voice. "Didn't you sleep well?"

"I slept very well!" I exclaimed, "But sneaking up behind me made me jump!"

"I didn't sneak up behind you!" Marge was all indignation. "I waved at you and called your name, but you were so absorbed in your book, you didn't even notice me! It must be a really good book, indeed!" Her last remark was a bit envious. "Maybe you could lend it to me once you're finished?"

I put my book down and looked a bit guilty. Marge was right, whenever I was reading a good book, the world around me ceased to exist. "Sure, you can have it, it's really fascinating!"

"Did you have lunch already?" Marge changed the subject. "John's still snoring happily in our cabin, so I was actually on my way to the restaurant, as I fancy something to eat."

I looked at the remains of my muffin, guessing its calories would easily make up for lunch. "Not really, but I had a chocolate chip muffin and that should be enough."

"Don't be a goose, darling, cruises aren't for slimming. Let's have something light, like a salad, your muffin won't last you long."

I must confess, Marge didn't really meet any real resistance on my part. Chatting animatedly about the previous evening's party we entered the airy restaurant where we settled for a light lunch. We ordered a salad, but were tempted by the waiter's recommendation to add the soup of the day (Minestrone) and the fact that he brought a wonderful bread basket accompanied by gourmet French butter didn't really count…

"Daniel was really brilliant, he almost beat me!" Marge opened the conversation as soon as we had placed our order. She laughed. "In truth, I think he let me win, he's really a great guy, and I'm quite sure my dear, he's got his eye on you."

I blushed and protested vehemently. "Don't be silly, Marge! I admit Daniel is handsome, but more importantly, he's witty. He's a nice chap but he's got more choice of single females on this ship than is actually good for him. I think he just likes talking to me because it's not my style to try to drag him into bed at the first opportunity."

"No need to get worked up, my darling. Although the idea of having Daniel in my bed would be a real temptation…"

Marge winked at me and continued in a whisper. "I will insist, of course, that I'm happily married to my John. But let's face it darling, passion fades once you've been married for so many years. Sometimes I'm scared that given the choice between a Budweiser and me he'd opt for his Budweiser."

Marge made a funny face as she professed this truth and I had to laugh. "I've heard this often enough; it must be the result of the routine of a long marriage. Maybe it's one of the reasons why I never dared to take this step. It would not be very reasonable to expect courtship to last forever!"

"How true, darling, it finishes earlier than you could ever imagine. During the first months it's 'honey' here, 'sweetheart' there – but soon enough he'll simply expect you to do things – and he'll not be pleased if you don't. But let's change the subject, or I'll be moaning on for hours. I couldn't help noticing that Professor Hopkins is showing a special interest in you as well. Time to face the truth, you're young and attractive and seem to be very popular."

I blushed again. This was becoming a bad habit. "That's kind of you, but don't tell fairy tales. Neil's an interesting man and we share a common interest: he's also very interested in French history. I'm reading an interesting historical novel and Neil was really interested when I explained the background to him. That's all, no romantic involvement at all!"

Marge made some soothing noises and just nodded knowingly. Then, making sure that nobody could listen in, she whispered (or at least she thought that she was whispering), "Wasn't it tragic how he lost his wife?"

I was completely taken aback. This was the first time I had heard about a wife. "What?" I shouted, more than I whispered back. "What happened, I've never heard about a wife!"

Marge shook her head in disbelief. If I had confessed to being totally illiterate, it might have had the same effect.

"The newspapers were full of the story!" she protested. "Professor Hopkins even dedicated his Nobel Prize to his late wife, he gave a very emotional speech."

"Then tell me, what happened?"

"Neil met his wife when both of them were quite young. Hopkins was a young aspiring assistant professor at Cambridge University at that time, whereas her father was one of the honorary members of the board, a big shot in the city. He must have dished out a lot of money to get this position as his academic achievements were not that renowned. They met and fell in love..." Marge's eyes suddenly became moist. She had a weakness for romantic stories.

"The famous 'coup de foudre'," I remarked.

"What's that?" Marge asked suspiciously. "Sounds very French to me!"

"It is!" I laughed. "The French say that love at first sight comes like a bolt of lightning."

"That's not stupid at all, there's certainly a lot of truth in the expression. The French are known to be experts when it comes to matters of love. But I'm straying from the subject: they got married and her money and her father's influence provided Neil Hopkins with the independence he needed to conduct his studies without having to bother about chasing for funds. Don't get me wrong, Professor Hopkins is absolutely brilliant, but I doubt that he'd have been able to see results so quickly if her money hadn't funded his extensive expeditions. You know what the reality is at universities, you must fill in forms, convince members on countless committees, fight against your jealous colleagues who all think that their own projects are more important..."

"You sound as if you've had a lot experience!" I was amazed. I hadn't expected this from Marge; I had thought that her expertise would be limited to spotting bargain-priced cruises or a Hermes bag in a boutique. It just goes to show how you can underestimate people.

"I happen to hold a master's degree in chemistry, believe it or not." Marge sighed. "I was stupid enough to stop my career after we married. I sometimes think it was the biggest mistake of my life. But they all told me that with Father's heritage and John's job, there would be no need to bury myself in a lab and pursue my studies. But I still understand enough to know that Professors Hopkins's research was revolutionary and the fact that he's fairly young to have received such a unique distinction only confirms this. But let's get back to his wife. In the beginning their marriage must have been quite happy but later she became depressive." Marge lowered her voice and looked suspiciously left and right before she continued. "Hooked on the bottle, she was, in the end. I know some details via a friend of mine who worked for him when Professor Hopkins was assigned to Yale for a year or two. It happened quite frequently that they'd have to call him to drag his drunken wife back home from a bar. He put on a brave face in public but rumours were flying around that he was planning to file for divorce. All the same, during that summer she accompanied him on an expedition into the rainforests, where she conveniently died, a relief to everybody!"

"How did she die?" I asked mechanically.

Marge looked around her, but the restaurant was almost empty and most of the other guests seemed to be busy talking.

"She was bitten by a snake, in fact it was one of the snakes he was rearing in his lab. They found her when she was already unconscious, and the anti-venom injection came too late. There was an official inquest, the Brazilian servants swore that they hadn't seen anybody and Neil Hopkins made a point of the fact that the keys to the vivarium had been hidden in a safe place, only known to the trained staff and himself – and his wife of course. The police came to the conclusion that his wife, under the influence of what they called anti-depressive medication, had opened the vivarium herself. If you ask me she was probably totally plastered and didn't know what she was doing. But maybe Neil helped a bit…"

"Marge!" I exclaimed. "That's a terrible assumption to make. You sound like Agatha Christie at her best, an infamous husband who can't get a divorce and finds no other way but to get rid of his wife. Neil is far too kind to do something hideous like that. Furthermore we live in different times, getting a divorce is so easy. Soon you'll be able to get them on the internet – there'll probably be a divorce app next to the dating app on every smartphone soon enough. Don't you think you're going too far?"

"Amanda, you're so clever and yet you're so naïve. Don't forget the money. I guess my John from time to time gets a bit tired of me. Most men do get tired of their wives. But I have the money, and I made sure that he won't see a penny if ever we divorce – and John knows this. From time to time I remind him, just to make sure."

Marge munched happily on her piece of bread as she voiced the most atrocious accusations. I was speechless. I simply couldn't imagine Neil as a killer. And yet, Marge had planted the seed of doubt – the opportunity and a strong motive had been there…

"If ever you're alone with Neil Hopkins, make sure there are no snakes are around!" Marge giggled – but I didn't think that this was very funny.

"Let's change the subject." I suggested. "Actually, Daniel is more of a riddle to me, if I'm honest. Do you know anything about him? He talks a lot, but never about himself."

"Sure, I do." Marge looked a bit smug. "If you didn't bury your nose in your musty history books, you'd know too. Who hasn't heard of Daniel Greenfield? He's in the tabloids often enough."

"Oh, that's his name then," I said lamely. "Oh, and by the way, my books are not musty!"

Marge waved at me with a dismissive gesture. "Who cares about things that happened ages ago? Daniel's certainly something special. I wouldn't know exactly where his money comes from but he's got plenty of it, old money, his family is rolling in it. In his youth he hung around the heiress of the Bulcatti fashion and jewellery empire for several years, then he fell for a Parisian model. He got carried away and they married – a spectacular marriage, if ever I saw one. They married in Bali – it was amazing. She looked beautiful, flowers in her hair, a romantic dream come true."

I felt as if someone had punched me in the stomach. A nice bunch of suitors I had – a potential killer and a married playboy! Definitely a cheery scenario. I grabbed a glass of water and downed it, but a vodka would have been of more use.

"Why's Daniel travelling on his own then, if he's married?" I managed to ask, trying to hold my emotions under control.

"Oh, don't you know? He's a widower as well. His wife got killed in a car crash, only two years after their marriage. But that was years ago and he's never been tempted by marriage again. Very tragic, but mind you, they had already started to have problems, and were quarrelling all the time. She was a beauty, but jealous as hell – and you have to admit it, Daniel is a true ladies' man. The newspapers were full of stories of his wife staging scenes in the fashionable clubs or restaurants they visited together. I once saw a photo where Daniel was dripping wet because she had thrown her cocktail glass at him; the paparazzi simply loved it. Every week a new story. I wonder if they didn't provoke some incidents deliberately, she had a quick temper, Russian blood…" Marge paused dramatically, revelling in her role of story teller.

"Daniel's wife died racing with some handsome nobody in Monaco – almost at the same spot where Grace Kelly met her end; the brakes of her car didn't work. I'm not sure if in the end it was a disaster or more of a relief for Daniel."

"Oh come on, Marge!" I protested, "that's a bit thick! First Neil, now Daniel!"

"Did I hear my name?" I looked into the smiling eyes of Daniel and all my doubts disappeared like the last snow under the rays of the sun.

"Oh, Daniel, how wonderful to see you!" Marge stood up so that he could kiss her cheek. Did she linger a bit longer in his arms than absolutely necessary? I decided to do the same – if Marge could linger, why shouldn't I?

"I was looking for Amanda, actually. Amanda, would you mind having dinner with me tonight? No excuses, unless of course you find me repulsive and I warn you, I intend to be utterly selfish. This invitation is only for you, no private parties or dance contests." He shot an apologetic smile at Marge, but his eyes were laughing at me. This was impossible to resist, how could I refuse?

86

"It's a deal!" I smiled back while I ran quickly through the contents of my wardrobe in my mind and felt an urgent need to visit the ship's salon (they wouldn't call it a simple hairdresser's here on the *Belgravia*) – even if I suspected that this decision would cost me a fortune.

"Great, I'll pick you up from your cabin at eight!" A quick kiss on the cheek and he was gone. I could still smell his eau de toilette, fresh and spicy, but it must have contained some special ingredient as it made me go weak at the knees.

"Oh, Amanda, that looks serious…" Marge sighed with delight. "Tomorrow, promise, you'll tell me all, every tiny detail!"

"Promise!" I answered. I hoped that she didn't notice that I had crossed my fingers behind my back.

***

Our lunch was finished and I walked back with Marge to our deck from where I continued to my cabin, as I had lots of things to ponder. I must have been walking like a robot as my mind was on overload. I needed a bit of peace and quiet.

Inside my cabin, I studied the discreet notice that explained how to access the internet on board – and the prices. I dropped it like a hot potato; nobody in their right mind would spend twenty pounds for only one hour. Minutes later I had logged my browser onto the net.

I don't know if the internet is a blessing or a curse. In no time I had zillions of results for 'Daniel Greenfield' on my screen – when I switched to 'Google images', I felt as if I had opened the society section of *Hello* magazine by accident. Daniel partying, Daniel with expensive sports cars, Daniel (a much younger Daniel, that was) surrounded by beautiful girls, Daniel dancing, Daniel receiving different cups (polo, rugby, racing – you name it, he must have won it), Daniel's marriage (his wife a dream come true, dressed deceptively simply in a white satin dream designed by Armani), Daniel and his wife on a yacht, a rigid-looking Daniel at her funeral. A celebrity life in fast motion, love, money, triumph, grief – every tiny detail recorded, privacy a thing of the past.

When I shut down the computer, my mind was in turmoil. There was a feeling of jealousy, seeing all these good-looking women around Daniel, but it was not only jealousy, I felt sobered. The truth dawned on me: Daniel and I had very little in common and my silly dreams were never to come true. Daniel came from a different world. I could only guess that he had invited me tonight as – for once – he didn't want to talk about Saint Tropez or a quick trip to Bali. I would provide a nice change from his usual dates. But I was not sure if I liked this idea.

I looked at myself in the mirror. Should I give up, call Daniel and invent an excuse, a convenient headache, for instance? I shook my head at my reflection. Amanda Lipton wouldn't give up so easily. I wouldn't waste this opportunity, and I had come to like Daniel very much, playboy or not.

'Come on, you've got a date with a celebrity playboy – make the most of it, don't be such an idiot!' I encouraged myself.

The Amanda in the mirror nodded enthusiastically. But I was at least lucid enough to see that this Amanda in the mirror needed to go to the hairdresser, and urgently so. Susan used to say, 'You deserve better, my dear…' and give me a long reflective glance. That's the moment I would know it was time to have my hair done.

I have a hairdresser's at home, around the corner. They know me, they don't try to sell me fancy colours or exotic shampoos, nobody ever suggests a head or neck massage. They wash and cut my hair and dry it, full stop. I hate going to a hairdresser's I'm not familiar with and the inevitable scenario that unfolds: I enter the shop to be greeted by patronizing assistants who might as well be pupils of mine, with dyed hair, varnished finger nails so long that they could be classed as dangerous weapons. They look at me and smirk secretly while they utter a bored 'How can we assist you, madam?' adding to themselves, 'this customer is hopeless, she'll never pay for extras'. They tackle my hair and I'm happy when the ordeal is over. But today I would have to endure this procedure. I wanted, no, I *needed* to look my best.

My mind made up, I strolled to the *Belgravia*'s salon and, breathing deeply to steel myself for the battle of wills that I would inevitably face, I entered. I was greeted by a young assistant (no surprise here) but not only did she greet me with a warm smile, she almost made me feel welcome. "Do you have an appointment, madam?"

I looked crestfallen. I had totally forgotten that you can't just walk into an exclusive salon and expect to be simply served on demand.

"I don't, I'm sorry, I totally forgot. But it's urgent, I mean I have a date – um, I mean, an appointment this evening…" I stuttered and blushed. I felt awkward in the extreme.

The girl smiled. "No need to apologize madam, if you don't wish to be served by Monsieur himself, I can take you right now. Would this be ok for you?"

"I don't need 'Monsieur'," I smiled back. "I'm sure you'll do a good job. I just want to look…. somehow better," I finished lamely.

"My name is Oksana, madam. Let me take care of you!"

I quickly discovered that Oksana was not only a very capable hairdresser, she was an extraordinary saleswoman as well! "Have mercy on me, Oksana!" I exclaimed. Not only had she convinced me that I needed a manicure, she moved on to explain that my hair needed golden highlights, a natural complement to the sparkle of my wonderful eyes… "I imagine everything here is very expensive, I'm not a millionaire, you know."

She laughed. "I will pay attention, madam, I promise!"

I thus gave in and accepted her suggestion of adding the highlights – it sounded so glamorous. Then she convinced me that my make-up needed a bit of improvement. By this stage I was already putty in her tiny but admittedly capable hands. When Oksana had finished with me, I must say I was more than pleased. For years I had cursed my mop of thick hair, but Oksana's haircut had transformed it into an asset. I don't know how she had done it, but I looked truly beautiful. My hair had a golden gloss I had never seen before and my eyes looked larger than usual, my lips had a sensual touch – I could have hugged her. I'd never be a model – but a new Amanda had been born, and I liked her!

When Oksana handed me the bill, she had kept her word, but beauty comes at a price. An African village could have happily feasted for a full year on the money I put on the counter that afternoon. All the same, I gave her a fat tip; Oksana had deserved it. I could face the evening with Daniel without feeling like a country bumpkin. I looked and I felt great.

Everybody knows that when you feel happy or beautiful, your whole body language changes. As I walked out of the salon, not even Veronique could have swayed her hips more elegantly. I was still walking on my little cloud of happiness when a voice behind called, "Amanda! What a stroke of luck meeting you here, I've been looking for you since lunchtime!"

Of course I recognized Neil's voice immediately. "Hey, did you survive the limbo dance or did your sciatica flare up?" I joked and looked at him affectionately. Today Neil was dressed in a bright blue polo shirt, almost perfect for this occasion.

Maybe he should just have considered removing the dry cleaning label before putting it on.

Neil looked at me with appraising eyes. "You look great today!"

I congratulated myself. If a man like Neil noticed my new hairstyle, Oksana must have performed a true miracle. I imagine normally you need to be brightly coloured and toxic to be noticed by Neil. Suddenly he smiled as he realized what had changed. " I think it's your blouse, first time I've seen you in pink, nice colour!" I just smiled back. No point mentioning that I had worn a similar blouse two days ago.

And then he asked the dreaded question, "Are you free tonight?"

"I'm afraid that I'm engaged already, Neil. Actually Daniel has invited me for dinner and I've accepted!" I tried to sound disappointed, but I'm not sure if I was very convincing. I had promised myself I would go out with Daniel, and not even a collision with an iceberg was going to stop me.

"Oh!" Neil looked lost, he hadn't foreseen this scenario. He cleared his throat. "Actually I had wanted to invite you to say thank you for rescuing me!"

"Why do you think that I rescued you?" I played the innocent.

"That ridiculous limbo competition – they wanted to make a fool of me, like a dancing bear or something. I was so grateful that you sacrificed yourself…"

"Oh, that was nothing!" I laughed. "That's what friends are for. In the end we had a lot of fun. I was amazed how agile Marge is, she beat me by a mile! I must have looked utterly inflexible."

Neil smiled affectionately. "You were great, don't belittle yourself. As you don't have time tonight, could you come over to my cabin right now?"

I swallowed. This was not a very subtle form of invitation. He noticed my hesitation and smiled. "No indecent proposal, but I do have a surprise for you!"

That was clever, he had me hooked. Not that I'm curious by nature – I love surprises, nice ones, that is. What could I do but accept his invitation? Chatting animatedly about the book that I was reading at the moment, we walked along the deck in the direction of the passenger cabins. I explained the plot of the story and immediately Neil wanted me to tell him how the evil cousin managed to escape from England. "Neil! I can't give away the plot! You'll have to read the book yourself, it's quite fun!"

"I prefer to hear the story from you, it's even more fun," he insisted. "You don't simply tell a story, you seem to live it!"

"Oh I do, I sometimes I wish I had a magic wand that could take me back into the seventeenth century. Just imagine, meeting Cardinal Richelieu or King Charles…"

"Before or after his execution?" Neil quipped.

"You're horrid!" I exclaimed. "Poor King Charles – and you make jokes about him…"

"He made a lot of stupid mistakes. The king never understood the rising power of Parliament and he had to pay for this. He didn't have a Richelieu to shield him from his opponents – and the Duke of Buckingham made things worse while he still lived…"

I was stunned. Neil was really well informed about that exciting period just before the Civil War ravaged Britain.

"What do you think about Richelieu?" he asked me.

"I think he was a genius, but an odious one." My verdict was clear.

We had been so deeply immersed in our discussion that we were surprised to have reached Neil's cabin already. Neil stopped and insisted that I should close my eyes before I entered – by now I was really curious!

Seconds later he pressed a bouquet of flowers and an envelope into my hands. I cried out in delight – the bouquet was truly beautiful, a bunch of roses in different shades of red and creamy pink. Then I opened the envelope. It contained a card, which said simply: 'Thank you, I'm glad that I had the chance to meet you. Your friend forever, Neil.'

I can get a bit emotional from time to time, and tears were rolling down my cheeks before I could stop them and I just managed to whisper, "Thank you, Neil, that's lovely! I'm glad that I met you, too!"

Neil blushed like a small boy. Quickly I turned to the vivarium that housed his snakes to avoid this potentially dangerous moment. I mean, I simply couldn't allow myself to fall into Neil's arms and kiss him (which actually I longed to do) when I was planning a date with Daniel that evening.

One of Neil's poisonous snakes was moving. It seemed to be mocking me, its arrogant eyes staring straight into mine. I'm glad that snakes can't talk. I don't need a snake to tell me I'm behaving foolishly. In order to calm down, I started to count the snakes: one, two, three, four… one, two, three, four… My heart beat faster. There should have been five.

"Neil…" I said in a thin voice. "Is it possible that one of your snakes might be missing? Last time I counted five, now I can see only four."

"Oh, don't worry, Amanda. They like to play games and coil up so you don't know if it's one or two. There were five of them when I fed them this morning."

I counted again. I could only make out four, but if Neil was so sure, who was I to insist further on this issue? But the idea that a snake could have escaped gave me the creeps. I couldn't forget Marge's hair-raising story about Neil's unfortunate late wife.

"Thanks again, Neil, that was a lovely idea. I'll hurry to my cabin now, the flowers need water. I inhaled the scent. "They smell lovely as well!" I planted a quick kiss on his cheek and pulled the door shut behind me. Was I afraid of the snakes or of getting to like Neil more than I should?

Back in my cabin, I buried myself in my book. I didn't want to think about Neil, nor about Daniel, nor about the murder I had witnessed. The trick worked better than intended. I only came back to reality when Kenneth arrived with an ice bucket for the champagne and a selection of mouth- watering canapés.

"Oh my goodness, it's seven already!" I exclaimed.

"A quarter past," Kenneth corrected me. "Anything amiss, madam?"

"I must be ready in half an hour, and for any woman, that's got to be a challenge," I answered as I hastened to the bathroom to start preparations. As I studied my face in the mirror, I came to the conclusion that Oksana's work of art was still perfect in my eyes, and I would only make things worse. I took a quick shower (tepid to avoid any steam damaging my expensive hairdo). Then came the most complicated part: what should I wear tonight? The images of Daniel surrounded by skinny models were still lingering in my head, all of them with tanned skin, perfect hair, long legs, perfect teeth… it was frustrating. Most of them had been wearing black – this seemed to be the colour of elegance and understatement in high society. Automatically my hands moved forward to take down the only black dress I had acquired for this trip.

'Don't be stupid, Amanda!' I chided myself. 'Be yourself, stop trying to be someone else!'

As I looked through the wardrobe, I suddenly noticed a dress that had been my favourite evening attire for years, but hadn't been worn too often – in school I didn't have many opportunities to do so. Elegantly cut, it had been tailored for me in Bangkok from local Thai silk, a silk that changes colour from rich plum blue to a lighter turquoise whenever it moves or the light changes. I simply loved this dress, and so it was a decision that only took seconds (unusual for me). Then I added the earrings and a necklace, a gift from my mother – I was ready! A last look in the mirror confirmed that my choice had been right. The silk was shimmering in the subdued cabin light, competing with the new golden shimmer of my hair. My green eyes were bright with pleasurable anticipation – no bored sophistication on my side! 'Daniel, here I come', I said to myself.

At eight o'clock on the dot, the bell rang and Daniel stood at my door. What is it that makes men look so much better in formal dress? Daniel always looked great in his usual casual attire, but in his dinner jacket he looked stunning. He grinned at me. I think my face betrayed me. As he entered my cabin he gave me an appraising look. "You look fantastic, Amanda. What a wonderful dress, Thai silk, a rarity! You'll have to tell me where you bought it." He stopped, looked at me again and smiled. "And may I congratulate you on your new hair style, I really like it, you look stunning!"

I blushed with delight. It's good to know yourself that you look nice, but so much better if someone else notices your efforts.

In the best of moods I joined Daniel and we took the lift that whisked us to the Westminster Grill. Daniel had reserved a table for the two of us only. From far off I could see Marge and John sitting at our usual table. Marge waved at me, discreetly, at least that's what she thought, but thanks to her waving, half of the restaurant turned their heads to try to identify the couple that had entered.

In the meantime we were greeted by the head waiter, of course; Daniel wouldn't expect to be served by a mere minion. I don't even think Daniel ever invested any thought on this, I guess he simply took it for granted that he would be treated like royalty. But tonight I felt like a VIP as well – and I loved it!

We started by ordering an aperitif. That was fairly easy, you can never go wrong with a Kir Royale, unless the barman adds too much cassis. But – how could it be otherwise – the drink was perfect and the frosted redcurrants in the glass gave it a decorative touch.

Then came the moment I always dreaded – the menu was presented to us. Not just the usual single sheet of paper, the *Belgravia* had opted for handcrafted sheets of paper of unusual size while the waiter read out at least a dozen special recommendations that could be found handwritten on a blackboard he had proudly positioned close to us. The immediate effect on me was that I was lost. It would have been easier to mention what kind of dish was *not* available or *not* recommended. Should I opt for something light or something sophisticated? For some stupid reason, women are always expected to order 'light' or healthy dishes. Life is so unfair.

Suddenly I noticed the words 'Cordon Bleu' – since childhood one of my favourite dishes. But I simply couldn't order a 'Cordon Bleu'! Being Daniel's guest I ought to order something sophisticated like 'Loup de mer au gratin de betraves avec sa garniture de perles de caviar'. The waiter waited patiently for my order but I needed to buy more time. "Daniel, please start, I always need a bit of time and I'd love to know your choice first!"

Daniel shot me a quick smile. It seemed that my reaction was not *that* unusual. He ordered scallops to start and then the loup de mer to follow. I knew that I should follow his lead – didn't I aspire tonight to be a sophisticated lady of society? As the waiter looked at me expectantly, I started with 'foie gras'. Then – and I swear I had the best intentions – somehow my mouth formed the words 'Cordon Bleu' before I could stop them.

"Can I change the side-dish, actually I'd love to have potatoes au gratin to go with it…" Rarely do I order a dish without changing my mind. It's compulsory, probably genetic. Anyhow, it was too late, I had betrayed my unsophisticated tastes.

Daniel looked startled. "That's a great idea, I haven't eaten Cordon Bleu for years. But it's really good when it's made by a good chef. Waiter, I'll change to Cordon Bleu for the two of us – but ask the chef to make it thin and the crust must be crispy and golden!"

"And for the goose liver paté, please don't serve it with the usual brioche, I prefer toast – and instead of the jelly, I'd prefer some sel de Guerande," I added, feeling bold now.

"I guess I shouldn't be ordering foie gras and cordon bleu," I said in a small voice as soon as the waiter had left. "It's loaded with calories and the waiter will think that I'm fattening myself up…"

"I don't recall when I bothered the last time about what a waiter might think." Daniel just shrugged. He could be very arrogant at times, an attribute I didn't really care for. "I must say, it's fun to dine with someone who likes to eat and won't just nibble on a lettuce leaf the whole evening. I hate it when people don't appreciate good food!"

"No chance of that with me, salads are reserved for home. I guess after this trip I'll be doomed to two months of nothing but lettuce leaves, but it's worth it!" I added in a cheerful voice. I had discovered the oven-fresh focaccia and had started working my way through it.

A different waiter appeared. It was obvious that he was the sommelier as he proudly displayed the silver cup hanging from his apron, the badge of his profession. Automatically he addressed Daniel in order to know which wine had been chosen but Daniel pointed to me. "Madame will choose tonight, I'm sure that she'll surprise me once again."

"Je préfère un vin rouge de Graves," I answered automatically in French. I had noticed that the sommelier spoke with a heavy French accent.

"Oh, Madame, vous parlez français!"

The sommelier was pleased and we entered into an animated discussion about the pros and cons of the different regions of Bordeaux before he recommended a wine from a small chateau located in the region of Graves Supérieur.

"Et un verre de Sauternes pour accompagner le foie gras," Daniel added. I guess he had to prove that he spoke French as well.

"Excellent, I love Sauternes!"

"How come you speak fluent French?" Daniel asked curiously as soon as we were alone again.

"I could ask you the same," I answered. "But let me answer your question first. I almost chose French as my second subject but history was my first love. As I didn't have to do a lot of work for English, thanks to my father, I visited lots of university courses in French, but it's become a bit rusty, I don't have much opportunity to talk French. Now you!"

"I was born in the USA, later my parents moved to England when I was about twelve years old. After school I studied economics at Oxford and spent a year during my masters in Lausanne, which is where I learnt French. I love it, I don't think that there is a more elegant language."

Soon we were discussing the various cities in France we had visited. From France we went on to the USA, then Germany and soon found ourselves in deep – and often controversial – discussions about world politics. Rarely have I spent a more fascinating evening. As the remains of our desserts were cleared from the table and Daniel was finishing his brandy, I suddenly realized that it was approaching midnight. The Westminster Grill was almost empty.

All of a sudden, Daniel took my hands in his. I was fighting hard not to drown in his wonderful brown eyes, but I managed to withdraw my hands. In a small voice I heard myself saying, "I'm afraid we have to stop here, Daniel. It has been the most wonderful evening." I took a deep breath. "But the truth is that you and I, we live in different worlds. I'm not part of your world. Thank you for this lovely evening, I'll never forget it, but it's better if we stop here."

Daniel looked as if he had been struck by a bolt of lightning. Could it be that I was the first woman ever to turn him down? He smiled at me crookedly. "You're adorable, you don't talk nonsense. Don't you like me, just a little bit?"

I sighed. Prince Charming was playing his tricks on me, and to be truthful, they were working. "Of course I like you, Daniel, that's exactly my problem, I like you too much. Now let's be sensible and say good night!"

I had just finished my brave little speech when suddenly the loudspeakers echoed through the empty restaurant: "Calling Professor Hopkins, calling Professor Hopkins! Professor Hopkins is *urgently* requested to come to the Queen's Suite. I repeat, Professor Hopkins, please come urgently the Queen's Suite, and bring your doctor's bag!" The voice on the loudspeaker tried to sound matter-of-fact, but I could detect a hint of urgency, even panic.

"Oh no!" I exclaimed.

"What's the matter?" Daniel asked me, "This doesn't sound good, for sure, but you sound really worried – anything amiss?"

"It could be the snake," I exclaimed, wringing my hands.

"The snake?"

"Professor Hopkins is travelling with a vivarium of coral snakes from the Amazon in order to continue his studies together with his colleagues in the USA. Yesterday I counted five snakes, but this afternoon I could only see four of them, but Neil wasn't worried, he just said that they like to play hide and seek. But what if

I had been right... Just imagine! These snakes are very dangerous. If they bite, the victim dies within twenty minutes. He explained it all to me."

Daniel gave me a long reflective glance. "I'm afraid that Professor Hopkins should have paid a bit more attention to your counting skills. One snake more or less makes a big difference. I'll take you back to your cabin now. I'm not feeling very romantic any longer and I don't need to be clairvoyant to see it's the same for you."

I answered with a wry smile. Indeed, my mind was no longer on romance right now. Daniel was true to his word and not only did he take me back to my cabin, he insisted on checking thoroughly to make sure no vicious snake was hiding underneath or in the folds of my bed. He gave me a quick kiss and left the cabin, where I stayed – alone, but I felt scared and my hands were shaking.

I undressed and started to destroy Oksana's work with the help of my make-up remover pads. As a plainer version of Amanda re-emerged, I couldn't have cared less. I was imagining the dramatic scene that must be unfolding right now in the Queen's Suite if my assumptions were right. I could only pray that Neil would arrive on time to inject the anti-venom. Wasn't this the only logical explanation for the urgent request to present himself with his doctor's bag? But how could a snake reach the Queen's Suite, on a different deck, located hundreds of yards from Neil's cabin? Another 'accident'?

Somehow I didn't feel like going to bed, even if the voice of logic and reason told me that no snake would be waiting there. I settled into my comfortable armchair and snuggled into a blanket, trying to calm down. But images kept racing through my mind, of snakes and hooded murderers with hidden faces; Veronique, maybe Tom or his father lying on the ground, Neil trying desperately to inject the anti-venom into a lifeless body. I simply couldn't close my eyes. In order to distract myself I grabbed my historical novel, but tonight the story failed to hold my attention and I just flicked aimlessly through the pages. It suddenly seemed so silly and meaningless.

Countless minutes later the phone rang. I almost slipped and kissed the floor as I rushed to the small table next to my bed where the phone was still ringing. "Hello?"

"Hi Amanda, this is Daniel. I imagined you probably wouldn't mind if I called. I suppose you can't sleep anyhow."

This man shouldn't be wasting his time as a playboy; he should be working as psychotherapist.

"You're right, I tried, but I'm still far too worried!" I replied, while a silly tear suddenly rolled down my face. I was a nervous wreck.

"That's why I'm calling you, Amanda. I just wanted to tell you that the missing snake has been found. All is under control now." Somehow I felt strangely relieved. I must have been expecting until that very moment to see a snake slithering in my direction. I'm not a very brave kind of person.

"And – did the snake bite anyone?" I asked, dreading the reply. Logically, the snake must have been smuggled into the Queen's Suite, certainly not with the intention of pleasing anyone.

"Yes." Daniel paused. "A nasty story. The snake bit Veronique and Professor Hopkins couldn't do anything, his anti-venom had been taken as well. Very thoughtful of the killer, indeed."

I swallowed hard. "You mean, Veronique is…"

"Yes, Amanda, she's dead; another 'accident'. You know of course what this means: we have a ruthless murderer on board. Tomorrow we'll have to meet up and discuss, something has to be done. I do have a request to make though – would you mind looking after Professor Hopkins? He needs to be taken care of. To be frank, it's not easy for me to ask you, as I know…" His voice faltered. "I know that Neil has also shown a lot of interest in you. But he's devastated. The doctor of the *Belgravia* gave him an injection to calm him down. But someone has to look after him, he's taken it very badly! Veronique died in front of his eyes, just like his wife."

I was feeling numb. Sometimes in life you don't even know what to think, everything just seems to be in a huge mess. On the one side, the mean side of me was relieved that Veronique had been the victim and not Tom or Sir Walter. No good beating around the bush, I had never liked her. And yet one murder had been one too many already for my taste and facing a second case made things even worse. The idea that a murderer was loose on the *Belgravia* did nothing to calm my nerves.

"I guess they're calling the police now, maybe they can come by helicopter from New York?" I asked hopefully. The idea of a band of policemen descending on our ship held a comforting notion.

"No chance of that, didn't you notice? The engines have almost stopped working. The hurricane that was going to hit Virginia has been reported as drifting north. New York is closed from tomorrow and we'll be delayed for at least two days – and in the meantime, it's impossible to get any help from the outside."

As Daniel was mentioning it, I suddenly realized that the humming of the engines had almost died down. "I don't like this," I commented, trying to sound brave.

"Who would, with the exception of the killer?" answered Daniel.

Daniel had a valid point there. Only one of the passengers would be happy that no police could board the ship.

Day 6 – Rough Seas and a Killer On Board

Kenneth brought breakfast but he was strangely taciturn this morning, although I'd have been willing to bet that he must be bursting to discuss the gruesome news.

I opened the discussion. "I've heard that something terrible has happened in the Queen's Suite."

"Who told you that, madam?" he replied, very much surprised.

"I was in the Westminster Grill yesterday evening when the paging system went off and Professor Hopkins was requested to come urgently to the Queen's Suite – with his doctor's bag."

"Yes, there has been an accident," Kenneth admitted, "but we've received strict orders from the captain, we're not supposed to talk about it."

An clam would have been talkative compared to Kenneth today. Quickly and in silence he arranged the breakfast on my table before he fled from my cabin. I don't know what the captain had said and what he had threatened to do, but the effect was clear, a news ban had been imposed.

I sipped at my coffee and nibbled at my croissant. I was surprised to feel suddenly quite hungry. I could have sworn I would never be able to touch a morsel of food again after learning of the second murder, but apparently human nature is more resilient to disaster than we think. In no time I had cleared half of the breakfast tray. Now I felt fortified and ready to tackle the world.

There is the old saying, 'mens sana in corpore sano' – in my situation it meant that finally I should kick myself into action and go to the gym. This decision was immediately reconfirmed as I did up my jeans – the fit was definitely tight, maybe sexy, but far too tight to be comfortable.

The ship's decks appeared less crowded than usual as it was raining heavily and the sea had become rough. There was no more Mediterranean feeling as strong gusts of winds reminded me that a hurricane must be ravaging the American coast – luckily more than a thousand miles away from us. As Daniel had foretold, the *Belgravia News* had announced this morning that the captain had decided to make a detour and slow down the engines in order to avoid the effects of the hurricane that would be moving north from Virginia to New Jersey, meaning that we'd be oceanbound for at least three more days. Then followed the sentence that inevitably follows in vacuous modern communications: 'We apologize for any inconvenience caused'. There must be a system shortcut to generate this hollow phrase, repeated thousands of times on any given occasion, although in truth nobody really bothers. What other option did the captain actually have – sail straight into the hurricane?

The gym was quite busy, and as usual I felt ill at ease. It starts with the fact that eighty percent of the people there look fabulous already. Why do they have to go to the gym at all? These people simply look great in their tight-fitting lycra and while I'm sweating, panting and puffing like a rusty steam engine, those athletic fellow passengers keep on chatting, breathing evenly, and even if they do happen to perspire, it somehow looks different, the proud perspiration of the accomplished athlete, not the steamy sweat of a random visitor like me.

Gritting my teeth, I attacked the treadmill. I ignored the break-neck speed of my neighbour and chose a speed setting and up-hill gradient that would be compatible with my limited skills. There's something about moving though, it makes your brain work faster.

'Who would want to kill Veronique?' I mused, as my legs found a rhythm of their own. 'And how was Veronique linked to Frank, the first victim?'

By now my brain was working at full speed – but I must admit, not very successfully so. The only link between the two of them that I could see was Tom, obviously, but why the hell should Tom first kill his friend and then his stepmother? Maybe he was jealous? Had Veronique been romantically involved with Frank? I shook my head. This was total nonsense. I wasn't even sure if Veronique had ever bothered to recognize Frank at our table. And yet, women can be great at misleading others, I should know. I had seen enough examples of it in my school.

Running time finished, it was time to do some spinning on the high-tech bicycle. Motivated by my successful running experience, I decided to go for a more ambitious setting, a mountainous course. It took only five minutes to convince me that I'm not the mountain-bike type of person. I was not only panting, I was close to dying.

"Aren't you overdoing things a bit, darling?" I could hear the cheerful voice of Marge next to me.

"How do you do it? You're not even out of breath!" I gasped, trying desperately to fill my lungs with precious oxygen in order to survive.

"Oh, that's easy enough, darling! I always choose the lowest setting, after all this should be fun – and I want to look good when there are gentlemen around, not a complete wreck. And there are some very nice specimens here..." She looked around her, appraising the group of fit-looking men around us, even if most of them were young enough to have been her son.

I swallowed. It didn't take much imagination to see who the wreck was here. A quick look in the mirror in front of me confirmed the depressing truth of Marge's statement.

"I always finish my sessions with a short sprint at the end," I lied quickly. "I was just preparing to take a shower, go back to my cabin and have a rest."

"Have your shower, darling, but join me for a smoothie and a chocolate cookie, I think we've earned it, after all, we *have* been very sporty today."

"You're not feeling sea-sick, I assume from your suggestion?" Due to the storm the ship had been rolling more and more vigorously during the last hour.

"Not at all! But you should see John, he thinks that he's about to die," she giggled. "It may sound mean, but frankly speaking, I love it when he's confined to the cabin from time to time. John's acquired the bad habit of following me everywhere, like a puppy. Cute, but annoying. My erotic horoscope in the Cosmopolitan promised me an interesting encounter for this week – how will I have one with John trailing behind me all the time? "

It took me twenty minutes to be restored to something that at least resembled my usual self before I left with Marge. Marge had continued to calmly push the pedals of her bike at a slow pace – she looked healthy and not a single hair was out of place.

We decided to go to my favourite café. Even if we couldn't see a lot under the rainy sky it still felt good to sit in the daylight.

"You don't really look very fresh, darling, if I may say so." Marge didn't mince her words. "Has Daniel been tiring you out?" she giggled.

"I wish... But two murders are more than anybody can take, it's been haunting me all night!" I answered before I had really given it a further thought. Me and my big mouth. I should think before I open it.

Marge's eyes became as large as saucers. I realized that she couldn't possibility have known about any murders, as Frank's disappearance had been declared an 'accident' to all of the other passengers. "Murder?" she whispered and looked around her in panic, as if a bunch of serial killers might be hiding in the café.

"Can you keep a secret?"

"Sure, darling, nothing will ever leave these lips, they're sealed!"

I still don't know why I told Marge that there had been two murders. I guess I must still have been in shock, and I was very tired. The combination of a lack of sleep and the strenuous gym session must have softened my brain. I explained to a rapt Marge that I had seen Frank being thrown overboard and that I knew from Daniel that Veronique had been the victim of a poisonous snake – an unlikely coincidence, given the fact that her cabin was located hundreds of yards and several decks away from the snakes' vivarium.

"Who's the murderer then?" Marge asked me. I couldn't suppress the feeling that she was relishing the situation.

"How should I know? I'm a teacher, not a sleuth!"

Marge dismissed this with a wave of her hand. "Darling, you cannot simply let a murderer run wild on this ship, you must do something! I mean, there can't be any rational relationship between those two victims, so it's fairly simple…"

I looked at Marge in fascination. "It's simple? Tell me then, who did it?"

"Either Neil Hopkins did or an outsider – someone who's escaped the loony bin!"

"The loony bin?"

"Whatever they call it nowadays, hospital for the mentally handicapped. It's clear that a person who runs around killing other people must be insane. You just need to identify him or her and the case is solved!"

Marge looked at me triumphantly. It sounded easy enough.

"How do you identify such a person?" I was curious now. Maybe Marge had a solution to this problem too.

"Look into his eyes! They can't hold them steady!" and she rolled her eyes like a bad actor in a B-movie. I almost laughed – it didn't even look crazy, it just looked funny.

"You're smiling, because you think it's funny, but it's not." Marge was offended.

"Oh no! Don't get me wrong, Marge! But just imagine, please, having to stare more than two thousand passengers in the eyes – that's a bit of a tall order!"

Marge was somewhat mollified. "You have a point there, I didn't think about that. When you travel first class you sort of forget about the others. I'll have to give it some thought and find another method. But don't forget about Professor Hopkins, he's the toxin specialist here on board! "

"I must confess that this worries me. He did have the opportunity. Marge, wouldn't that be terrible? But I can't come up with a motive – why should Neil go running around killing fellow passengers who he barely knows, it doesn't make sense!"

"That's true, it doesn't make sense. But you never know, do you?"

Our good relationship restored we ordered smoothies (strawberry for me, mango and banana for Marge) and a cookie (chocolate walnut). As the size of the cookie was gigantic (US style) we shared one between the two of us as best friends and left in good spirits.

"Pay attention!" I warned her. "If your horoscope mentioned an encounter, don't let it be the murderer!"

"You'd better pay attention!" Marge replied complacently. "You're the witness, you just told me. I wouldn't like to be in your shoes…"

I had meant it to be a joke, but Marge's reply was a sobering truth.

***

Back in my cabin, I tried once again to read my book. By now a dense curtain of rain was hammering against the large window and the sea had become very rough. The dark clouds and the foaming sea looked like a compact mass of grey misery while dense streams of rainwater poured like miniature Niagaras down the window panes.

I shuddered. This had not been my idea of a cruise when I had booked it. Well, when Susan had booked it. She had wanted some diversion for me and I must say, she had been successful. I'd had plenty of diversions so far.

Luckily I never get sea-sick. I simply try to imagine that I'm a kid, sitting a on a seesaw, enjoying myself. But today we were enjoying a bit too much of a seesaw ride, and the *Belgravia* was rocking on gigantic waves. There was no end in sight.

Luckily my book managed to occupy me again. Time passed quickly, and it was early afternoon when I finished it. Now all I needed to know was if the evil cousin would survive the last encounter – but this meant that I'd need to walk back to the library and pray that the sequel was available. Suddenly I felt a pang of guilt. Absorbed by my book, I had completely forgotten about Neil. He must be desperate – at least this was what Daniel had told me. I remembered my conversation with Marge, but came to the conclusion that Neil couldn't be the murderer. He needed my help!

Quickly I grabbed my coat and handbag and rushed to the mall. I needed to find a small gift for Neil. As the ship was still rolling and pitching I had expected the mall to be deserted, but maybe there were plenty of souls resistant to sea sickness like me, or who were benefiting from the wonders of modern medicine, as the mall was crowded with shoppers. It was a strange atmosphere though – a bit like a sort of party, with that British never-say-die attitude of carrying on regardless in the face of impending doom. My German compatriots on the other hand were probably sitting in their cabins, studying the emergency procedures with clammy hands.

As I browsed the gift store, I found exactly what I needed: a cute teddy bear with an embroidered 'Friends Forever'. This would cheer Neil up, I was sure. Then I made a quick stop in the flower shop where I bought a bunch of flowers in all kinds of bright colours. I wanted something cheerful, not necessarily chic. Armed with my bouquet and my gift, I knocked at Neil's cabin door and breathed deeply. I was really nervous. I had no idea in what state of mind I'd find Neil after this ordeal – and I certainly did not want him to think that I had decided to throw myself into his arms. It would be quite a challenge to find the right balance....

Neil opened the door and I almost gasped out loud. He looked ten years older. I guess he hadn't got any sleep since yesterday, as his eyes were bloodshot and he walked as if had been drinking heavily – I then remembered that he might still be under the influence of the tranquillizers that the ship's doctor had administered, according to Daniel. Neil's hair looked more mop-like than ever, and his shirt was untucked. He looked like a wreck of a human being.

I had rehearsed some elaborate speech but seeing Neil standing there in front of me I just dropped my gifts on his table and hugged him, as a mother would hug a child.

"Let me go, Amanda!" he said gently. "You'll soon learn the truth, you're hugging a murderer."

I had heard something similar from Charles Peltier before. I wouldn't walk into this trap again. "Daniel told me all about the snake and Veronique's death, but why would this make you a murderer?"

105

"Because I didn't listen when you told me that a snake might be missing... and because I failed to check if the anti-venom was stored properly. I couldn't save Veronique, she suffocated in front of my eyes, just like...." He started to cry.

"Just like your wife?" I asked gently. Neil just nodded, he couldn't answer.

"Neil, don't wallow in self-pity. My father always says that self-pity is as despicable as arrogance, and my father is a wise man!"

While I kept talking I spotted a glass jug that could be utilised as a vase for my flowers. The jug was a bit small but as the end justifies the means, I stuffed the flowers inside. They looked at bit strange, like soldiers standing to attention, but they lent a nice colourful touch to the cabin. I was content with my choice. As I looked around, I stopped, startled. There was a space where the vivarium had been.

Neil followed my glance. "I insisted that they take them away, they'll be guarded day and night from now on."

Then he seemed to realize that I had brought him some flowers and with a crooked smile he continued: 'Thank you, those flowers are lovely. One of them is actually slightly poisonous..."

"Who cares, as long as you promise not to eat them!"

"I promise!" he answered meekly. "So... you don't think that I'm guilty?"

"Neil, don't be stupid! I'm ready to swear that you've been used by a ruthless killer. I'm also sure that the murders of Frank and Veronique are related!"

"Frank's murder?" he exclaimed. "You mean, Frank's death wasn't an accident? I had heard that Frank had been drinking too much, lost his balance and fell overboard. It sounded a bit fishy though, I never saw him drinking heavily; Peltier does by the way, he drinks far too much."

"It was as much an accident as Veronique's death. I'm convinced that there must be a master plan behind all of this. Veronique's killer knew exactly how dangerous your snakes are and he knew that only you might be able to save her! He obviously left nothing to chance, as the anti-venom was stolen too. Well, maybe it was a woman, I don't know, I'm totally lost, I have no idea who's behind all of this."

Neil looked at me in surprise. I could also see that he was relieved that I hadn't accused him of being negligent. He must have been living a nightmare.

106

"Neil, I implore you, please keep this information secret. We're waiting for the police to sort out this riddle. Officially we're still dealing with two accidents. Only Daniel knows all the details so far." Suddenly I remembered my slip of the tongue earlier and added to myself, '...and Marge happens to know, as I was stupid enough to tell her.'

Neil nodded and as he sat down he discovered the teddy bear next to the flowers. He took the bear and smiled at me. "I think this is the nicest gift I've received since I won the Nobel Prize. Maybe even nicer."

I was embarrassed. I really didn't know what to answer!

"But you can forget about the police," Neil continued, coming back to his normal analytic self. "Nobody can come on board as long as we're in the middle of a tropical storm. We'll need to wrack our own brains as to who could have a valid motive to get rid of Frank and Veronique. I don't see any relationship. What could be the common denominator?" He looked puzzled.

We sat a moment in silence, but all of a sudden Neil seemed to wake up from his thoughts. "Amanda, I must look ghastly. Let me take a shower so I can feel human again. Thank God that you came. Last night all those terrifying memories came back – I saw my wife perish the same way. I'm not betraying any secrets when I tell you that Beth and I had been at odds; we had been quarrelling for months – lately I had even hated her. But all of this was forgotten the moment she was lying there helpless, fighting for breath. I tried my best, but the injection came too late. To see the panic in her eyes..." He stopped and took a deep breath. "Beth must have realized that I couldn't save her..." His voice broke. "It was horrible, all I wanted was to die with her."

Neil rubbed his eyes, cleared his throat, forcing himself to go on. "I was naïve, I thought that people would help me, be compassionate. But my eyes were opened. I had to realize that in truth I didn't possess a single friend among my fellow colleagues. Maybe that's normal, maybe I was expecting too much. We're all competitors at the university, fighting for funds like dogs fighting over the best bones. The tongues started wagging: 'First he married her for her money, now he's killed her'. I pretended not to notice, but it started to wear me down, and in the end I was desperate. This is why I was planning to leave England and to live in Brazil. I'm taking the snakes to the USA to allow my colleagues in Yale to finish my research."

"It must have been a very difficult time for you," I said softly. "People can be mean, I experienced that myself after I won a lot of money in the TV show. My colleagues were horrible to me."

Neil shrugged. "People are people, but I'm glad I met you. I'm not a great believer, but I'll say a little prayer tonight to say thank you that you've come along."

Neil took the teddy bear in his hands and looked at it with affection. "'Friends forever'! Thank you, Amanda!"

And then what did stupid Amanda do? Emotional me, I started to cry and hugged Neil. So much for wanting to keep my distance. I'm simply hopeless.

Back in my cabin, I came back down to earth. I could only pray that Neil had told me the truth – that he was innocent – for the simple reason that I wanted him to be innocent. Marge's words of warning still lingered in my mind. Who should I believe?

But Neil had seemed genuinely surprised to hear about Frank, therefore he must be innocent. Or he was a fantastic actor.

**

We met again at dinner, but as could have been expected, the general mood was melancholy – and that's an understatement. Everybody seemed to be whispering rather than talking. John had opted to stay in his cabin, as he was still feeling sea-sick. Tom and his father were absent, but Charles Peltier had chosen to show up. He barely ate a morsel of the delicious food but kept drinking heavily. I think he must have finished almost two bottles of Dom Pérignon before he left our table.

Daniel whispered into my ear, "I can see that you've done a marvellous job of resurrecting Professor Hopkins. I hope this was an act of pure charity…"

I turned a flaming red. Daniel just laughed, but his laughter sounded a bit forced – did I detect a hint of jealousy in his eyes? But quickly Daniel resumed his usual self-assured manner and continued in a brisk tone, "I need to talk with you, Amanda. I've spoken to the captain and we have a problem. There will be no police available before the remains of the hurricane have passed over New York – but we can't just sit around and do nothing!"

I thought of Marge's idea of searching for insane passengers with rolling eyes. I could only hope that Daniel would have a better idea. I was sure that he would.

As soon as our table had finished the last course in leaden silence, Daniel and I decided to meet for a drink in the Kensington bar and talk things over. As Daniel needed to finish some urgent emails back in his cabin I said I'd make my own way

108

to the bar, and he'd join me about half an hour later. Somehow I didn't fancy the idea of going back to my cabin through the dimly lit corridors without company, so going straight to the bar seemed to be the safer option.

The bar was busy, but not as packed as usual after dinner. I guess the rough sea was deterring all but the most ardent regulars from showing up. I was surprised though to meet Tom Olstrom; somehow I had expected him to stay with his father inside their lavish cabin, mourning. Well, not exactly mourning, as I was sure that Tom wouldn't grieve the loss of his stepmother, but I had expected him to stay close to his father, at least to keep up appearances. Sir Walter was devastated, Daniel had told me as much and his reaction seemed natural enough.

Tom must have been drinking heavily, as his face was flushed and his eyes were sparkling. This was a great opportunity to do some sleuthing. Wasn't Tom my prime suspect now, as his stepmother had been removed from my list of suspects (removed by fate, that was)? But how to approach Tom in a casual way? I must not arouse any suspicion. That was the difficult part – I couldn't simply walk into the bar, saying, 'Hi Tom, by the way, did you kill your stepmother? If yes, congrats, I never liked her anyhow…'

I was still trying to decide how to open the discussion when the bartender approached, leaning slightly over the counter. "Would you fancy some 'sex on the beach' today, madam?" He winked at me. He was a good-looking lad, and he knew it.

"Don't drink that stuff, Amanda!" Tom suddenly interjected. "It'll give you a terrible hangover tomorrow. Have something pure, like a good Scotch – this one is quite good."

"Thanks Tom, it's very kind of you to warn me!" I smiled at him. I still liked very much what I saw. Tom was a very handsome boy, well-mannered. Why would he have decided to embark on a career as a mass-murderer? That would be such a shame.

I cleared my throat. "Tom, please accept my sincere condolences for the loss of Veronique. I heard the terrible news from Daniel this morning; it must have been a terrible shock for you and your father."

Tom looked at me as if trying to focus on the person that was intruding in what he must consider rightly to be his private affairs. I tried hard not to shrink under his glance, as he spluttered, "Spare me the bullshit, Amanda. It might have been a shock, but not a terrible one, I can assure you! I'm glad the bitch is gone forever!" He raised his glass in a mock salute and looked to the ceiling. "Cheers, lovely Veronique, sometimes life holds an unpleasant surprise in store even for those who think that they'll always be a winner!"

I was shocked. I had expected Tom to at least respect the usual codes of behaviour. I didn't know what to say.

"Don't look at me like that, Amanda! Veronique was a bitch, if ever I met one. Father dropped my mom like a hot potato when darling Veronique moved her cute little ass into view. Since then she's done everything to kick me out as well. Her last scheme was to convince father to try in vitro fertilization – apparently the desired new heir wouldn't come the natural way..." He bristled with anger.

'Oh, Tom,' I thought, 'You're hopeless, you're digging your own grave. Plenty of motive here.' My sleuthing instincts had led me to the right person, I was sure. What a pity, he was such a nice boy! I was at a loss as to how to continue the conversation, as Tom didn't look at all intimidated or inclined to talk further. There was no chance that he'd confess to murder here and now.

"It's already the second tragedy on this trip," I finally continued, trying to keep the conversation going.

Suddenly Tom looked sad. "You're right. I still don't understand how this could have happened." He paused for a moment before looking straight into my eyes. "You seem very curious, Amanda!"

Suddenly he must have realized that he had committed a social faux-pas with this remark and blushed. "I mean, you communicate easily with your fellow passengers. I have problems doing this. Maybe it comes with owning too much money. The people I tend to meet are never interested in me as a person, it's just the Olstrom money they're after, brazen gold-diggers most of them." He realized that he had lost the trail of his first sentence. It happens when you drink too much. After a minute or two of silence he must have remembered that we were talking about Frank and he resumed the focus of his initial conversation. "I mean, have you heard anybody talking about why Frank might have thrown himself overboard? He was a nice chap, a bit on the queer side, but alright. I don't think that he took any drugs, maybe a bit of coke from time to time, but it seems they all do in the fashion world."

I was still smarting from being labelled 'curious'. Well, I am, I admit it, but I don't like people telling me. Tom was apparently waiting for my answer, but was he just playing naïve? He should have known best of all that Frank's death hadn't been an accident.

"I have no idea, Tom. I did talk with Charles Peltier, but he seemed to be lost for an explanation as well."

"Peltier was dead jealous!" Tom grinned, suddenly full of mischief. "That old pervert probably thought I was shagging Frank on the quiet. You should have seen his expression when I left the table together with Frank, quite murderous! I wasn't – of course – but Frank was only too happy to get rid of Peltier from time to time. It seems that Peltier needed constant attention and admiration, a tiring kind of personality, a bit like my father."

Once more I didn't really know what to answer, therefore I changed the subject. "You're reading *The Economist*?" I admit, it was a stupid question as the open magazine lay on the counter next to Tom.

"Yep, one of the best journals in this field, if you ask me. This article is excellent, they really do their research. Usually I read it on my tablet, but having it in print is a nice change from time to time."

I bent forward to look at the article. 'Richard Wu – from Russian Dream to Nightmare' – I had heard this name before. Then I remembered that Kenneth had mentioned the name before, and later Tom had talked about Richard Wu as well. I now remembered that Wu must be on the ship together with us, as he had given a fat tip to Kenneth.

"Have you ever met Richard Wu? What is he like and what does this article say? He must be a real Hong Kong tycoon, rolling in money."

"How come you know Richard Wu?" Tom looked at me, surprised.

"My cabin steward mentioned that he's on board – and you discussed Mr. Wu with your father when you were sitting at our table."

Tom looked at me with respect. "You don't miss much, that's for sure. Richard Wu is actually our most dangerous competitor. A man in his early sixties, quite obese, which is something of an exception in China, they tend to be skinny. Wu's my number one enemy, to be blunt. If you're interested, have a look at the article. I have to be going now, anyhow. I know now that we'll need to be even more watchful. Cheers."

Tom called the bar tender for the bill – I was surprised, somehow I had assumed that he wouldn't even bother to ask for the bill. I had thought that the son of a billionaire wouldn't care about such trivial matters and have a secretary on hand to pay for him. Tom checked his bill thoroughly before he signed it and left a moderate tip – no big spender in the making here, I concluded.

"Did you make your mind up, madam?" the bartender reminded me politely. Ignoring Tom's advice to stay with whisky, I chose a fancy cocktail and settled in the corner of the bar where I sank into one of the soft leather armchairs.

Sipping my drink and nibbling roasted almonds I tackled *The Economist*. The article was interesting, Tom had been right. Richard Wu held a fifty percent stake in a Russian oil company, a risky investment. It became more and more obvious that his Russian shareholders were following their own (not always very ethical) agenda. The article concluded that the Wu empire might soon be suffering from a shortage of funds if Russia didn't allow him to sell some shares or get hold of the sizeable dividends that had been conveniently (at least from the point of view of the Russians) frozen by the Russian high court. Wu owned a lot of companies but what looked impressive at a first glance had mostly been mortgaged to the hilt if you looked closer. There was one remaining free precious asset, his last trump card. The Wu holding possessed large strips of lands in Canada where shale gas could be extracted, worth billions of dollars in the near future.

And yet, lately Wu had encountered a streak of bad luck in Canada as well. The Canadian government had flatly refused to grant building permission for the pipelines that would have to be constructed to transport the precious gas through the bordering National Parks – and the only available access meant crossing land that belonged to the competing Canadian Imperial Petrol & Gas PLC. He'd need to come to an agreement with his enemy in order to survive – and fast.

Suddenly a hand touched me from behind and I dropped my magazine as I turned around to see who was the owner of the hand. Daniel was grinning at me, then he looked at *The Economist*.

"Must be exciting reading. Planning to invest your millions – maybe you can advise me?" he drawled.

"Daniel Greenfield!" I used my stern teacher's voice. "Stop teasing me. You told me yesterday that you have a masters in economics."

"The problem with you, Amanda, is that you never seem to forget anything. Most annoying, I'll have to watch what I tell you!"

"You better had, Daniel."

But Daniel wasn't listening. He picked up the article and started reading it at speed but also with great attention. Somebody could have kidnapped me right next to him and he wouldn't even have noticed. Only after he had finished reading the article did he drop the journal onto the low table.

"Most interesting," he said in a strange tone. "I think I may have to change some of my ideas."

"You mean that you've invested in Wu's company?"

"I was planning to; he invited me to do so recently. But as you've certainly read for yourself, his company seems to be in a rather shaky situation at present. I guess Mr. Wu urgently needs to raise some cash and get results. This all sounds a bit desperate."

Daniel ordered a Bloody Mary and we changed to small talk, as a noisy group of American youngsters had occupied the table next to us, making it impossible to discuss any serious matters. As soon as our drinks were finished, Daniel proposed moving to his cabin in order to discuss things in privacy.

I looked at him with suspicion. "Daniel, we agreed to be just good friends yesterday. You're sure, it's only to discuss things?"

"I swear, Amanda, I have only the purest of intentions!"

Before I could react, Daniel had already settled our bill and we walked – or should I say swayed – in the direction of his cabin. The *Belgravia* was still rolling heavily, but I consoled myself with the thought that it would be rather unlikely we should encounter any icebergs at this latitude.

We arrived safely at Daniel's cabin, an even bigger version of mine. He had opted for a suite with a rather large, separate bedroom. It was a comforting thought to know that his bed was in a different room and we headed to the couch where I sat down. Daniel, playing the host, opened the mini bar and offered me a drink.

"Sparkling water would be lovely."

"That sounds a bit extravagant. I hope I can afford such extravagant whims."

"I can leave you a tip, Daniel, it's quite common on a boat to reward good service."

Oh, me and my big mouth! This might sound like a double entendre to his ears, exactly the kind of comment I should *not* be making.

Daniel laughed. "You seem to be experienced… But I think I can offer my services without having to ask for a tip."

He filled two glasses with sparkling water and swayed back to the couch, holding the glasses and trying to tune his balance to the motion of the rocking ship. The *Belgravia* chose this very moment to play roller coaster and dived deep into a valley of water. Daniel stumbled and ended up on my lap – with two empty glasses. Both of us were dripping wet. Still balancing the glasses in his hands he profited from my surprise and kissed me before he stumbled back onto his feet.

"Daniel, you swore that you'd keep your distance!" I exclaimed, still a bit out of breath. The worst thing was that I wouldn't have minded continuing, he smelled so good.

"I didn't!" Daniel protested. "I just said that my intentions were pure, but intentions are intentions…"

"Are you a lawyer by any chance?" I asked suspiciously.

"I might have forgotten to mention that I studied law and economics. Well, usually I don't mention it because it tends to confuse people."

I digested this information while Daniel disappeared into the bathroom. He came back minutes later, clad in a bathrobe, and handed me some fluffy towels. "Dry yourself, otherwise you'll catch a cold!" he advised. I followed his suggestion but ignored the second bathrobe he had brought for me. Having Daniel sitting there with bare legs and a tanned chest was dangerous enough.

"We wanted to discuss serious matters – the murders…?" I reminded him.

"Oh, yes. The murders. I had completely forgotten about them." He sent me a long reflective glance that I chose to ignore.

"Daniel, that's serious enough. I talked with Tom before you came. I really like the lad, but he admitted that he hated Veronique – and he has a motive!"

Daniel had been sitting relaxed, ready for small talk, or a bit of flirting, but immediately his attitude changed, and I could see that he was alert.

"Everybody could see that Tom loathed Veronique, that's not really surprising. But if you have found a genuine motive, that's interesting! Please continue, what did he say?"

I couldn't quite hide my triumph that my amateur sleuthing had yielded a spectacular result and repeated with glee the conversation we had in the Kensington bar: "…and then he told me that Veronique had convinced Sir Walter to try in vitro fertilization– she wanted a child – and of course she'd want her child to become the heir of the Olstrom fortune!"

Daniel whistled. "That's a strong motive indeed, the Olstrom fortune must be worth billions. But I still have problems seeing Tom as a culprit – and what about Frank, why should Tom have killed Frank?"

"I have no idea," I answered, trying to come up with a reply that made sense, "and I have to admit, despite my suspicion, I still rather like Tom. But as you just said, people have been killed for less money already and he really hated Veronique, that was obvious enough. The nice-boy façade may hide a very sinister character."

"I can see that life in school has made you suspicious. Did you consider the possibility that the killer might have made a mistake and smuggled the snake into the wrong cabin?" Daniel suggested.

"That's an interesting idea," I conceded. "Can you find out tomorrow who's staying next door?"

"That's easy enough, I know the answer already. Charles Peltier is residing there in regal splendour."

"Maybe there's a motive there." I was getting excited, we had a fresh scent. "First Frank, now the murderer wants to get rid of Peltier, maybe the link is Peltier, he's a known collector of art, he might possess a priceless painting and doesn't want to sell it…"

Daniel looked at me, but I wasn't sure he wasn't finding my enthusiasm entertaining. He was looking a bit smug.

"Don't look at me like that! Have you got any better ideas?"

"Oh, sorry, I was just amazed at what kind of fruitful imagination you have; I wouldn't have thought that teachers possessed such fertile minds. I do have some ideas, but if I'm wrong, I'd provoke such a scandal that the captain would need to throw me overboard here and now, and rightfully so. So I need to wait a bit before I can tell you."

If there's something I hate, it's people who hint at something that makes me curious and then shut up like an clam the moment things are getting really interesting. Offended, I rose and looked down at Daniel. "If you don't trust me and don't want to tell me, that's fine with me. I was going to leave anyhow."

With a last scornful look I said good-bye, ignoring the fact that the flap of his bath robe had opened. He could save these cheap tricks for others. Maybe running around half-naked would work for the battalion of teenage girl friends that might long to be noticed by him.

But Daniel somehow didn't seem to be bothered too much about my cool good-bye. He rose and kissed my cheek like an old friend and wished me good night. "What about seeing you tomorrow morning at breakfast?"

"Maybe, it all depends if I'm in the mood," I answered a bit crossly and closed the door behind me. I was not satisfied. This encounter had been a battle of wills – and I was not sure if Daniel hadn't won in the end.

Damn it, he had looked really sexy in his bathrobe. 'Amanda,' my inner voice suddenly started arguing, 'stop meddling with playboys. Daniel is too rich and far too good-looking, he's just playing games, wake up or you'll regret it!' As usual my inner voice was right, and yet…

Deep in my thoughts I walked back to the safe haven of my cabin and opened the door. Back inside, I went through the usual motions of undressing and getting ready for bed. I was still fuming at Daniel's arrogance. This man urgently needed a lesson in decent behaviour and modesty! I was mentally going through various agreeable and very satisfying options on how to punish Daniel while I sat down on my inviting bed, ready to snuggle into the soft pillows.

It was at this moment that I noticed an innocent-looking sheet of paper on the floor, close to the door. Sleepily I wondered who had slipped it underneath – maybe it was a special note from the ship's bridge related to the tropical storm? I could have remained in my bed, but curiosity got the better of me, and the fact that a note was lying there couldn't simply be ignored. Cursing myself, I unravelled myself from the blanket and picked up the piece of paper.

A message from the ship's bridge it was not! The blood froze in my veins. I had to read the text several times, hoping that the message might change or that I was just in the grip of a nightmare. But of course I wasn't, and I didn't need to pinch myself in order to face the truth. No matter how often I read the message, the text didn't change. Printed in bold script were the following words:

'Amanda, stop meddling, or the next accident will be yours.'

116

Day 7 – Waiting for the Storm to Pass

I don't remember how I managed to get to sleep that night. My instinctive reaction had been to rush to the phone and call Daniel. But how could I show such weakness after I had stormed out of his cabin in a huff? I was an independent woman, I didn't need an arrogant macho-man to manage my affairs. I secured my cabin door by fastening the metal chain, then I locked it from inside – at least this action made me feel a bit safer. I needed time to think.

The next morning a tired and worried-looking woman greeted me in the mirror – I didn't like the look of her and it would take more than the mere application of lipstick to make her look half decent, no doubt about that. Twenty minutes later, Amanda looked better. Not the work of art that Oksana had created, but at least the shadows of a sleepless night had disappeared under thick layers of make-up. There would be no luxurious breakfast inside my cabin this morning. I needed to talk with Daniel. From today's perspective my behaviour yesterday looked a bit childish. Daniel must have thought that I'm a moody specimen. Maybe I am – but no worse than others.

I stuffed the threatening sheet of paper into my handbag and headed to the Westminster Grill where the usual buffet breakfast was served. Luckily the sea had calmed during the night, and I could almost walk normally without the risk of bumping into my fellow passengers. The wonderful aroma of freshly brewed coffee already greeted me from afar, to be matched by the smell of eggs and bacon as I approached the restaurant. This cheered me up considerably – any diet would have to wait another day. I needed to fortify myself.

Daniel was already sitting at our usual table. I took this as a good omen. As I greeted him, I couldn't suppress a feeling of annoyance. How dare he look so relaxed and cheerful – this was a clear lack of empathy!

"What's the matter, Amanda? You look as if you haven't had a wink of sleep! Did the rough sea trouble you?"

So much for my make-up skills! I could only conclude that I must look positively hideous. Luckily the waiter chose this very moment to fill my cup with coffee and offer some freshly squeezed juice to accompany my croissants and I was spared an immediate reply. Just as I was about to open the conversation, Neil arrived at our table, his plate loaded with toast, fried eggs, bacon and baked beans, the staple foods that had helped Britain to create and maintain an empire.

"Good morning, Amanda!" he greeted me. "You look splendid! How do you do this? I had a difficult night, I kept rolling in my bed from left to right, damned hurricane." I smiled broadly at Neil and invited him to take a seat next to me, ignoring Daniel's smirk. At least Neil knew how to greet a lady correctly.

I hesitated as to how I should continue. I had no desire to plunge head-on into a somewhat delicate conversation. But most of the surrounding tables weren't occupied and the few passengers sitting close-by appeared to be too busy to pay any attention to us. No need to procrastinate, I could talk freely.

"In truth, I spent a terrible night!" I started, hoping for the appropriate feed-back. Any female listener would have known that this phrase was an invitation to ask me why I had spent such a bad night. But I was to be disappointed.

Neil just nodded and silently shovelled the food into his mouth and Daniel seemed totally absent-minded. Maybe breakfast was not the right time to start a serious discussion. I tried once again – it's a general rule that you need to be patient when it comes to eliciting male sympathy.

I thus cleared my throat and repeated with a bit more emphasis: "I had a *really* terrible night!"

Finally my statement filtered through to the minds of both men and they exclaimed, almost simultaneously, "Sorry to hear that! Anything amiss?"

"Look at this!" With a dramatic move I opened my handbag and presented the note. At least this was what I intended to do. But my dramatic gesture lost its impact as I opened my handbag with too much verve and a lipstick, keys and a small calculator chose to escape their confinement and roll underneath the table. My precious possessions were soon retrieved, but the dramatic moment had evaporated.

"As I was just about to explain, I found this piece of paper, it was shoved underneath my cabin door."

The interruption had been a good thing, as I could talk normally now, in an almost detached manner, about the horrid note. Sitting in broad daylight in the Westminster Grill, it seemed somehow unbelievable that I could be the next target of this lunatic murderer – and yet, the menacing piece of paper lay on the table, right in front of me.

Daniel whistled softly as he handed the sheet of paper to Neil, who took out his reading glasses, although the letters were of such a size that even a mole could have read it.

"Now you're speechless!" I said triumphantly to Daniel – which was a bit silly as there was nothing to feel triumphant about.

"I am – it blows away my whole idea about the murders!" Daniel looked really troubled, which warmed my heart a little. Maybe he felt worried about me?

"It must be a psychopath then!" I stated the obvious. "And I don't like it," I added in a small voice.

"This might explain why the first murders might not be linked after all," Neil intervened. "I've been wracking my brains to find a motive since Amanda told me yesterday that Frank's disappearance was not an accident after all – but I haven't come to any satisfying conclusion!"

"I don't like it either," said Daniel curtly. "Let's arrange a meeting with the captain later today – we must do something, we can't wait for the police to arrive in three or four days. It was never a joking matter, but the situation is getting out of hand. This is becoming highly dangerous!"

"Do you think this is really serious?" I suddenly had a queer feeling in my stomach. "Not just a tasteless joke?"

"A joke?" Neil was upset. "Nobody would joke about something like that!"

"Some people would…" Daniel took the piece of paper into his hands as if it would yield more clues. "But only very few people know that Amanda saw the murderer. How come he knows about it?" He looked puzzled. "Amanda was sure that neither of the two boys had seen her. Nothing adds up! Let me arrange a meeting with the captain – and in the meantime, behave normally. Be relaxed, it's just a warning."

"Thanks so much for this valuable advice, I feel much better already!" I was fuming. "'Be relaxed', what great advice! It will make a nice inscription on my tombstone!"

But I failed to impress Daniel. He just grinned at me. "I'll ask the crew to look after you. Don't forget to wave at them when you spot a camera!" In a hurry he stood up and left the table, leaving me alone with Neil.

Neil looked behind him. "All very dynamic, but does he really understand that someone insane is after you?"

I sighed. "I don't think so, but sitting here, I'm starting to think that it's just a fantasy, a Hitchcock movie – maybe I'll bump into Cary Grant in a minute or so."

"Unlikely, Amanda, he's been dead for some time now."

"Oh Neil, it was just a manner of speaking, of course, that was long ago. I think I'll have one more go at the buffet, there's really no use sitting here fretting. Let's change the subject and look on the bright side of life."

This is what we did and Neil succeeded in cheering me up considerably. But even the most wonderful and most sumptuous breakfast has to end at some time and finally it was time to leave the Westminster Grill.

"Let me accompany you back to your cabin," Neil offered, a true gentleman.

"Neil, I've been living and coping on my own very well since I left home. This is very kind of you, but really, I can walk back on my own!"

"Bullshit, Amanda, let's walk together, anyhow it's a pleasure for me. I think you're the first female acquaintance I have made during the past two years who didn't want to know immediately how the Swedish Queen was dressed for the Nobel Prize dinner, neither have you consulted me about your health problems – or worse –those of your pets."

I laughed. "I have no pets – a pity because I'd love to have a dog, and I feel fine, unless I've received any nasty letters, that is. But as to the Swedish Queen, I was just waiting for the right opportunity... would you remember what kind of tiara she was wearing, was it diamond or sapphire?" I teased him.

He groaned; of course he didn't remember. He did remember though that they had had a long and very detailed discussion about the Amazon. "She's charming and very bright, Sweden can be proud to have a queen like her," he concluded, a compliment indeed from a Nobel Prize winner! And if I'm honest, I felt a just a teeny bit jealous.

He walked me back to my cabin where I stayed for a good hour and flicked at random through some magazines. Actually I was very much tempted to call Susan but dropped this idea and opened several books instead, flicking through the pages, only to close them again impatiently. I had difficulty concentrating on anything. I looked around my gilded prison and suddenly I became angry, really angry. This trip had been supposed to be the journey of a lifetime, the journey I wanted to remember when I was old and would probably have forgotten most other things. I would *not* stay here, locked in my (admittedly very nice) cabin simply because I had received a stupid letter. I would take action.

Just taking this decision felt good!

'All you need is a bit of physical exercise, a bit of sport to get your mind back on track and feeling positive,' my inner voice told me. I had once read in a newspaper article that sport encourages the body to produce the kind of hormones that make you feel happy and give you the right kick (Neil would know how this works and rattle off all of those endocrine processes) – this was exactly what I needed. I slipped into my leggings and put on a t-shirt in my favourite turquoise colour. I glanced into the mirror close to the entrance and liked what I saw. I would never be a model, but I looked good, so much better than Amanda in her sloppy old teacher's clothes. A comfortable soft sweater would have to do against the chilly gusts of wind, a distant reminder of the hurricane that must be hitting the shores of New Jersey today. I winked at my image in the mirror to cheer me up and I was gone.

I don't know if I had expected anybody to follow me or something spectacular to happen as soon as I stepped out of my cabin into the corridor, but all was silent, and nothing happened. I reached the gym and the only incident en route was an encounter with a group of French youngsters (the same kind of adolescent boy-monsters I've had plenty of teaching encounters with in school) who were exchanging some flippant 'youth-speak' about my physique, especially the size of my breasts. I answered in kind, comparing parts of their physique to peanuts and saw them trot away with red faces – they hadn't expected to be understood, or to receive a sharp answer in their own language.

I arrived in the gym where I bumped into Marge. Same as last time, she was sitting on a bicycle, pedalling at her modest pace when she saw me. "Amanda, darling, how great to see you! Let's go and have a coffee together, I have something weird that I want to show you!" she shouted across the gym, which had the effect of making everyone crane their necks to see who had arrived. I could have done without this kind of attention.

I could see that Marge was not at ease, although I couldn't precisely define what gave me this impression. And yet I had no intention of leaving the gym without having performed a single exercise. I needed to move my body, that's why I had come here!

"Marge, have mercy, I've just arrived, and I know your coffee habits by now. Don't tell me that you won't order one of those chocolate chip cookies to come with it. I'd love to have a coffee with you, but let me finish my exercise first, please," I pleaded.

Marge looked a bit sulky and tried to persuade me to leave early but I remained resolute and tackled my running programme. I did follow Marge's advice though not to overdo things like last time; you never know, maybe Daniel would choose this very moment to walk in… Therefore I went through my physical exercises in considerably better style than last time. I steadfastly ignored Marge's attempts to start a conversation and was rewarded as she looked for a new victim after some minutes. Marge's silence gave me the opportunity to think about the letter that was still troubling me greatly while my feet were moving as if they had a life of their own, a sort of auto-pilot driving my limbs.

The next time I glanced in Marge's direction, I watched fascinated at how Marge had succeeded in getting her neighbour to talk, a man in his late forties. Like a spider, she was wrapping her helpless victim in her net of questions. Marge's interrogation skills were worthy of those of a ruthless secret agent. While I was going through my exercises she extracted all kinds of information from the poor man – I was surprised that he didn't hand over his personal bank details to Marge at the end. This little interlude had the effect that Marge was still glowing with glee as we took a shower and dressed for our coffee break.

The gym had cheered me up considerably, and now I felt perfectly capable of dealing with any lunatic at large. Marge and I followed our newly established routine of sharing a cookie with our coffee when I reminded her that she had wanted to talk to me about some strange occurrence. Suddenly Marge's face fell, the animated look draining from her face as if I had pulled a plug.

"It's a terrible thing, darling, I haven't even found the courage yet to talk with John about it!" Her eyes were a tell-tale red and suddenly a single tear ran down her cheek. I was alarmed; nothing in Marge's behaviour had prepared me for the advent of a new drama.

"Tell me, Marge, what has happened to make you so upset, maybe I can help you?"

Marge didn't answer but seized her big sports bag and dug into the chaos of sneakers, towels, T-shirts and an impressive variety of expensive cosmetics (she favoured Nina Ricci and Dior, I noted almost automatically). Finally she found what she had been searching for and banged a crumpled sheet of paper on the table.

'Stop meddling, you old witch - or the next accident will be yours.'

I gasped. I was not the only victim.

"That's horrible, Marge! You must feel dreadful!"

Marge nodded. "I didn't get a wink of sleep last night. I found this horrid note late in the evening. First I wanted to show the note to John, but he'd worry himself to death, he's such a dear and always wants to protect me. Amanda, I needed to talk to someone, that's why I thought about you, darling!" Marge suddenly looked very fragile, like one of my mother's delicate Meissen figures, her most precious treasures. But should I feel flattered that everybody seemed to be discussing their problems with me, expecting me to deal with them – or should I merely feel irritated?

"Marge, if it is any consolation to you, I received a similar note yesterday evening. I really do understand how you must feel. It's horrid, you were right from the beginning, there must be a lunatic on this boat, there's no other explanation!"

"Yes, of course I remember what I told you yesterday!" Marge sounded offended. "But you were just laughing at me, next time you'd better listen!" she finished, with an accusing look.

"I wasn't laughing! I just told you that it might prove difficult to check out two thousand fellow passengers," I protested hotly.

"You've got a valid point there," Marge conceded. I could see that she had decided to forgive me and be magnanimous. "Just imagine, this morning a young man followed me from the deck to the breakfast. Later, when I was helping myself from the breakfast buffet, he was almost breathing down my neck!" she shuddered. I tried to look suitably impressed, being aware that Marge liked a bit of melodrama.

"Can you describe him?"

"He was young..." Marge frowned. She closed her eyes and tried to concentrate. "Medium height, almost tall, brown hair, maybe more on the fair side, I mean, I'm not *that* sure... And he wore a red Lacoste sweater!" The latter came triumphantly. "This should be easy enough to recognize!"

I sighed. There must be a good hundred young men on this boat potentially fitting her description. The *Belgravia* was quite popular for honeymoon cruises, I had discovered.

"It's good that you're paying attention, Marge!" I tried to be positive. "I told Daniel about my note this morning, and he's considering talking to the captain to see what we can do to stop this."

Marge looked sceptical. "It's good that you believe in the superior wisdom of our captain, but how can he do anything, he's not the police? Do you expect him to

124

search every single cabin? I think we'll have to take this matter into our own hands!"

I didn't like to admit it, but deep inside, I knew that Marge was right. We'd probably better rely on our own resources. Marge and I continued discussing several wild ideas but apart from deciding to spend more time together and watch out for each other, our coffee break yielded no tangible results. Marge then drifted into reminiscences of her youth, but I suddenly felt dead tired; the sleepless night was taking its toll. I had to suppress a yawn and all I was longing to do was to sneak back to my cabin and have a nice nap there.

I heard a familiar voice behind me. "My inner voice told me: 'If you want to find Amanda, try the library or the coffee shop'."

"Daniel!'" I exclaimed, suddenly wide-awake. "Guess what, Marge has received the same kind of threatening note as I did!"

Daniel looked at us. I was pleased to note that I had caught him unprepared. He was genuinely surprised. If there's something I dislike in Daniel, it's his supreme self-confidence. It felt good to surprise him. "You didn't expect this?" I asked, trying (without success) to hide my glee.

"Not really, at least not so soon." He frowned, then turned towards Marge and switched on his Mr. Nice Guy smile. "Hi Marge, I hope this hasn't upset you too much. How did you receive your note?"

Marge glowed under his sudden attention and purred with satisfaction. I had always suspected that she had a bit of a crush on Daniel.

"It must have been shoved underneath my door at night. I only noticed it this morning."

"But Marge, you told me that you didn't sleep the whole night, because you saw it last thing!" I couldn't help blurting out.

Marge looked confused and turned flaming red. "How silly of me, this horrid story is making my brain go soft! Of course, you're right, it was in the early morning but it was still dark, when I had to get up to... you know what I mean." Luckily she spared us more details. "And afterwards I couldn't get to sleep, I lay in my bed, but sleep wouldn't come."

"I'm sorry to hear that, Marge. I was looking for Amanda as the captain wants to meet her because of her note. I'll certainly mention yours as well. We'll discuss our plan of action, so promise me not to worry too much! Sorry to break up your cosy coffee break."

I saw myself being dragged away from the table, but I didn't mind. The conversation with Marge had ended in deadlock. Apart from the hint with the young man in a red sweater, we hadn't come up with any tangible lead or concrete plan of action. Did I believe this red sweater story? Not really – what else had he done but have his breakfast close to Marge? It was hardly a hot lead.

Daniel led me straight to the deck where the captain was waiting for us. I had expected to return to the bridge but was led into a plain office – I could have been sitting in a hospital waiting room. The atmosphere was frosty, almost clinical, not even a cup of tea or coffee was waiting for us.

The ensuing discussion was swift and efficient. I told my little story and presented Marge's letter, holding it with a Kleenex. I could see Daniel smile, as usual, a bit supercilious.

"Why are you grinning? I want to make sure that the police will be able to identify the finger prints!" I remarked in a cool tone.

"That's very smart of you, the police will appreciate your precaution very much," the captain's voice could be heard. I thanked him with my brightest smile.

"I'm willing to bet that the police will only find two traces of finger prints on those notes – those of Marge and yours," Daniel muttered.

"We're not taking bets here. I think Miss Lipton's action is very wise!" The captain came to my defence and stored the paper carefully in a plastic wallet.

Daniel smirked but declined to enter into an argument. "The question remains, how can we identify the author of this note and how precisely is it linked to both murders?" Daniel asked instead.

But as Marge had predicted, our discussion didn't yield any brilliant results either. The captain reassured me that he'd organize special vigilance for me and would include Marge as well. I could be sure that I'd be under constant supervision; nobody would be able to approach me or my cabin without being noticed.

I thanked him – but I wasn't sure if I felt really so thankful, deep inside. I hated the knowledge that I was under constant supervision; somehow I had imagined my holidays to be a bit more relaxed. Once we had left the captain's office, I complained, "This is leading nowhere, Daniel. We can't solve two cases of murder and stop a lunatic by doing nothing. At least Marge will be relieved when I tell her that she's under special protection as of now."

"May I ask you a favour, Amanda?"

"Of course you may! Unless you want me to act as bait for the murderer, in which case it's a flat refusal – and that's final!" I hope that I sounded witty.

Daniel laughed. "Do you really think that I'd be capable of using you as bait for the killer? Nice impression that I must have made on you! I wonder you're still talking to me. Don't worry, my request isn't dangerous at all. I just wanted to ask you *not* to tell Marge that she's been placed under special protection from now on."

"Why? She's really terrified by the whole experience, expecting the worst to happen, poor dear. She'll be so relieved to know this. I simply have to tell her!"

"You know Marge, she's a bit melodramatic! Once she knows that she's under special observation she'll behave as if she's in a soap opera, waving to the cameras and telling everybody on the ship how secret and hush-hush this all is. It'll be impossible to nail down the blackmailer if she's boasting about being under special protection to every single human being that happens to come close to her. We must keep the surveillance low-key, make the culprit write new letters and catch him on the spot. That's the course of action I have already discussed with the captain!"

"Daniel, you're a monster!" I was almost shouting. "First you tell me that you'd never dream of exposing me to any kind of danger, but in fact you're messing around with me. I'm supposed to act the innocent until this madman uses the first opportunity either to slide a new note underneath my door or strangle me if he fancies a bit of a change. But if this is what you expect from me, my last service to mankind, so be it. I hope you feel comfortable with this."

"Amanda, you're every bit as melodramatic as Marge," came the dampener. "Nothing is expected of you, just don't tell Marge."

It may not have come as a total surprise that I remained unusually taciturn when Daniel accompanied me to the library, my next stop. When he said good-bye, he surprised me again. "I'll come at half past seven tonight to your cabin and fetch you for dinner."

"If this statement is supposed to serve as an invitation for another romantic evening, I don't think that I'm in the mood."

127

Prince Charming just grinned. Probably when you've dated women by the dozen, you become immune to such kinds of spiteful remarks.

"Sorry to disappoint you, Amanda, I've nothing special planned for tonight, just the usual dinner with our fellow passengers – unless… Well, we'll see."

With these obscure words he left me and I had ample time to hate him. What did he mean by his last remark? He had aroused my curiosity, which annoyed me. But browsing along the book shelves rewarded me with the discovery of a new book and I sank into one of the comfortable armchairs, forgetting Daniel, Marge and all the lunatics of this world.

Only much later did I become aware that I should have paid more attention to Daniel's remarks.

***

The evening came and Daniel rang the door bell on time, well, almost on time. Actually he was five minutes early, an unforgiveable crime when it comes to a date with a lady – a lapse worsened by the fact that I was a bit late. I had been lost in my new book and had forgotten the world around me. Thus I was still clad in my bathrobe when I opened the door and asked Daniel to take a seat, rather breathlessly as I had rushed to the door from my bathroom. "Daniel, I'm so sorry, I thought it was room service with fresh towels. A thousand apologies, I was reading a new book and totally forgot about the time! Can I offer you a glass of champagne and canapés in the meantime?" (Luckily the faithful Kenneth had passed by thirty minutes before with fresh supplies).

"Thanks, that's a nice idea. But how can my ego survive the thought that you forgot about me – and all because of a stupid book!"

I bent down and filled his glass. "First of all, my book is *not* stupid, it's historical and very edifying! Secondly, I think that's just the kind of treatment your ego needs from time to time. I guess your mother must have doted a bit too much on you. An exercise in downsizing your ego seems just to be the right thing to do!" I remarked, using my stern teacher's tone.

"That's ok, Amanda, as long as you promise to compensate your moral lectures with an exciting view to cheer me up. Nice bra, by the way, Victoria's Secret…?" His grin was downright salacious.

I yelped, as following his glance I noticed that a flap of my bathrobe had opened, revealing more than I had ever intended to do and in my confusion I fled back into the safe haven of my bathroom. It took me more than twenty minutes to re-appear. Getting dressed and applying my make-up seemed to be a difficult task this evening, and my hands were not very steady. Finally I managed to get my act together and was ready to leave the bathroom, hoping to look cool and composed.

"You look a bit flushed, Amanda. Let me pour you a glass of champagne."

I almost flung the costly liquid in his face, but probably a bit of champagne would do me good. I grasped the glass and I downed it.

"Let's go, Daniel, sorry to keep you waiting!" I played it cool, and would not give in. Tonight I'd play by my own rules!

Gallantly he opened the door. "It was a pleasure, Amanda, it's always so revealing, when people offer you a glimpse into the intimacy of… their souls," he said, with a smile.

I choked. It had been the wrong decision to drink the champagne – I should have flung the stuff right in his smug face!

We reached the Westminster Grill where we were greeted and led to our usual table by the head waiter. Oddly, this was one of the things that always annoyed me. The moment Daniel appeared anywhere on this ship, people just seemed to pop up, ready and eager to be of service for him. I don't think that the head waiter had ever bothered to bestow more than a punctilious nod whenever I had arrived in the restaurant on my own. But tonight he was ready to kiss the ground on which Daniel walked. No wonder Daniel must think that he was special. It was time to teach him a lesson!

I was still trying to cope with my indignation when Marge looked up and noticed our arrival. "Hello, darling, I see that you're still alive! No wonder, with such wonderful and caring protection…" She winked at me in a way she probably assumed to be discreet, the kind of message you'd exchange with your best friend at college.

But Daniel – of course – had noticed and whispered, "Anything I should know?"

"Nothing, I can assure you," I answered through gritted teeth, suppressing the urge to first strangle Marge and then do the same to Daniel. If it was my destiny to end my life in prison, why not make a thorough job of it?

Daniel didn't reply. He just smiled, the kind of knowing smile that made me mad. Daniel probably did not realize how close I was to committing murder.

I was still fuming with indignation when I noticed that our table had been set for seven people – something was wrong here!

"Don't you think that it would have been more considerate to set the table for six people only, the crew must be aware of what has happened to Veronique?" I whispered to Daniel, forgetting about my plan to punish him by a prolonged period of silence.

"I asked them to lay the table for seven guests tonight as I took the liberty of inviting some guests. Sir Walter has excused himself, he'll be dining in his cabin, therefore I thought it might be interesting for us if I invited Richard Wu and his, well, let's call her 'his assistant', to join us tonight. I hope that Tom won't mind too much, but a couple of fresh faces and change of topic will do us good. We seem to have discussed Frank and Veronique's disappearance from all angles by now."

"We have indeed, but we haven't really made any progress, or did I miss something? We've not been desperately efficient so far."

"We haven't! You're right, but it's not my fault. I'm trying my best, but I'm just a guest here." He shrugged.

"I really hope that our captain comes up with some bright ideas. It's not only very frustrating – it frightens me a bit…"

Daniel took my hand and squeezed it gently to reassure me. A nice gesture; maybe I could consider forgiving him after all.

"A change of topic will do us all good. I happen to know Richard Wu from the past. He may look a bit odd but he's a fascinating character, a brilliant strategist and amazing entrepreneur, but judge for yourself."

I tried not to feel impressed. I had already been thrilled to dine with Sir Walter, but in Daniel's world dining with billionaires seemed to be nothing special. My thoughts were quickly diverted by Neil who had chosen this very moment to arrive. No head waiter had showed up to guide him to our table and my heart warmed to him – welcome to a fellow soul from the ordinary world. All right, not *that* ordinary, you could argue, after all, he had won a Nobel Prize.

As Neil came closer, I tried hard to ignore the flashy pink polka dots on Neil's baby-blue bow-tie, but at least he had remembered to use his comb tonight and came close to my idea of looking presentable.

I noticed with satisfaction that Neil looked less haggard than yesterday. Apparently my efforts to boost his morale had been fruitful. He kissed Marge and me before he sat down and ordered a whisky to start. Soon Marge and I were listening rapt to Neil's narrative of a hair-raising episode in Borneo where he had escaped by a whisker a close encounter with a bunch of extremely excited natives who had shown no understanding of his passion for toxic frogs.

Neil laughed. "I guess they needed the frogs more than I did – they use their poison for their daily hunting forays. I was very unwelcome competition – and they didn't appreciate my arrival at all. But I was lucky, they made a lot of noise, but must have run out of poisonous darts that day, otherwise I guess I'd not be sitting here tonight."

I heard Marge utter, "For goodness sake!" but I wasn't sure if she was commenting on Neil's story or the entrance of a very odd couple.

A murmur of noise rippled through the restaurant. A royal entrance couldn't have looked any different. The pompous head waiter, followed by a trail of no less than three of his subalterns, accompanied the two persons I could easily identify as Richard Wu and his assistant to our table. The assistant alone would have created a commotion in her own right, for she was not only beautiful, but stunningly so. Lustrous hair, dark as a raven, made a perfect framework for her pale skin. She was perfect from her almond-shaped eyes to her tiny nose and sensual red lips. She could have leapt out of the pages of *Vogue*.

The head waiter bowed deeply as he moved the chairs while our fellow passengers craned their necks to catch a glimpse of the VIP couple that had condescended to visit our table. Satisfied, I noticed that I was by far not the only curious soul on this ship.

Wu ignored the general attention and dropped onto his chair like a shapeless sack of potatoes. He was not merely fat, he was obese. His face glistened with perspiration and I could hear him breathing hard. The short walk must have been exhausting for him. But his beady eyes were attentive, darting left and right, examining and assessing all of us.

I felt a shiver running down my spine. Richard Wu looked like a fat human beetle, a Kafkaesque version of mankind. Instinctively I understood that it would be a fatal error to end up on the list of his enemies. Here was a man who wouldn't take any prisoners.

Daniel didn't seem to be at all intimidated by this strange couple and opened light conversation with ease, evidencing his well-oiled and experienced social skills. I was impressed but suddenly my cursed inner voice reminded me, 'Isn't it strange that your Daniel is such an intimate friend of a man who looks like evil incarnate?

What do you know about your Daniel – nothing. And yet you melt as soon as he sets his eyes on you.'

'It's not 'my' Daniel!' I argued with myself, 'and stop thinking the worst about everybody. He's been extremely considerate and very caring.'

'Pfft!' answered my inner voice. 'You're so naïve, it's hopeless, you'll see!'

In the meantime Daniel and Wu had started to exchange polite small talk. But Wu's assistant didn't participate. I heard her giving orders in her high-pitched voice to a waiter. Almost instantly the waiter returned with a hot towel on a silver plate and while Wu kept on talking, his assistant dabbed Wu's face with the towel as slowly and as delicately as if she were caring for a baby. Wu totally ignored her administrations as if she were just a minion. I was disgusted – how could someone accept being treated like this?

In the course of the discussion I learnt that the beauty's name was Angela. With her delicate Chinese beauty she could have been a sister of Veronique. But whereas Veronique had been attractive in a robust and dynamic way, Angela looked much more like a doll, exquisite and delicate. Tonight she was wearing a tight bright red silk top embroidered with golden dragons. Her top was styled in the traditional Chinese fashion which made her dress look even more exotic.

I was still trying to digest Angela's colourful appearance when I noticed something else. She was adorned from head to toe in precious jewels, mostly gold, jade and diamonds, certainly not the sort of costume jewellery I could afford. I knew from a Chinese friend that there are almost no limits when it comes to jade, as this stone holds a special magic for its Asian collectors. Richard Wu might not treat her well, but there could be no doubt that he paid handsomely.

During dinner my feeling of unease continued to grow, and finally I started to despise Richard Wu and Angela. I couldn't decide whom I disliked more. Angela spoke in an abrasive high-pitched yet submissive voice. I guess her way of speaking was chosen deliberately to sound attractive to Mr. Wu. To me it sounded like a meowing cat.

The first course was served and I hardly could believe my eyes. Angela had ordered chop sticks and used them not only for herself, but made a great show of selecting the best morsels and feeding them to Richard Wu. This seemed to be an established part of their dining routine as Wu didn't pay any more attention to Angela than he paid to the waiters who kept filling his plate and glasses.

While we were drinking wine, Wu had switched from vintage champagne served in a crystal bottle to a rare XO cognac. I watched fascinated as he drank the cognac at the speed I'd drink water, while Angela kept feeding him or dabbing his face lovingly from time to time.

"The Russian president's position and power seems unassailable," I heard Daniel say.

Richard Wu laughed, a short asthmatic sound. "Not only in Russia," Wu answered. "It's no secret that he's trying to resurrect the former Russian Empire."

"You're well positioned to know that," Daniel commented with a wry smile. "It's not always easy to deal with stubborn business partners in these regions."

Wu shook his head and sipped at his glass of cognac. "I can count on my government's support," he stated simply. "Otherwise I agree, my shareholding would be pretty worthless and my shares have been long pocketed by the usual suspects. But trust me, I'm in a very strong position, I'll be the winner in the end. Nobody will dare to irritate the Chinese Dragon. China is the super power of this century, forget about Russia and America or Japan, only India will ever be able to challenge China."

Wu belched and I grinned at Marge's disgusted face. As if nothing had happened, Wu continued, "India could be a challenge, but only if the Indians ever get rid of their stupid democracy. It's outdated and inefficient. Look at China, we can build an airport in the time it takes the Indians to start discussions in parliament. No, Russia needs China, as there's no real competitor to China in the world."

As if to confirm Wu's statement, Angela started to coo and feed him a huge bite of braised pink salmon glazed with a layer of creamy caviar sauce that had been served on silver plates among several other delicacies. Wu snapped at it like a piranha and the pink bite was gone, only leaving a reminder in the form of a bright spot on his chin as the fat dribbled slowly from his lips.

I shuddered. Just the idea of having to spend a minute of my time alone with Richard Wu made my skin crawl. And yet I was fascinated, he was a powerful personality. Daniel seemed as well informed about politics as he was about the petrol, gas and coal markets. Richard Wu might be disgusting – but he was clever, devilishly clever. I sent a small prayer of gratitude to heaven that I had read the article in *The Economist*, allowing me to follow the discussions closely.

Tom joined our dinner table a little later. I saw him hesitating at the entrance, apparently unsure if he should join us or not. I think in the end his curiosity got the better of him and he sat down close to me, making sure that Marge and John formed a buffer between him and Richard Wu. To no surprise Tom followed the discussion with keen interest. Wu's beady eyes had opened for a second in surprise, taking stock of the enemy's son at a short distance. But after the shortest possible greetings had been exchanged, the minimum of politeness dictated by good manners, Wu chose to ignore Tom and concentrate his attention solely on Daniel.

It was not hard to understand that Richard Wu was in fact trying to sell the idea of investing in his company to Daniel. Daniel pretended to be interested, doing so in a very credible way, although I knew that the article in the magazine had probably changed his view. I was amazed. I had never imagined that business on such a scale could be the subject of a dinner meeting – and that Richard Wu might consider Daniel to be wealthy enough to invest in his venture. Either Daniel was an excellent actor, or he must be by far wealthier than I had ever imagined.

It then happened that I committed a severe faux-pas. Daniel and Richard Wu were discussing the possibility of extracting shale gas in Canada when I interjected, "Is it correct that your company has recently encountered problems in exploiting the Canadian gas fields?"

The beady eyes shot bolts of lightning, and even Angela, who had followed our discussion, eyed me with obvious displeasure.

"Nothing of importance, nothing that couldn't be solved – and believe me, it will be solved," Wu answered, but I felt that he was not only irritated by my remark, he was furious. I was sure that I had been moved to his list of potential enemies tonight, and this notion wasn't a very comforting one. My intuition told me that men like Richard Wu never tolerated any obstacles. I retreated but I heard a faint snicker from Tom. Apparently he found it highly amusing that I had dared to challenge the mighty tycoon.

Dinner ended with dessert being served from a trolley that made me forget all of my best intentions about starting a diet and after having ploughed through an impressive pile of different pastries and fruit, our Chinese guests followed Daniel's invitation to join him in the bar – Richard Wu loved to smoke a cigar after dinner, as he let us know. I politely declined. I had had enough of Wu and his assistant for one evening.

I watched this odd couple walking out of the restaurant next to Daniel – one of them waddling, the other one floating on her ethereal high heels. Suddenly Angela seemed to stumble – her heel must have got caught in the carpet. While Mr. Wu kept on waddling in front of her without taking any notice, Daniel rushed to her rescue and gallantly offered his arm. Angela accepted it with an inviting smile and leaned heavily on Daniel – if ever a featherweight can do such thing. I sighed. The manoeuvre had been a bit too transparent for my taste. Are men really so blind?

But then I discovered that Daniel was not blind at all, but on the contrary, he seemed to be encouraging Angela to stay close to him. There could be no doubt, he was a very willing victim of her charms. I was not amused.

"Are you impressed by the great tycoon?" I heard Tom's sardonic voice say.

"More irritated than impressed. How can a woman like Angela debase like that? Just imagine it, feeding this fat crocodile like a child? It's disgusting!" I hissed, trying hard to ignore that I had seen Daniel's arm around her shoulders as they went through the door of the restaurant.

Tom laughed. "Money, Amanda, it's all about money. Why do you think Veronique married my father? For the beauty of his blue eyes? I just don't understand why my father and Wu turn into brainless fools when it comes to women."

"Richard Wu is no fool." Marge suddenly joined the conversation. "Angela's playing the submissive geisha because he expects her to play by the rules, that's what he pays for. But it's not difficult to see that he's a master of the game, not at all like your father. If I may say so, Sir Walter was totally smitten by your step-mom." I was astonished. Marge had analysed their relationships so clearly. She was a much more perceptive observer than I had expected.

"I guess you're right. My father loved Veronique, but the relationship between Angela and Richard Wu is different, she's just one of his mistresses as far as I know. And I've heard that he loves to change them regularly."

"His assistant!" I smirked.

"With *very* special skills, that's obvious." Neil Hopkins joined our discussion. "Scientifically speaking though, there's no valid explanation for how she can walk on those high heels at all, it seems against all the laws of gravity."

"Which proves that science doesn't answer all life's questions," I dropped in. "I think I'll walk back to my cabin now. I can't get the smell of Angela's perfume out of my nose. I think I need to take a shower, it's sickening. It seems to have been following me since I shook her hand." Angela's perfume had an overpowering note of vanilla; my stomach was starting to churn.

"Let me walk you back to your cabin!" Neil proposed.

"I'd be delighted!" And I truly was. In the course of the evening I had forgotten all about the threatening letters, but now I remembered and walking back in Neil's company would give me a much safer feeling.

We reached my cabin and as I opened the door, I glanced with apprehension at the floor. I couldn't help it. But there was nothing to see but an innocent-looking carpet. I couldn't suppress a sigh of relief; I had almost been sure of finding another message. Neil must have noticed my reaction as he suddenly took my hand, a kind and somehow reassuring gesture.

"Come in, Neil!" All of a sudden I didn't like the idea of staying on my own. "I think there must be a bottle of champagne left. I didn't drink any before I left for the Westminster Grill. I'm finding it rather difficult not to become addicted or to turn into an alcoholic on this ship."

Neil laughed. "That's for sure, I saw some passengers starting their breakfast with a good dose of champagne already. For me it's tea, nothing else in the morning!"

"For me it's coffee, which means we have already disagreed!" I added and smiled.

"Nothing that couldn't be solved easily, Amanda. I feel already that I'm warming quickly to the idea of drinking coffee in the morning."

Not only did Neil follow my invitation to stay for a drink, he also set to the task of opening the bottle of champagne waiting in the ice bucket (to be precise, it resembled more an iced water bucket by now). He took off his dinner jacket and tackled the task quite professionally, and seconds later a loud popping sound announced the success of his labours. We drank to each other's health but the smell of Angela's sickly perfume was still lingering in my nostrils. It was not only disturbing, it was nauseating.

"Neil, would you give me a second, I really need to take a shower. The smell of Angela's perfume is following me, it's even mingling with the taste of the champagne. I'll just rush under the shower, you can pick something to read in the meantime, make yourself comfortable."

"No problem, I'm grown up, I can cope with five minutes on my own."

"Have you ever met a woman who honestly managed to have a shower in five minutes?" I asked suspiciously.

136

"I have indeed. It was in Poland in the winter and the heating in the hotel bathroom had broken down," he laughed, "but that was about the only time I can remember. You're right, just take your time."

I flashed a broad smile at Neil and vanished into the bathroom where I soaked in the warm water of the shower, happy to get rid of the penetrating smell. Stepping out of the shower I overlooked a towel on the floor and slipped – the bathroom on a ship is not the size of a ballroom, after all. I therefore bumped with a loud bang against the bathroom door. It didn't hurt at all but the room vibrated as if I had triggered the trumpets of Jericho. Seconds later the door was flung open and a very worried-looking Neil stood in the doorframe.

"Is everything all right, Amanda?"

I shrieked and grabbed the first available towel, but it was far too small to cover me. I could only hope that the floor would open up and swallow me – but of course it didn't, it never does when you need it to.

I wrote this story as I wanted to tell the tale of my cruise of a lifetime. Only in cheap romances, written by underpaid authors with grubby minds, would this little accident end in a sexually explicit bedroom scene. I'm a serious woman, and a discreet one.

But I can tell you this – some Nobel Prize winners do know how to kiss a girl…

Day 8 – A Birthday Party

The next day I awoke alone in my bed, relieved that Neil had suggested returning to his cabin during the night. Somehow I didn't wish Kenneth to find me with a man in my bed who didn't belong there – first of all I had to come to terms with it myself. How had I managed to end up in this impossible situation? Why does life tend to be so complicated?

'You're amazing!' my hated inner voice chided me. 'You worship Daniel, play the frosty virgin with him and at the first opportunity you hop into bed with somebody else? How on earth could you do this?'

How on earth could I do this? I had no clue. I must have drunk too much champagne, this could be my only excuse.

'Amanda, this can't go on, be more careful, don't lose your self-respect,' the nagging voice continued and although I hate my inner voice, we were in total agreement this time. I was prey to a weird mix of emotions. A part of me felt terrible (the sane one), and the insane part of me felt just wonderful. Try sorting that out!

I urgently needed to get some order and logic back into my mind. The best course of action therefore would be to skip breakfast and take some physical exercise. I'd follow my new routine of visiting the gym. As I opened the curtains, I could see that the weather had cleared, the sea was no longer grey and foreboding, and a bright sun was playing with the foam on the tops of the waves. The cheerful humming of the engines announced that the *Belgravia* was back on course, heading to New York, full steam ahead. We had weathered the storm.

Although the sea was much smoother and the morning sky was showing large and very inviting patches of blue, I didn't see myself running five times around the boat on the jogging circuit or playing golf by hitting balls against a gigantic net, so the gym it would be.

My night-time adventure with Neil had occupied all of my attention, and only as I stepped out of my cabin did I realize that I had been spared a new note. This meant that I could start my morning without an additional worry and it cheered me up considerably.

Soon I arrived at the torture chamber – also known as the gym – and I was in luck. Marge had chosen not to show up today. Probably I had arrived far too early for her – the hand on my watch hadn't even moved to the eight. Not that I didn't like Marge, but I simply didn't want to talk to anybody this morning – and not talking to

Marge was a mission impossible. I needed to run or cycle in order to calm down and get some sense of order into my mind. I needed to be on my own!

Deep in my thoughts, I started to run faster and faster on the treadmill. A quick glance around me assured me that the few passengers who had ventured into the gym at this early hour didn't seem to care about me or to bother at all how attractive I looked, so I decided to increase the treadmill speed by another notch and was soon puffing away like a steam engine – it felt good to get rid of the tension.

I liked Neil very much, but I had a crush on Daniel, there was no use denying this annoying fact. And yet Neil was really quite attractive as well, once you forgot his terrible taste in clothes. Both men were highly intelligent, both of them charming. My thoughts were turning in circles, repeating themselves, but I was incapable of making a decision. I guess the ugly truth was that I didn't want to decide at all, I liked both of them – and once we arrived in New York, the whole story would be at an end anyhow. Amanda would go back to her old boring life, so why not savour every second of my adventure?

I have never understood the devious minds that decide to place mirrors on every available wall in a gym. As I looked up from the screen in front of me I could admire myself from at least three different perspectives – but none of those looked particularly flattering. My face was flushed a vivid red and my puffed cheeks did nothing to improve my image. Sweat was running down my forehead; the fact that I kept wiping it away regularly with a towel didn't change much. There was only one thing I could do: ignore those stupid mirrors or pretend that the Amanda in the mirrors was an entirely different person. Anyhow what did it matter, I was here on my own, and I needed the exercise to help me come to a decision, a decision that somehow moved further out of reach the harder I tried to make up my mind.

I lowered my glance to continue watching an old episode of 'Friends' on my screen (the TV series from the last century – clearly I was the right target group) when ice-cold hands came from behind and covered my eyes.

I shrieked.

"Don't get excited, I have no dishonourable intentions – not yet, anyway." I heard Daniel's amused voice. He lowered his hands and once again I hoped that the floor would open up and swallow me, but of course, when you need it to…

Daniel looked sleek and elegant, even in his shorts. There was no sign of the wobbly bulge most men carry at his age. And here I was, looking simply hideous. I decided that it was about time to hate Daniel – Neil would have been more considerate. He wouldn't have surprised me in the gym.

"Daniel, do me a great favour please!" I begged.

"Anything you wish, consider it done."

"Just close your eyes and leave the gym and forget that you ever saw me in this state. I look terrible and there's no use denying it, the mirrors all around me are telling the truth."

"You're becoming melodramatic, Amanda. Maybe it's your job as a teacher – I've heard that it's quite challenging for the nerves in the long term. You look great, how do you think people should look when they're running? "

Gently he took my towel and started to dab my forehead, assuming the role of a caring friend. My glance roamed around the gym and I detected a pair of innocent-looking dumbells; those would be ideal tools to dispatch Daniel into the next world. He must have followed my glance though as I heard him laughing.

"Don't give in to temptation, Amanda. It would be so crude and just imagine, my blood splattered everywhere. And what a mess to clean up afterwards! Ok, I'll leave you now if you promise to join me for lunch at noon, and by the way, I reconfirm that I like very much what I see."

He rewarded me with a long glance measuring me from head to toe, lingering a bit too long for my taste on some parts more than others. "I used to have a girlfriend who'd stop running when the first bead of perspiration formed on her forehead and might ruin her make-up. I never understood why she joined me in the gym at all. She had a black belt in shopping though, nobody could beat her at that. Honestly, I prefer your style of exercising."

Maybe there was hope, but I wouldn't be deceived by his smooth talk. "I expect that with advancing age your memory is becoming selective. I bet you forgot to mention those girlfriends that looked great even when they were doing some form of exhausting sports," I gloated.

I liked the mention of his advanced age. Cheap revenge maybe, but satisfying.

"That's perfectly possible, Amanda. You know that advancing age is a scourge that hits all of us at a certain point. Now, as you mention it, I suddenly remember, there did happen to be one or two."

"Daniel, I hate you! I really shouldn't reward blackmail, but I'll see you at lunch, and now go with my blessing, but go!"

He blew me a quick kiss and was gone the next minute. But my mind – which was supposed to have become calm, logical and structured after some strenuous exercise – had returned to its state of complete disarray, and I, poor feeble Amanda, still had no clue as to how to sort this out or fit the pieces back together. Daniel's sudden appearance hadn't helped at all.

There was Neil, and there was Daniel, but all the time I was aware that this adventure would remain only a short episode and Cinderella would soon be back in her two-room apartment, teaching listless pupils – unless of course the killer on board chose to make me his next victim. I started to warm to this idea – it would certainly solve a lot of issues.

Finally I discarded those dark thoughts, as in truth I'm a born optimist. I did some spinning, hoping in vain that some more exercise would help me to soothe the turmoil of my brain. Finally, tired and soaked in sweat, I staggered to the showers, ignoring the mirrors. It wasn't me anyhow, this strange person heading to the showers.

As I entered the women's changing rooms I noticed that the Turkish bath was empty. I had read often enough about the beneficial effects of steam for the skin. Why not try it today and iron out the last effects of a sleepless night? Minutes later I was sitting in the steam room, inhaling the warm steam, my mind still occupied in finding a way out of my emotional mess. I relaxed on the marble bench but it didn't take long before I started to feel dizzy as my energetic running had left me feeling quite hot even before I had entered the steam room, and now, having inhaled the steam for some time, I couldn't fail to notice that the temperature inside the cubicle was rising to uncomfortable levels. Steam might be good for the skin, but in here there was definitely too much of it. I'd soon be looking like a boiled lobster which meant it was about time to leave my confinement and hop under a cool shower! A lovely idea!

I wrapped my towel around me as tightly as possible, hoping fervently that the hot steam had yielded its promised effects. Then I turned the door knob and pushed at the door. The door wouldn't move.

'Silly me, I must have moved the knob in the wrong direction,' I admonished myself.

I turned the knob again, pushed, but once again nothing happened. Slowly I started to panic as more and more steam filled the room and my situation was becoming very uncomfortable. I rattled at the door, pushed it hard and turned the knob with all of my force, as hard as I could, but the door remained stuck. Cursing loudly, I bumped the full weight of my body against it – but to no effect, the door remained firmly closed. The steam room had become my prison.

The heat was becoming unbearable. I was having difficulty breathing and the steam was suffocating me. As I sank down helplessly on the marble bench, I was terrified. This could be no coincidence, was I about to become the next victim on the list of fatalities on the *Belgravia*? Just another accident?

While my heart was racing with a crazy rhythm and speed, thoughts were spinning in my head: would this be the end? But I wasn't ready to give up yet. I dragged myself once again to the door with the small glass window and I hammered against it with all the force I could muster. I tried hard to smash the glass, but to no avail. The door simply wouldn't yield.

The intense heat spread through my body like ink on blotting paper. It numbed my brain, it was cooking me alive. My last memory was the view out of the small window onto the deserted corridor from where no help would come.

***

Later the attendant told me that she had heard me hammering at the door and found me unconscious in the steam cabin. She had no clue as to why I hadn't been able to open the door; she said that she had found the door unlocked.

Close to tears the young attendant apologized profusely, breaking into some incomprehensible language of Slavic origin, but I knew of course that this incident hadn't been her fault at all. Greedily I drank the cold water she handed to me with trembling hands while my thoughts raced along. I was sure by now that the murderer hadn't limited himself to just sending me a message. Somehow he must have come to know that I was the only eye witness to the first crime. Amanda Lipton had become an obstacle that needed to be removed. This sounded very logical but I was finding this assertion hard to digest. I needed to be on my own and come back to my senses. One thing was clear: from now on I'd need to be extremely careful.

About ten minutes later I had recovered and I was able to take a shower under the attentive eyes of the attendant and got dressed. On my way back to the cabin I was still walking as if in a bubble, not yet fully in control of my senses. In truth a whole bunch of villains could have leapt on me then, and I'm not sure if I'd have noticed them. So much for being more careful.

142

Back at my cabin the next surprise was already waiting for me. As I opened the door a new note was waiting for me, a sheet of white paper lying on the carpet with a single sentence screaming at me:

'You prying bitch, last warning.'

I grabbed the piece of paper and sank onto my sofa. Had the attack in the gym been this last 'warning'? Had the unknown villain arranged this note as his perfidious last reminder, would his next attack be swift and deadly? Or should I have received this message earlier? My hands were shaking. These messages were like poison, administered in daily doses, hurting but so far not hurting enough to kill. Until the final day when the dose might be increased to a lethal one, a terrifying thought indeed.

I looked once again at the piece of paper, hoping to get some kind of clue or inspiration from it. But like the first time, no matter how many times I might turn the page and read it again, nothing changed. I was dealing not only with someone who was insane, but someone who must be cruel as well. Frightening me to death must have given my stealthy enemy a devious kind of pleasure. It was sick.

Suddenly I remembered that I had promised to meet Daniel for lunch.

'Here you go again,' intervened my cursed inner voice. 'Daniel was around, wasn't he? Just like the first time… but of course you trust him, because he's gentle, he's amusing and handsome. Amanda, you're so naïve that it hurts, behaving like one of your schoolgirls with a crush.'

Furious, I dumped the note back on the table. Was Daniel capable of playing such cruel games with me? I simply couldn't imagine him doing this, but whom could I really trust?

I had to talk with Daniel, see his reaction. I had to clarify the situation. I couldn't live with this horrid suspicion. Deep in my heart, I hoped that he'd be able to help and protect me, so maybe I was really unbelievably naive. And then there was Neil. I was sure that he'd be ready to protect me as well, I'd just need to say the word.

Daniel and Neil… Neil or Daniel…?

I needed a coffee. This was an emergency!

On my way to the coffee shop I hurried through the silent corridors, making sure that I walked in full view of the cameras, knowing that some officer on duty had been assigned to watch over me right now. This calmed my nerves and reassured me greatly.

My coffee break, accompanied by a flaky croissant, brought me back to my senses. As the delicious hot beverage spread its warmth and the caffeine kicked my brain into action, I came to the conclusion that I'd test Daniel by asking him to help me. It would be silly to spurn him just because he had been around at the wrong time ('or the right time,' interjected my hated inner voice).

As the *Belgravia* was heading towards New York now, the police would soon be taking over. I had also come to the conclusion that it would be much wiser to shut my mouth and keep Neil out of this for the time being as – especially after last night – he'd worry far too much about me. Neil had developed a very chivalrous attitude towards me, a bit old fashioned, but very nice and comforting. It was a strange feeling, having to take two men into consideration. Having lived on my own for several years, I wasn't used to the comfort of being looked after or cared for. And worst, I wasn't accustomed or skilled enough to date two men. If I wasn't careful I'd end up creating havoc. I really needed to make my mind up, a difficult thing to do.

I was still pondering the emotional mess that I had ended up in when I noticed John standing at the counter. He looked worn out – he must have had a sleepless night. So I had not been the only one.

"Hi John, want to join me for a cup of coffee?" I asked. A bit of a chat with John would do me good. My mind had ended tangled in a maze with no exit in sight. A change of subject could only help.

John flashed me a smile and minutes later he came over with a gigantic cup filled with coffee and cream which emanated a strong smell of vanilla and fudge. A quick estimate of the calorie input of this told me that drinking one cup would be enough to make my new leggings burst. It smelled delicious but I placed it immediately on my list of forbidden beverages. Unaware of my thoughts on his caramel latte, John took a large sip and sighed happily. If it tasted as good as it smelled, he was right to be happy. I was just a little bit envious.

"You look a bit tired." I opened the conversation cautiously. "Didn't you sleep well with the rough seas last night?"

John sighed again, but unhappily this time. "It's about Marge."

He gave a long pause. Unless it concerned football, John was no great talker.

"Anything I could help with?" I proposed discreetly.

"That's very kind of you, Amanda, but I'll have to sort this out myself. I told you already that Marge isn't always very stable emotionally – and lately something must have happened that is preying on her mind. There's nothing you can do, but thanks again for wanting to help!"

I almost told him about the threatening messages, but then I remembered that Marge had insisted on not saying anything to John. I was still at odds to understand whom to believe or not to believe in this couple, but I felt bound to honour my promise. Therefore I just replied, "I imagine it's nothing very serious. Marge may have her moods, but I think that she's quite shrewd actually. Don't worry too much about her, John!"

"Yes, my Marge is a clever little girl, but that's exactly part of my problem."

We changed the subject and discussed when the ship would arrive in New York. "The engines are humming," I said cheerfully. "I would guess in two days at the latest we'll arrive in port."

John shook his head. "The engines are not yet working at full speed and after a storm like that the port authorities will need to catch up with a huge backlog. I think three days at the earliest, but there are worse things in life than being trapped on the *Belgravia*."

I would have readily agreed with this statement, if it wasn't for the tiny nuisance that a murderer had chosen to share the pleasures of our cruise – which brought me back to my message and my prolonged but rather involuntary sojourn in the steam room. I needed to tell Daniel all about this, which then made me remember I had promised to have lunch with Daniel.

As I looked out of the windows that looked onto the mall, I realized that the woman reflected in the glass was (a) me, Amanda Lipton, and (b) not looking as appealing as she had done yesterday.

I simply couldn't stomach meeting Daniel for lunch looking like I had been dragged through a hedge backwards. He might have mentioned in the gym that he liked my natural style, but did he really mean it? His statement had been made a bit too quickly and far too smoothly in order to be true.

I couldn't leave such an important issue entirely to chance, and a bit of help to restore my looks would do me good. Suddenly the thought of Oksana's magic hands flashed through my mind. Her magic touch would restore my looks, my nerves, and (last but not least) my confidence.

"John, I'm so sorry, but I've completely forgotten the time. I booked an appointment with the hairdresser's in ten minutes, I have to rush now," I exclaimed and planted a quick kiss on the cheek of a totally surprised John. In a flash I was gone and raced out of the coffee shop, praying that Oksana would be on duty, and available. Breathless, I arrived at the small salon but my heart sank as I could only see a new assistant at the counter, the kind of Barbie I despise, legs perfectly shaped, hair platinum blonde, blue eyes, a pouting mouth with a thick layer of violent red lip gloss.

"Can I help you, madam?" came the bored question while Miss Platinum inspected her red nails, which were three inches long, at least, and perfectly matched the red of her glossy lips. Had she put nail varnish on her lips instead of lip gloss? I disliked the assistant at first sight.

"I'm Amanda Lipton, I booked an appointment with Oksana at 9.30, I'm sorry, I'm aware that I'm a bit late," I lied shamelessly.

Miss Platinum frowned and tried to decipher the hieroglyphs that had been scribbled into a diary in front of her. I could see that the mere act of reading demanded considerable effort; I've had several girls of this type in my classes. My fingers were itching to rip the diary out of her manicured fingers but I had to be careful – her long finger nails might turn into lethal weapons.

"I don't see any appointment with your name and Oksana has been booked, her customer will be arriving shortly." She finally pronounced her judgement, voice still bored.

"That's really not my fault. Please ask Oksana to come here immediately, I don't see why I should be left standing here!" I was using my teacher's voice now, which often worked.

The model recognized the voice of authority and stopped arguing. She walked to the room at the back of the salon, hips swaying as if she were training for the catwalk. A minute later Oksana arrived and listened with a mild expression to my lengthy explanations that apparently someone had forgotten to scribble down my appointment.

"Would you take over Madame de la Rue? She should be arriving at any minute, and she also booked a manicure," Oksana asked Barbie. The latter only shrugged. An appointment with Monsieur de la Rue would probably have been more her type of thing.

"Thank you, Oksana," I whispered, "you must understand, it's an emergency!"

"Tell me more," she answered as she led me to the chair. Oksana started to wash my hair while I unburdened my heart about this morning's unfortunate encounter in the gym. We agreed quickly that meeting any eligible bachelor drenched in perspiration and in a state of total disarray was not just a calamity, it ranked as a major disaster.

"I'll make sure that you look glamorous for lunch," Oksana promised with a conspiratorial smile.

"Don't overdo it," I pleaded. "After all it's just a lunch appointment, it has to look natural."

Oksana laughed. "I understand, just make him forget that he ever saw you any other way. I'll do my best."

She did and was true to her word. After my hair had been shampooed and the hair dryer had done its duty, make-up was skilfully applied and a new Amanda with an exciting golden glow in her hair looked at me in the mirror. My green eyes were shining, larger than I had ever seen them before in any mirror. I hugged Oksana and my enthusiasm was only dampened when she handed me the bill. I nearly dropped my handbag.

"That's a lot of money…"

"I know." Oksana looked guilty. "But I have to charge you the full prices otherwise I'll end up in trouble with Monsieur. I already skipped the mandatory head massage which Monsieur expects us to sell after every hair colour …"

I gathered that 'Monsieur' was the owner of the salon and that he was very revenue-driven indeed.

"You're worth it, Oksana, and I was really desperate." I sighed and pulled out my credit card. I added a nice tip and left the salon, a very attractive but much poorer Amanda. Some people might say that you can't buy beauty, but then they've probably never met an Oksana.

Time in the salon had flown by and I had to race back to my cabin. The good thing about my interlude at the hairdresser's had been that my scary confinement in

147

the steam room had lost some of its impact. Had the infamous villain tried to scare me – or had it just been a silly accident after all? Doors can get stuck, it does happen. Trying to be positive I came to the conclusion that I must have been dead tired and simply over-reacted.

Now it was time to get dressed properly. Easier said than done, as a critical review of my clothes left me undecided; they seemed either too formal or too casual. Finally I settled for a navy blazer with discreet stripes and white trousers – smart casual, they call it on invitations. But I had lost valuable time and consequently I arrived more than fifteen minutes late.

For an Italian or Spanish soul this would mean that I had arrived far too early for any kind of appointment but if you're born and raised in northern spheres, being on time becomes a sort of obsession. Daniel seemed to think the same way as he was already sitting at a table set for two with an empty drink standing in front of him – he must have arrived quite early.

"Oh Daniel, I'm so sorry I'm late!" I exclaimed as the waiter showed me to the table, feeling a bit guilty, but only a bit, as I was congratulating myself on having made the detour via the hairdresser's. In the end, making Daniel wait might only do him good as I was convinced that his ego needed a dampener from time to time.

"Don't worry, Amanda, I don't mind as long as it wasn't Professor Hopkins who detained you."

My face went pink. This man must surely possess a sixth sense. Luckily Daniel spared me an answer. "Let me tell you, you look fantastic!"

I rewarded his compliment with a broad smile. It's nice when your efforts don't go unnoticed, and I love compliments. In truth I felt a bit overdressed compared to Daniel who was wearing a pair of comfortable jeans and a simple sweatshirt. Daniel was one of those hateful persons who always look good in whatever they choose to wear. The fact that his jeans carried a discreet Armani logo and the sweatshirt was designed by Ralph Lauren offered no consolation.

"I just dropped in at the hairdresser's on my way," I admitted. "After the gym I looked dreadful, they could have cast me as a witch in a new Hollywood release."

Daniel smiled at me wistfully. "Amanda, promise me that you'll never change. Be sure that I'd admire you even if you did play a witch. But I will admit, this is much better."

148

"Let's change the subject, Daniel, we've talked enough about my looks. I received another one of those damned messages." I dug the piece of paper out of my handbag where I had stored it carefully – among a myriad other things. But this time I didn't take the pains to touch it with a handkerchief, but simply unfolded the sheet of paper and banged it on the table.

Daniel made a face and studied it for a minute. I guess he was hoping for some sort of inspiration just by holding the paper. I saw that he was frowning, then he looked at me. "That's very upsetting, I'm surprised you're so calm. When did you receive this love-letter?"

"This morning, coming back from the gym. I found the paper on the floor. Someone must have shoved it underneath the cabin door. "

"That's fairly obvious then. I guess we should find out very soon who's the author of this piece of soap opera poetry. The cameras should have captured him this time."

I shuddered. "I really hope so, Daniel. It feels weird to be followed by someone, a secret stranger. It sounds so pathetic, just like bad fiction. What makes it worse, I know that he's got no qualms at hoisting his victims overboard or placing a poisonous snake in their bedroom whenever he feels it might suit his plans. I'm trying to put on a brave face, but if I'm honest, I'm scared…especially as I had a strange incident in the steam room this morning."

Daniel looked at me, his face a question mark. Quickly I told him about my adventure. Daniel looked scandalized; it was very comforting to see his reaction. "Why are you so sure that our suspect is a man? It could just as well be a mad woman?"

I shrugged my shoulders. In my mind it had been clear that the villain must be a man, but admittedly, nothing was clear and Daniel was right, we couldn't discard this option.

Daniel sat a minute in silence, then he looked into my eyes. "This insanity has to stop! It's time for action now."

Speaking to me, Daniel grasped my hand to reassure me, which was nice, but a bit unfortunate, as Neil had chosen this very moment to enter the restaurant. There was no way for me to become invisible and simply disappear. I had to ride this one out.

Of course Neil had noticed us and gave me a long and very thoughtful glance. I had the grace to blush and shrink under his blistering regard.

"Nice to meet you here," he said. "I'm sorry if I'm interrupting you, I can see that you're busy. I was looking for Amanda actually, but I guess it's not the right moment to… talk." He paused, then added, speaking directly to Daniel, "Well, let me tell you that I envy you having the privilege of sharing such an intimate… ah, lunch with Amanda."

Before Daniel could answer, I intervened quickly. Neil no longer looked angry; he had changed strategy and had taken on the appearance of a hurt puppy. I couldn't stand this; I simply had to say something.

"Neil, this is not a romantic rendezvous. In fact the same lunatic who is running around killing people on this boat has sent me two threatening messages already and I'm sitting here with Daniel to discuss what can be done. Daniel was kind enough to listen to my pleas. I didn't intend to tell you as you've had enough worries yesterday. I didn't want to add mine on top. Now we're talking about what can be done as we both feel that something has to be done urgently."

It had been a long speech and I was a bit out of breath at the end, but I simply didn't want Neil to think that I was sitting here, ready to sink into Daniel's arms, just hours after I had been in his. This may sound illogical, as part of me had of course been willing to commit exactly this kind of folly. I was in a total emotional mess, in fact, I had no clue what I wanted or what I didn't want. But I was still sensible enough to know that I didn't want to hurt Neil; he deserved better.

Neil gave me a very thoughtful glance. I felt highly uncomfortable – how can people look at you like that? I felt as if my mind was being x-rayed, or whatever scientific method they use nowadays to analyse people's brains.

"Am I allowed to have a look as well?" Not waiting for our reply, Neil grabbed a chair and sat down next to me. He scrutinized the paper carefully and handed it back to Daniel. "Printed on a laser printer, probably here on board. Either it's a tasteless joke or a real threat. What's your impression?"

He had addressed his last question solely to Daniel, as if I were non-existent. So much for my concerns that I shouldn't involve Neil as he might be inclined to feel too chivalrous, to worry far too much about me. I should have known that a man of science would always be fascinated by any kind of mystery.

"Yes, nothing special, even the paper is standard printer paper at first glance," Daniel conceded.

"Must be a cool customer if he dares to print his messages under the nose of the stewardess in charge of the business centre."

"Not much of a risk," Daniel replied. "I also go there from time to time, the girl at the reception never seems to bother what kind of documents I'm printing."

"Which makes you a prime suspect!" I thought it time to come back into the picture, after all, this story was about me, I was the one being targeted!

"Which makes me a prime suspect, that's right," Daniel grinned and grabbed his mobile. "Maybe I should already be talking with my lawyers at this stage and checking if I'm still allowed to talk to you…"

"Ha ha, very funny!" I was not amused. "Any concrete ideas from you two gentlemen on what to do now?"

"Yes, actually I do have some, but the first step will be to order our lunch! I can't think properly when I'm hungry."

I couldn't agree more; my stomach was rumbling. Daniel opened the menu and started to study it. But if he had hoped that his move would discourage Neil from pursuing the discussion and leave us alone, he was wrong.

"Great idea, that's exactly what I need. I'm hungry too, don't know what made me so hungry though. I think I have been overdoing my exercises lately. Let me treat you, be my guests! Waiter, one more menu please!"

Neil winked at me and I had to fight the urge to empty my glass of water over his head. The hurt puppy look had gone and he was a man ready for battle now.

Unsurprisingly, lunch was not a very successful social event. Our small talk was conducted with a politeness beyond any possible reproach but in the end I was totally exhausted. I had the impression of keeping two dogs at bay – fighting for a juicy bone. Only that I seemed to be the juicy bone in this case – a new experience for me. But admittedly, never in my life had I dated two men at the same time. I hadn't ever intended to get myself in such a situation. If I was to keep a sane mind and my self-respect, I must put a stop to this crazy situation.

But as our lunch slowly drew to its tedious end, I was still incapable of making a clear decision. I felt totally worn out, ready to stop seeing either of them just to recover my peace of mind. This might be the best solution after all.

It was Daniel who surprised us at the end of the meal. "Actually, I wanted to invite you out tonight. I'm organizing a small party in the Kensington bar after

151

dinner. I'd be delighted if you could join me." Daniel looked deeply into my eyes, the kind of look that made my knees go weak. My decision to stop seeing him was immediately postponed to a later date – don't they say that one should avoid rush decisions?

Daniel remembered that there were three of us sitting at the table and added lamely, "Of course, you're invited as well, Neil."

"I'll come with pleasure," Neil replied immediately. I was more and more amazed; my scientist had decided to leave his ivory tower and take part in a social life here on earth, what a change!

"Thank you, I'll be delighted to come!" I added quickly. "May I know if there's a special occasion?"

"Nothing too special," Daniel smiled. "It just happens to be my birthday today. That's settled then, I'll come to pick you up at your cabin before dinner time. Better be ready on time tonight," and he winked at me.

Then Daniel's mood became more serious. "Amanda, do me a great favour please, stay in your cabin this afternoon – or in public places among other passengers until we've sorted out the identity of your stalker. It seems that he means business."

I had been so involved in trying to sort out my private life that I had totally forgotten about the letters. But Daniel was right, I must be more careful.

If Neil was upset because Daniel had elegantly taken the lead for tonight, he didn't show it. He called the waiter to bring us three glasses of champagne and we toasted Daniel's health, although Daniel wouldn't tell us his age: "Beyond forty, but luckily not yet approaching fifty," was all Daniel would tell us. I concluded that Mr. Perfect had a sensitive spot after all – his age.

Daniel left us after lunch. He wanted urgently to speak with the captain to discuss possible plans of action and therefore I remained alone with Neil. In the beginning there was a long and very uneasy silence, and I had no idea what to say – or what not to say.

Finally Neil started to talk. "I'm sorry if I put you in a somewhat awkward situation, Amanda. I've come because I wanted to thank you for last night. Please don't worry, I don't intend to stick to you like a leech in the future. I admit I was jealous when I saw you sitting here having a tête-à-tête with Daniel, but I concede that I have no right at all to feel jealous and all I can hope for is to keep your friendship. I want you to know that this would be very valuable to me."

I felt tears stinging my eyes. Why did I always become so sentimental? But I managed to hold back my tears and replied, "That's very kind of you, Neil. I'm still at a loss as to understand what happened yesterday – it's not my style at all. The worst is that I don't regret anything. I mean, I probably should feel guilty, but I don't. And I do hope that we can stay friends."

I hated my silly little speech, but how could I explain something that I didn't understand either?

Neil took my hand with surprising delicacy and kissed it. "Thank you, Amanda. I do understand you and – it means that there's some hope for me."

Later, sitting in my cabin, I tried to come to terms with our weird lunch meeting. I was still unable to sort out my own feelings. Both Neil and Daniel seemed to be falling for me and yet they were so different – each of them fascinating in his own way. And what did I really want? I had no idea. I liked and admired Neil, but this feeling was not love, at least not the kind of love you read about in the romantic novels I liked to devour curled up in my armchair.

As for Daniel, if I was honest, he made my heart race and made me behave as foolishly as my sixteen-year-old schoolgirls, but the small residue of mental sanity that I had been able to retain told me that my situation was hopeless – it was clearly insanity on my part, a severe case of a midlife crisis infatuation – but this was not true love either. The picture of Daniel taking Angela in his arm when they left the Westminster Grill appeared in front of my eyes. I hadn't liked it at all and I knew instinctively that a man like Daniel would always appear on the radar of some sort of femme fatale, it was inevitable. I wasn't really prepared to accept or to live with this.

For a person who had never received any formal training in analytical psychology, I think I was making good progress, but it didn't help me in the end. From whatever perspective I looked at my situation, I was at an impasse and I had no idea how to deal with it. If I was entirely honest with myself, I didn't even want to deal with it. Cinderella was prepared to cherish every second until she was destined to leave the *Belgravia* and return to her old and regrettably very boring life.

I was stuck – mentally speaking, at least. Trying to find some distraction, I took the *Belgravia News* and had a look at the long list of entertainments that were on offer for the passengers. There was a lecture on life in the depths of the Atlantic Ocean – probably edifying, maybe even verging on being interesting, but not interesting enough to motivate me to spend ninety minutes looking at pictures dedicated to diverse species of sea-life. I prefer my fish on a plate.

There was a chess tournament – no option at all with my present state of mental chaos. My finger followed the index: Zumba! That would be great – I love to dance and Zumba is great fun. Even people endowed with moderate talent (like me) can participate. But then I remembered that I had paid a fortune that morning to allow Oksana to restore my gym-wrecked looks and Zumba would ruin all of this again – no way!

My finger moved on and suddenly it came to me: Bingo! It must have been ages since I'd played bingo, that would do. Daniel had recommended staying in public places, and I couldn't imagine anything less dangerous.

One hour later I arrived at the bingo tables that had been prepared in one of the main restaurants and found myself surrounded in no time by a good fifty fellow passengers, eighty percent female, well beyond their sixties – old pussies, as my pupils would have called them. At least this had one positive side effect – I felt like a teenager among them. Soon I discovered that they were a well-rehearsed group, and everyone knew their place exactly. Consequently I earned some openly hostile stares as I steered by accident towards a seat reserved for one of the senior members of this exclusive club. Realizing my error I smiled, and murmuring apologies I withdrew to one of the rear seats, well aware of the pecking order by now. A man smiled back at me, inviting me to sit close to him. I had made a new conquest – pity that he must be well over seventy years old.

'I simply must drag Marge along tomorrow, this is a fabulous hunting ground for her,' I thought, as I installed myself comfortably but soon the excitement of the game took over and I forgot all the worries of my private life. I even won a voucher for a cocktail at the swimming pool bar – could I have asked for more?

After the bingo was finished I convinced myself that I had earned a cup of coffee and a piece of cheesecake. There's nothing quite like chocolate or cheesecake to strengthen one's morale. On my way to my favourite coffee shop I bumped into Tom, literally, as I was looking in a shopwindow and wasn't paying attention.

"I'm so sorry!" I exclaimed. Looking up I saw that it was Tom who had been my victim and I added, "Oh, it's you, Tom! I'm terribly sorry, I must have been blind."

Tom laughed. "No collateral damage, Amanda, don't worry! How's your amateur sleuthing progressing? Any news on the murderer – I hope he hasn't had a go at you in the meantime?"

Tom sounded a bit too cheerful for my taste. He was taking a very serious issue a bit too lightly. Murder is always a nasty business, not a subject suitable for jest. I'd always had a soft spot for Tom, but his reply made me frown. Why did he ask me about sleuthing? What did he, how could he, know about my recent adventures?

I suddenly remembered that Tom was still on the top of my list of suspects. He must have been reading my thoughts as he laughed softly. "Don't look at me like that, Amanda. Do you suspect me of being involved in getting rid of Veronique? In truth I'd have loved to. You never know, Amanda, appearances can be so deceptive. Better take care and don't trust anybody! Maybe another murder will follow soon enough, be careful. I'm not joking!"

In a flash he was gone, leaving me with very mixed feelings – and relieved that this encounter hadn't happened in a dark corner of the boat or close to a railing.

***

Daniel called at my cabin on time but tonight I had made sure that I was dressed and ready on time as well! I had chosen an elegant black designer dress with a low neckline, a dress that looked classy in a subtle way. I was wearing the ancient green family tourmaline necklace set in diamonds, a loan from my mother. She had insisted that I should take it on this trip – she had been so excited after she saw me on television; I'm a star now in her eyes. I was happy that I had accepted it; the diamonds looked fabulous, sparkling in the cabin light, a nice contrast to the elegant but sober dress.

Since lunchtime I had been debating what I could give as a birthday present to Daniel. He belonged to the class of people who have enough money to satisfy whatever whim might come to their mind, which made him a terrible friend to choose a present for. It was a daunting, if not frustrating task.

Wracking my brain to find something original hadn't been very rewarding. I hadn't come up with any truly satisfying ideas. Finally I had chosen a book about Alexander the Great and an eau de toilette from Hermes. If he didn't like it, he could always recycle it as a gift for his valet. I simply assumed that he must have a valet waiting for him somewhere, as you always read in books that rich people do have valets, either the dedicated and faithful or the deceitful type.

But my concerns that Daniel might not like my gifts quickly evaporated. I could see that Daniel was genuinely delighted that I had thought about his birthday and bought him some presents. Like a child he tore off the wrapping, not bothering to notice the artistic bows I had affixed with much effort.

"Alexander the Great!" he exclaimed. "How on earth did you know that I'm fascinated by him?"

"Easy," I replied. "I was sure that you wouldn't settle for a lesser personality."

Daniel flashed me a grin while I went on, "The man in the bookshop told me that it's a new edition and that the author Alvin Goldstein is recognized as being the best in this field at the moment."

Daniel nodded. "Yes, I've heard about him. He's got some shortcomings, but I've heard that he knows a lot about his stuff. Thanks a lot, it's a lovely idea! "

He tore the next parcel open and sniffed at the eau de toilette, declaring that this was a fantastic scent as he had been tired of his present eau de toilette but had never found the time to test a new one. I was delighted as it would have been a bit expensive to be wasted on his valet. Daniel kissed me – but it was just a social 'thank-you' kiss between friends.

I didn't know if I should feel relieved or disappointed.

***

Dinner tonight passed quickly. We were our usual circle of passengers, and even Sir Walter had made his mind up to join us. I was shocked when I first set eyes on him; he had grown old in a matter of days. His shoulders were hunched, the aggressive rugby-player attitude gone. Absent-mindedly he just nibbled at his food and he drank heavily. Painstakingly we avoided the touchy subject of his wife's sudden death and I was once again amazed to witness Daniel's social skills as he managed to keep the conversation moving with the ease of long practice.

Tonight it was Tom who did most of the talking; roles between father and son had changed. Tom looked self-assured and competent, even a bit arrogant at times towards his father. Veronique's death had been all to his advantage and I couldn't help feeling more and more uneasy about this obvious fact.

Charles Peltier had also found his old personality. Charming and witty, he was full of plans for his forthcoming fashion show in New York, a show to be dedicated to the memory of Frank. Marge blossomed in this atmosphere of animated conversation, talking a lot with Neil and John. I also heard her discussing share prices of petrol companies with Tom – she commented on the latest developments like a true professional. I was amazed. Marge was a riddle to me –

156

was she just playing the helpless female? There was no doubt that she was highly intelligent and that she knew exactly what she wanted.

***

After dinner our little crowd walked together to the Kensington bar, which had been reserved for Daniel's private party. The bar filled with amazing speed. Apparently Daniel had plenty of friends and acquaintances on the boat. The hum of animated small talk in numerous languages filled the bar, accompanied by the sound of low-key piano music and the familiar clink of glasses. The champagne was flowing and colourful cocktails were being served. John looked with disgust at the pink cocktail offered to him by a waiter. He whispered something in his ear and minutes later he was holding a Budweiser in his hand.

The party had been going on for some time already when I noticed that new guests were approaching the entrance of the bar. The crowd made space for the newcomers: the bulging figure of Richard Wu followed by his ethereal assistant Angela. Today she wore an updo with a sort of tiara which made her look like an incarnation from *Vogue* magazine, an oriental version of Audrey Hepburn. To me she looked the perfect Asian beauty.

Angela was wearing a deceptively simple black dress with a dragon in golden embroidery, made in the traditional Chinese style with a slender shape and a high cut that had the advantage of showing her fabulous long legs whenever she walked. Every move she made was followed with awe by the men who surrounded her – and with barely hidden contempt by the women. I was sure that Angela would not possess a lot of girl friends.

"Sir Walter will not like this!" Marge whispered, at least she thought that she was whispering. But as the noise level was deafening, it didn't matter. "They've been worst enemies forever," she continued, "but lately Sir Walter's business has been doing much better. I bought some shares in his company and sold my stake in Wu's and I'd be surprised if I were wrong in my assessment."

"I didn't know that you managed your fortune yourself." I had always imagined that Marge frittered her time away playing cards or shopping.

"Of course I do!" Marge was all indignation. "I'm not one of those indolent heiresses squandering away the money their forefathers toiled so hard for. I certainly can't rely on John or I'd end up owning several football clubs and be bankrupt in no time. He's too good-hearted anyhow. And as to banks with their private wealth mantra, they're absolute crooks, that's what they are!"

157

Before I could reply, Neil grabbed my attention and we kept talking for quite some time, at least half an hour, I guess. Neil was a good entertainer once he came down to earth. From time to time I noticed that Daniel was looking at us. Maybe I was only imagining things, but I was almost sure that he looked a bit jealous. I did feel a bit guilty but rather liked this thought.

But then Neil was greeted by an old friend from Oxford and he had to release me. I wandered off thinking it was time to speak with Daniel now, after all, it was his birthday and I owed him some attention. As I moved through the crowd I drifted towards Tom who had been monopolized in the meantime by Angela, Richard Wu's assistant.

It was fairly obvious what she had on her mind. Her eyes were wide open, sensuous red lips lightly parted, her body language not at all subtle. She had also made sure that a well shaped, extremely long leg was showing through the slit in her dress while her adoring eyes seemed to swallow Tom up. The latter didn't seem to mind this attention – on the contrary. Both of them held a cocktail glass in their hands, a fancy drink of a striking emerald colour. The bartender had added a Caribbean touch with coloured drinking straws and slices of exotic fruit .

"Oh Mr. Olstrom," I heard her say in her high-pitched voice. "We surely must talk more, what you're telling me is *absolutely* fascinating! Both of our companies can only profit, it's a sure win-win situation! Mr. Wu so very much regrets that he hasn't been able to talk privately with your father but we understand, of course, that circumstances are a bit difficult."

"I think Mr. Wu should be talking to me," Tom replied, strangely relaxed for someone who had just lost a close relative. "My father is still in shock from his sudden bereavement, but we share the same opinions and visions. When we're back in Canada, I'll be taking over the management of some of our divisions."

"A joint venture between our companies can only yield advantages," Angela went on. Apparently Sir Walter's sudden bereavement didn't matter to her either. "The combined operation would control half of Canada's petrol reserves, we could dictate the prices."

Tom smiled, but his smile was not a pleasant one. "But you know our conditions, Angela. Canadian Imperial must have the majority. We'd be bringing most to the party, we control the access to your gas and oil fields. There can be no question of becoming equal partners."

Fascinated I watched Angela the cat suddenly flash bolts of lightning from her eyes. She tried hard to keep her alluring pose but not hard enough. She looked extremely rigid now.

"You should know that this attitude is totally unacceptable to Mr. Wu," she hissed more than said. "Our proven and testified gas reserves are much bigger than yours!"

Tom laughed softly. "I can only suggest then, he should find a way to exploit them. Good luck!"

Angela looked as if she was choking. A small period of silence ensued while Tom sipped at his drink, watching Angela with amused detachment. As he tasted his cocktail he made a face, it must be very sweet. But as their conversation had become a battle of wills by now, Tom probably wouldn't really have noticed what kind of cocktail he was drinking anyhow. I was satisfied to state that Angela's efforts to turn him on didn't have the desired effect. Tom was proving to be a cool customer.

Swiftly Angela regained her composure. "I might be able to convince Mr. Wu to throw in a sizeable shareholding of his Russian petrol interests; you know that those are worth billions of dollars."

Tom didn't look impressed. "It's an open secret that your assets there are frozen. I agree that they could be worth billions – but for the foreseeable future Mr. Wu's shares are worthless, and you can't even exercise your voting rights. There's no flow of dividends, your shares can't be traded. Angela, you know that you're offering me printed paper, Monopoly money, that's all. Forget it."

Angela tried hard to maintain her smile but her eyes were burning with fury. I was impressed. Tom was no longer the small boy or the simpleton his stepmother had wanted him to look like. Once again I became uncomfortably aware that he had gained most from the sudden departure of Veronique. In a matter of days he had become a real man and he was ready to fight for his father's empire. Tom was a tiger in the making, a dangerous tiger.

"Nobody would dare to challenge a shareholder who has excellent relations with the highest circles of the Central Government in Beijing," Angela replied arrogantly. "And you, you have nothing. Your government is kowtowing to the USA, they'd never intervene to help you. Mr. Wu can talk to the prime minister of China at any moment – and he'll be listened to! The Russians will not be able to ignore the wishes of Beijing."

"Maybe the Chinese Government is calling the wrong phone number in Russia, as nothing is happening?" Tom replied in the same arrogant tone. "And maybe Mr. Wu can call the prime minster at any time, but at the moment he's got nothing that puts him on equal terms with us. He needs us to make his Canadian oil and gas fields profitable, it's an open secret that you're running out of cash."

Angela's face was a frozen mask. The discussion hadn't turned out to be very successful for her. "Without China, you're nothing! We know that Sir Walter is trying to hammer out an agreement to sell his gas to China, but without Mr. Wu's backing, you'll never get there. You've got no chance, zero!" There was an unpleasant edge to Angela's voice .

"Then let me reveal a secret to you," Tom sneered back at her. "It'll be all over the news tomorrow morning anyhow. SINOPEC signed a deal last week and they're becoming not only our strategic partner, they'll be a strategic shareholder in Imperial Canadian. Your offer has come too late, sorry, Angela. I had no love for my stepmother but I must admit that her negotiation skills were simply superb when it came to forging deals with China. She masterminded this agreement. We'll liquefy the gas and ship it to China for at least two decades. This deal is worth billions, we don't need your shares or your Russian oil fields."

I could see that Angela was nearly having a fit. Later I would find out on the internet that SINOPEC was China's biggest oil company, directly controlled by the Chinese Government. No wonder Tom was radiating satisfaction – his family had outsmarted Wu and his assistant.

Angela however showed remarkably skill at keeping her control. "Let me congratulate you then, Mr. Olstrom. I will tell you though, I would have loved to work more closely with you." She looked deeply into his eyes. " Not just for reasons of business…"

She brushed his hand, flashing Tom a seductive smile while she changed the topic to our chances of arriving tomorrow in New York. Her voice was seductive and mellow now. I could only admire the way Angela had not only accepted defeat – it was impressive how rapidly she could switch over to small talk. Only seconds later Angela was talking animatedly about a typhoon she had once experienced back in Hong Kong. While recounting her dread of being trapped in a car with floods all around her, she was gesticulating with her small handbag, a black designer bag studded with expensive crystals. It matched a diamond necklace that must have cost a fortune. Angela was certainly an expense for Mr. Wu, I concluded, probably working to his greatest satisfaction in several fields, not only in business. Putting a bit too much élan into her gestures she sent her bag spinning through the crowd.

160

Angela shrieked – not too loud though – expressing her surprise and consternation that she should have been clumsy enough as to have lost her handbag and graciously accepted Tom's offer to get it back to her. What else could he do – he was a gentleman. She offered to hold his glass as Tom prepared to make his way through the dense crowd and retrieve it.

From my corner I watched Angela's little show with disgust; if Veronique had been a gold digger, this woman was even worse! It was clear that she wouldn't give up. Tom's announcement that a deal had been done with a competitor just seemed to have spurred her ambition to reach her goal with all the weapons that are at the disposal of every beautiful woman. I could only hope that Tom would be lucid enough to keep his distance, as he had done so far.

In the meantime Angela placed both glasses on one of the high tables dotted around the room. She looked reflective; I guessed she was planning her next move to seduce the rich heir. I was fighting with myself. Should I drop a word of warning to Tom? I guess it's the teacher in me. We like to meddle, we think it's our job, it's in our blood. But instinctively I knew that I'd be interfering with something that was not just a private issue and I was sure that the new Tom wouldn't like it. He wanted to manage his own agenda.

Angela planted a kiss on Tom's cheek as he came back with the bag and cried, "Oh Tom, you're my hero, I love this bag so much. I bought it in Beijing when Versace was opening their new boutique there. Thanks for bringing it back."

Tom blushed. "It was nothing, don't bother Angela! I did it with pleasure."

Both had their backs to me now and I decided to leave them alone. I had seen enough of Angela's talents.

"Cheers, my hero!" Angela turned and handed Tom his glass.

Suddenly Daniel grabbed my hand. "Here you are! It's my birthday and I think I deserve a bit of attention!"

How could I ignore his request? I left my corner and in no time forgot about Tom and Angela as Daniel drew me into a merry crowd. I soon found out that two of his illustrious guests were holders of a chair in history at Oxford.

"Let me introduce you to Amanda, she's an expert in history!" Daniel declared with a wink, knowing exactly that I had no chance of survival amid genuine professors in this area.

"Always nice to meet someone who's a real expert, we mostly just pretend to be experts, history can be so confusing," one of his friends, I think his name was Professor Golding, remarked to me with a forgiving smile.

"I'm certainly no expert!" I replied nervously. "It's just Daniel's strange sense of humour. I do like history very much though!"

Before I could escape I was drawn into a discussion about Julius Cesar and his time, an interesting subject, but soon I discovered that my knowledge of this period was nothing compared to theirs, and I was treading on thin ice. They agreed after a lengthy discussion that the whole period should be regarded from the perspective of a clan struggle. I must confess that I hadn't even noticed the extent to which all of these people had intermarried and were linked to each other. If it wasn't an uncle or nephew who was involved, it must be a brother- or sister-in-law – very confusing, especially as the Romans liked to use almost identical names over the generations.

"Daniel is actually quite an expert in history," Professor Golding remarked casually.

"I'm not surprised, but I imagine he's quite an amateur compared to you, just as I am," I replied.

"Oh no!" Golding protested. "Daniel's a real expert. He even publishes books on a variety of subjects. His last one was on Alexander the Great, but he chose to publish under the name of…"

"…Alvin Goldstein?" I asked, as my knees threatened to give way beneath me.

"Yes, did he tell you? Normally Daniel likes to keep it a secret. Interesting theory actually. He posits that Alexander's father, King Philip, did in fact encourage Alexander to rule, but many authors would contradict this theory. "

Seconds later I was standing close to Daniel.

"I hate you!" I declared, coming straight to the point.

"There could be many reasons to hate me," Daniel answered indulgently. "Tell me please, what's the reason today?"

"I gave you a book for your birthday, the very book you wrote yourself and you didn't say a word, I made myself look totally ridiculous!" I was all indignation.

Daniel wasn't very impressed. "I found it very sweet and I was amazed that after knowing me for only a week you really found out about the things that I like. It was surprising, actually, and very touching! I don't think that any of my previous acquaintances ever invested so much time thinking about a gift for me. Normally it would be a tie from Hermes."

"Which means that you have ties in all colours of the rainbow probably!" I snapped back. I was still licking my mental wounds.

"I certainly have a nice collection," Daniel conceded. "If you fancy, I could offer to show them to you, maybe even tonight…?"

This man was simply impossible – maybe this was the reason why I felt so attracted to him?

"Thank you, there's no need."

"I do have a surprise for you." Daniel grinned unabashed. But I didn't like that grin, it was a bit cheeky. He dragged me close to the piano and I noticed that a screen had been placed close to it. Daniel suddenly took the microphone. "Ladies and gentlemen, it's karaoke time now! I have the honour of opening the competition with Amanda. Oh, and by the way, we're both open to serious negotiations if anyone wants to sign us up, but we'll not consider anything below a million US dollars, so please don't insult us with any lesser offers. You'll quickly understand why, this will be an experience beyond anything you've ever listened to!"

Why does the floor never open up and swallow you when you most need it to? I blushed like a teenager and became uncomfortably aware that around 200 people must be staring at me. Well, maybe only 198 as I saw Richard Wu waddling out of the bar, Angela walking next to him, holding on to her boss. Beauty and the beast, I thought, before I concentrated again on the terrible ordeal that was now waiting for me.

Daniel had chosen the evergreen 'Summer Wine', and I tried my best to imitate Nancy Sinatra. Luckily I like to sing, so my performance could have been worse. It didn't come as a surprise that Daniel had a pleasant voice – why else would he have dragged me to the microphone?

Suddenly I decided to make the most of the comedy of this performance and started to put on a show, playing the famous star ready to collect her Grammy awards. The crowd started to cheer as I moved my hips and sent inviting glances to the audience, then, like a true entertainer, I grabbed an innocent bystander (poor Professor Golding) and made him sing with us. The crowd went crazy and

163

everybody joined in, finishing the song together with us. I don't know if it was the effect of the cocktails or if I wanted to show to Daniel that I was not the boring teacher that in fact I am – but I rocked the crowd that night. Another song followed and I must say that I have rarely spent such a wonderful time. The whole bar went on singing and dancing during the night and it was far beyond four in the morning before Daniel delivered me to my cabin door – well, to be true, I was delivered there by two gentlemen, as Neil had insisted joining us. He reminded me of a jealous dog.

Therefore I just exchanged chaste kisses with both of them before I went to my bed.

"Thank you Amanda," Daniel kissed my hand once again. "This was probably the nicest birthday that I've ever had!"

"It was certainly the most entertaining one I have been invited to for many years!" I smiled back, and gave him another quick kiss before Neil could protest and closed my door. A quick glance at the floor told me that no threatening notes would mar my dreams tonight and minutes later I was sound asleep.

But things can happen while you're sleeping.

Day 9 – Approaching New York

I slept late, so late in fact that my personal steward Kenneth woke me up. He entered my cabin with a trolley loaded with a full American breakfast. Under normal circumstances I would have welcomed this initiative, but as I was still suffering from an overdose of fancy cocktails, my stomach didn't appreciate the smell of fried eggs and bacon.

"Kenneth!" I groaned. "That's very kind, but I didn't I order any breakfast, at least I can't remember doing so."

Kenneth seemed a bit nervous. "You did not, Madam, but I took the liberty of waking you as it's already a quarter past ten!"

"That doesn't seem so unusual, it was quite late last night," I yawned and stretched while my eyes tried to adapt to the daylight that was flooding my cabin as Kenneth opened one of the blinds.

"What's the matter, you look upset?"

Kenneth didn't reply immediately. He seemed to be unsure how to go on. Suddenly he seemed to make up his mind and blurted out, "You'll hear soon enough. There has been another 'accident' – and I wanted to make sure that you were all right!"

"Another 'accident'?" I felt as if someone had punched me in the stomach – the very stomach that was already feeling a bit delicate this morning. It didn't feel good, not good at all.

"You mean, there's been another murder?"

"I don't know for sure, Madam, but last night, Miss Angela, the assistant of Richard Wu, fell violently ill and passed away before the ship's doctor could help her; rumour has it that it looks like poison. I think I'll be leaving this ship in New York! As soon as the police allow us to leave, that is." Kenneth looked positively sick now. "There's bad Feng Shui on this boat, they can pay me whatever they want, I won't stay!"

"Thanks anyhow for looking after me, Kenneth, this was a very kind thought of you. I'm fine, as you can see. But I'll be much better if you remove the bacon and the eggs, a coffee and croissant will be more than enough."

Kenneth took the hint and withdrew with the dishes that had been assailing my nostrils. I took the tray, poured some coffee and withdrew to the sanctuary of my bed. I needed to think. It could have been me, the victim yesterday, and yet this was a very different turn of events.

A quarter of an hour later I was still pondering what to do. I may be a slow thinker or might shy away from responsibilities but it's quite a decision to come clean, especially if the subject is not a very pleasant one.

I finished my breakfast and took a hot shower, then I scanned my wardrobe. I needed something sober and serious, after all it's not every day that you have to declare in public that you've killed somebody. But there could be no more excuses and no more denying it, as we were approaching the port of New York. I needed to be ready to face my guilt; hiding from it was no option.

After I had finished dressing I looked in the mirror. A very nervous Amanda looked back at me. I had looked better, though. I breathed deeply before I picked up the phone and called reception.

"Can you put me through to Mr. Greenfield? I need to talk to him urgently!"

"Of course, Madam, I'll put your call through…"

A very tired voice answered me. Daniel must have been sleeping.

"Hi Daniel, it's Amanda. I must talk to you, urgently!" I tried to sound competent and positive.

"I hope so, otherwise I'd have to kill you for waking me up. By the way, I was having quite a pleasant dream, want me to go into details?"

He might be tired, but this didn't stop Daniel from being brazen. Well, soon enough he'd understand that there was no time for joking. I could only hope that he had good lawyers to help me; I had heard dreadful stories about American jails. Maybe I could plead insanity? I was sure that my colleague Claudia would fervently support this notion. Whenever American movie stars do something silly, they put it down to the influence of drugs, check into a specialized clinic and re-appear looking ten years younger about six months later. I could try that.

"No, I don't want you to go into details, I have an inkling what your kind of pleasant dreams are about. Daniel, it's serious, there's no time for joking, please come to my cabin as soon as possible."

I didn't wait for his reply. I clicked the red button and the phone went dead.

166

There was not a lot that I could do in the meantime, at least I didn't have the nerve to do anything but drink a second cup of coffee, and then another one.

I must say this for Daniel, he rang at my door only ten minutes later. He hadn't shaved yet, which had the perverse effect of making him even look more attractive than ever. It's stupid that you still notice these kinds of details even if you know that your fate is at stake.

"Good morning, Amanda," he greeted me and kissed my cheeks. Then he looked critically at me. "I'm aware that a gentleman is not supposed to mention this, but I've seen you look better – anything amiss?"

"Everything!" I replied and tried to hold back my tears. So much for appearing composed and competent.

"Tell me what's bugging you, but if you could spare me a cup of coffee first, I'd be grateful. I rushed immediately from my bed to see you. It sounds a bit pathetic but there you go, I need a cup of coffee to wake up."

Feeling guilty that I had forgotten the basic rules of being a good hostess, I quickly poured a cup of coffee. It would be his first and his last as there wasn't any more left. Daniel took a large gulp and declared himself ready to face any kind of disaster now.

"It's no joking matter, Daniel. I have a confession to make, I've killed somebody."

I had done it, I had told the truth. Strange, how calm and relieved I suddenly felt. The confession had been relatively easy. I was just a bit disappointed at Daniel's reaction. I mean, it doesn't happen daily that a friend confesses to a capital offence. He could have looked a bit frightened, or taken aback. But Daniel just eyed me with slight suspicion and the kind of look you give a naughty dog that has just chewed your favourite slipper.

"Hmm," he finally said. "That sounds a bit strange. Can you tell me a bit more, for instance the name of your last victim?"

"Don't take it lightly!" I snapped. "I killed Angela, Richard Wu's assistant. My steward just confirmed that she died last night, from poison, and it's all my fault."

Daniel looked suddenly as if he'd finally grasped the seriousness of our discussion. "Angela died last night?" he shouted. "And nobody informed me?"

"Why should they inform you? Do you think that everything revolves around you on this boat? She wasn't your assistant, unless…"

"Unless I was involved with her in… let's call it… a different way?" Daniel grinned. "Your imagination is a bit grubby, but very impressive! I can put your mind at ease though, I don't sleep with every beauty that crosses my path. But you know me, I always need to know things first…"

"Can't you be serious for a second?"

"I am now. Tell me why you think that you murdered her then. I saw that you disliked Angela greatly – but that's not enough to go and kill her. I think you owe me an explanation."

I sighed. "I was very silly yesterday. I saw that Angela tried to make a pass at Tom and I couldn't refrain from listening to their conversation, I don't think they noticed me. She tried to convince Tom to arrange a joint venture with Richard Wu."

"And what did Tom reply? I guess he was smart enough to refuse?" Daniel was all attention now.

"He did, he turned her down and told her that they had signed an agreement with a competitor, SINOPEC, if this rings a bell with you."

"Indeed it does, quite a loud bell actually."

"Angela was furious although she tried hard to hide her true feelings. All of a sudden she changed tactics and tried to befriend Tom. It was all far too transparent for me. Finally she made quite a fuss, gesticulating with her bag and sent it spinning across the bar. Tom offered to bring it back and left her for a moment. I saw from my corner that she dropped something into his glass that was on the high table next to them. The moment she turned her back, I switched the coloured straws and the position of the glasses." I had to pause, I was running out of breath.

"I thought that she had added a sedative to drag Tom into bed that night – I never thought about poison. I've heard these stories before from my pupils, girls being made unconscious, ending up in bed with boys they never fancied. But I should have told you immediately. It's all my fault!"

"Hmm… quite difficult to have a go at a man when he's unconscious. But what do they say: all's well that ends well."

Daniel suddenly jumped up and kissed me. "You're a genius, are you aware that you just solved all the mysterious deaths that occurred since we left London? I always suspected that Angela was involved, but now we have proof, you're fabulous!"

He raised his coffee cup to me while I felt completely lost. My rash intervention had killed a young and beautiful woman and Daniel looked almost cheerful. I didn't understand a word of what he was saying!

"But now we need to speak to the captain and I need to organize some things. Let's go, we have no more time to lose!"

"Daniel, you cannot just go and see the captain at any time, he's a busy man, just remember what happened on the Titanic!" I intervened nervously.

"Oh, don't worry, he'll find time for us. And just to reassure you, the nearest icebergs are at least a good five thousand miles north of us."

There was not a lot to say and nervously I followed Daniel. His words 'we have no more time to lose' echoed in my mind. Who'd be the next victim, could it be me? How did Angela fit into this picture? Had she killed Veronique? This could be a lead, maybe she had been because Veronique had succeeded in capturing Sir Walter? But if Angela was the murderer, who else could be involved?

Soon we reached the lift that would bring us to the upper deck. But I could see that this deck was only accessible by means of a special key card.

"Ha, you see, even you can't reach your captain. You need a special card to reach the control deck. Let's go down to the reception and announce ourselves properly!" I couldn't hide my triumph. Men always think that they can conquer the world but never think about the next logical step.

"Thanks for reminding me," Daniel replied and pressed a key card against the metal plate of the control board. Immediately the lift zoomed upwards. I declined to comment.

The door of the lift opened noiselessly and we found ourselves in the inner sanctum of the captain, the undisputed ruler of our small world.

"Hi Alberto," Daniel said to an officer who approached us in the corridor. "I need to speak to Tony urgently. Please ask him to join us in the small office."

Why was Daniel so familiar with the crew? Did he travel with the *Belgravia* so often? I would have to ask him later, but this was not the right moment for such questions.

"Sure, Daniel, please wait in the small office, I'll send Tony right away!"

Daniel's key card went into action again and we entered a small cabin. It looked like an office but it was as cosy and inviting as a prison cell. Bright neon lamps shed cold light on white functional furniture. There was no gleaming mahogany or brass here in this part of the ship; a hospital would look homely compared to this space. We had just taken a seat when the captain arrived.

"Hi Tony, thanks for coming so quickly, but you'll understand that it's urgent."

"That's ok, Daniel, always at your service!"

Daniel's voice suddenly developed a steely edge. "I heard that we had another fatality last night. Why did I have to hear this from Amanda, why did nobody bother to inform me?"

Tony, the captain, looked ill at ease. "I wanted to be sure that the results of the analysis showed something unusual. I didn't want to bother you without any clear evidence."

"And, what's the result?"

"More than a strong suspicion of arsenic poisoning, in fact we have evidence," followed the unhappy answer. "We've informed the New York police already, and I'm preparing an announcement for the passengers right now. Nobody will be allowed to disembark until the police have interviewed the passengers. They want us even to seal all restaurants and bars, but this is ridiculous, I've refused this request, we're still discussing the procedures! But let's face it, three deaths in a row, that's a real nightmare!"

"Having the police here turning everything upside down sounds like a lot of fun!" Daniel remarked drily.

"That's not even the worst of it. I brought a print-out from today's headline in the *Evening Star* for you, my men showed it to me just minutes ago."

The captain opened a folder that he had brought along and showed Daniel the screen prints. 'Luxury Cruise, Destination Death' screamed the headlines. 'The curse of the *Belgravia*, who'll be the next victim?'

I gulped, this was certainly not good publicity for the *Belgravia*, but I could help by informing them that I had a great chance of being the next victim.

"How do they know?" Daniel asked curtly.

"Twitter, I guess. The crew is extremely nervous, you know, most are very superstitious. It's a miracle that nothing leaked out earlier."

"I guess the PR department of Astra Lines will be very busy during the next days and weeks to get this under control. We've been lucky though, Miss Lipton has in fact just told me that she discovered the truth. I need you to help us to organize a meeting. If we play it right, the case will be closed before the police take over."

Daniel explained his plans and the captain immediately called his officers to arrange everything as suggested by Daniel. I had stopped wondering why everybody seemed to jump at his command, but I would certainly ask him about it later.

***

It appeared that this meeting was to take place in the luxurious suite of Richard Wu. Like an oversized Buddha, Wu sat hunched in his armchair and examined with a slight frown the procession of strange visitors who dared to invade his cabin. There was Daniel, of course, the captain of the *Belgravia*, two of his officers, Tom, Sir Walter and me. I had insisted very much on being present.

"May I know why you have stampeded into my cabin and disturbed me in this painful hour of bereavement?" Wu spoke in a surprisingly mild voice, with an air of detachment from the pettiness of the world.

I couldn't detect any signs of bereavement though, no tears, no red or puffy eyes. He didn't look haggard in any way. A cup of Chinese tea had been placed beside his armchair, its herbal aroma filling the cabin. An empty plate with crumbs was a witness that Mr. Wu's appetite certainly hadn't suffered from his sudden bereavement.

"Please accept our heartfelt condolences at the passing of your wife." Daniel opened his speech, "But we need to clarify some matters quite urgently."

I stifled a cough. This was a new twist to the story.

"My wife?" asked Richard Wu, raising an eyebrow. I could see the consternation in the faces of Tom and Sir Walter.

"Yes, your wife. You married Angela two months ago in a private ceremony, no need to go on pretending that she was just an assistant."

171

"You seem to possess excellent intelligence sources," Wu sighed, trying hard to look sad. "Yes, we married, Angela insisted and she could be very obstinate when she wanted something. But it doesn't change much, she's gone now, my poor lamb."

A true love marriage, I concluded. She must have wanted his power and money, he probably must have hated the idea of needing to find a new assistant – very romantic indeed. I shuddered. Even a massive fortune could never have driven me into the arms of a man like him!

"May I remind you that we're still offshore and the captain of this ship therefore holds full juridical power. Captain, it's time for your little speech now!"

"I must inform you, Mr. Wu, that you're under arrest for masterminding and actively supporting the murder of two persons on my ship. You shall not be allowed to leave the cabin. Please also hand over your mobile phone to my staff and please be informed that we've cut all internet connections until the police in New York take over! You may, of course, contact your lawyers."

Wu ignored the captain. Like a turtle he slowly turned his head. "Daniel, you've gone too far. You'll regret this little comedy. By the way, what kind of charges can you bring?"

"Your company, Mr. Wu, is in a desperate situation. Your Russian assets are frozen, your Canadian company has no right to build and operate the pipelines you urgently need. Your only hope of survival was to come to an agreement and create a joint-venture company with your greatest enemy, Sir Walter's company, Canadian Imperial Petrol. As Sir Walter had rejected your last proposals, you decided to change tactics. You developed a plan to kill Sir Walter's wife and his heir in order to break your competitor and make him sign whatever agreement you'd present to him in his hour of distress. A devious plan, if I may say so."

Wu's expression remained impassive. Only his eyes mocked us; he seemed to find this speech slightly amusing. I could see though that Sir Walter was devastated. Tom just nodded; the truth didn't seem to come as a complete surprise to him.

I suddenly remembered his warning to be careful – he had meant himself! I owed him an apology.

Daniel basked in the attention that was centred on him. He was a first-class actor. "Mr. Wu, you used your wife for the dirty work that had to be done. She followed and attacked a person she had identified as Tom Olstrom and pushed him

172

overboard. In the twilight she could only see the fair hair, a hooded-sweatshirt she could identify as Tom's, and as the young man was about the same size as Tom, she was convinced she was striking the right target. But Tom was lucky, she pushed Frank Müller overboard, the young passenger travelling with Charles Peltier. A pity for Frank that he liked the same designer label as Tom did. We, of course, were at a loss as to an explanation for this 'accident'. To be honest, we all thought that Charles Peltier was involved – a young, attractive man travelling with an ageing designer – the papers are full of such stories, a 'crime passionnel'."

Daniel made a short dramatic pause and continued. "But the attack was filmed and thanks to the intervention of Miss Lipton, this footage was saved and shows that Frank was pushed overboard by your wife."

Wu shook his head slowly, as a teacher would address a mild reproach to a naughty child. "Daniel, if you have such wonderful and solid proof in your hands, I wonder why you didn't come forward to arrest Angela at that moment. Your behaviour seems a bit strange, to say the least. I can only swear that Angela was always at my side. I'm an old man and suffer from diabetes; I needed her constant presence."

'Touché', I thought. Daniel had failed to hit his target here.

"This murder might not have achieved its purpose," Daniel went on, unperturbed by this scathing remark, "but you decided to go on with your devious plan. The next victim would be Veronique Olstrom. The plan was perfidious in the extreme, as you placed a poisonous snake from the vivarium of Professor Hopkins in her bedroom. This time you succeeded and Veronique died a painful death. Essentially she suffocated, as the anti-venom that could have saved her had been removed beforehand from Professor Hopkins' safekeeping. This murder was planned and executed in cold blood."

Sir Walter jumped up and before anybody could react he hit Richard Wu's face with all his force. Immediately the officers sprang into action and withdrew the raging Sir Walter.

"Sir Walter, please restrain yourself or I will have to arrest you as well!" thundered the captain. Sir Walter fell back on his chair, looking ghastly.

"Thank you, Captain," Wu said. His cheek was starting to swell, but I had problems feeling any genuine compassion and refrained from rushing to put some ice on it.

"May I inform you that my wife suffered from a snake-phobia and she'd never have touched a snake. This story is just a bad piece of fiction, soap opera at its worst," Wu sneered, his speech somewhat distorted by his swelling cheek.

"Strangely enough your wife held a masters degree in biochemistry; she had worked some years ago on a project with Professor Hopkins. He recognized her when I showed him some old photos, photos that were taken before she underwent plastic surgery."

Wu didn't comment, but I saw his eyes flashing. A clear point for Daniel!

"Then came last night's reception. Your wife tried one last time to convince Tom to agree to a joint venture. When Tom refused and revealed that – even worse – SINOPEC would be stepping in as a major shareholder, she decided to act on the spot and dropped what we now know to have been poison into his drink. But Angela wasn't clever enough. Miss Lipton saw her dropping something into Tom's glass and swapped the drinks, not being aware though, that Angela had tried to poison Tom Olstrom. She thought that your wife just had the intention of adding a sedative. This is why your wife died, Mr. Wu. As we have a witness, your game is up. It's time to call your lawyers now. The USA are not known to be lenient towards this kind of crime."

Richard Wu slurped his cup of tea, the only sound that filled the cabin, followed by a loud belch. He set his cup down with a loud clatter and yawned. "Fairy tale finished?" he asked politely. "You'd make a first rate author of 5-cent trash novels. I happen to know a movie producer in Hong Kong, maybe I can recommend your services, but they'll probably add some kung fu scenes, maybe improve it with some action or a bit of sex…"

"For my taste there was enough action. Your game is up, Richard. Better come to terms with the truth."

"Daniel, you're so naïve, it hurts. Now, please leave me, all of you – and if you don't mind, I need some more hot tea, it will soothe my nerves. Angela's sudden passing has been quite a shock."

And so we were dismissed. I had to admire Richard Wu's sang-froid. Daniel's analysis had been brilliant, but basically the only tangible proof was my testimonial. I didn't even want to imagine what would happen if he was brought to justice in a country where judges could be influenced. Maybe I'd end up in prison then instead of Richard Wu – if I survived until then, that is. Richard Wu had eyed me like one of Neil's poisonous snakes. I was now definitely on his list of enemies, not a very comforting thought. In any case it was clear that Mr. Wu didn't seem too bothered about being tried and judged. I was sure that not only did he have a plan 'B' but even a plan 'C' up his sleeve. Worst case he'd blame Angela; her death provided him with a convenient excuse.

"I need a whisky!" I could hear Sir Walter's voice. "That horrendous ass, he really thinks he's above the law! I'll have him tried in Canada, we know how to deal with people like him."

Then he grasped his son's arm. "I still can't fully believe what I heard just now. I don't even want to imagine what could have happened to you." He had tears in his eyes.

Tom caressed his father's arm. I could see that he felt a bit awkward; it must have been quite some time since his father had been so close to him.

"I was almost certain that I was meant to be the victim when Frank went overboard," he whispered to Daniel, falling back a bit behind his father, "but I was convinced that Veronique was behind it. I hated her as she hated me and even if she's dead now and you're not supposed to speak ill of the dead, she was a ruthless bitch if ever I saw one. Only when she was murdered could I open my eyes and change my ideas. It's sort of comfortable if you only have one enemy to concentrate on. I think I've grown up over the past few days. I don't take everything at face value anymore."

"Yes, you've become a man." I couldn't help cutting in, though I hated myself for the patronizing tone of my reply.

"Good to know that I'm no longer on your list of favourite villains." Tom grinned at me.

"I really do apologize, Tom, but everything fitted, you profited most from the death of your stepmother. I disliked this line of thought profoundly but you have to admit, you had not only the motive but also the opportunity! The problem was, I couldn't stop liking you although you did everything to unnerve me!" I answered, a bit upset.

Tom laughed. "I'm sorry, but you made it so obvious that you suspected me, I couldn't help teasing you a bit. Please accept my apology."

He looked at me with those big eyes. How could I not have forgiven him!

***

175

Our small group dissolved quickly. Tony, the captain, had important things to attend to and Tom and his father needed to talk. This episode had given Sir Walter lots of things to think about.

Daniel offered to fetch me a coffee and gratefully I accepted his offer. I didn't really mind that he brought me an Irish coffee. The whisky and the cream were exactly what I needed to soothe my nerves.

"Since when did you suspect Mr. Wu and Angela?" I asked Daniel.

"Since the day Veronique was killed. When Frank died I thought that Charles Peltier might be involved, although his behaviour didn't seem to support this idea. But Veronique's death made it clear that the Olstrom family was targeted, and I spent some very uncomfortable days waiting daily for the next disaster to happen. But I knew that it would be impossible to accuse someone as important as Richard Wu unless I had some hard facts to hand. I knew that I must find proof, only too aware that Tom or Sir Walter might be the next victim. I was really worried."

"Why didn't you mention Angela's attack on me?" I felt a bit offended. "She almost killed me in the steam room. Doesn't this count as a crime?"

Daniel looked a bit uncomfortable. "I hate to say it, but there was no incident. You turned the knob in the wrong direction all the time in your panic. There is no key to this room, for reasons of security it cannot be locked. But I'll ask Tony to have the knob changed in any case."

Needless to say I felt like an idiot and a moment of silence ensued as I digested this information.

"I wonder though, why Angela printed these silly messages for Marge and me, it makes no sense at all."

"It doesn't. Actually Angela never pushed any message under your door."

"She didn't? Is there another lunatic loose on this boat?"

"Yes and no. No point beating around the bush, Marge was the author of those silly notes."

"Marge, you mean: our Marge?" I shouted so loud that the waiter looked at me in surprise. I must have looked as if I had finally lost it.

"Yes, it was Marge. She craved attention and came up with this daft idea after you told her that Frank had been murdered and you had seen it happen. She regrets this profoundly now and is waiting for you to come to her cabin. She wants to apologize."

I had to digest this first. "You mean, she's waiting now?"

"Yes, I guess so, like a nervous school-girl."

What could I do? I followed Daniel and ten minutes later we reached the cabin of Marge and her husband. John opened the door as soon as Daniel knocked and pointed at Marge who was sitting hunched on the sofa, crying silently into a damp handkerchief, a picture of misery.

As soon as I entered the cabin, Marge jumped up and threw herself into my arms. I felt as if I had landed in a bad soap opera, waiting for the audience to cheer or boo us at any second. Perhaps Oprah and her TV crew were hiding in the wardrobe?

"I was so foolish," Marge stammered. "I thought that we could share an adventure together, like best friends. I wanted so much to become your best friend. And I was a bit, well, bored."

She clung to me like a monkey, a surprisingly strong monkey. Did Marge do real exercises in the gym when nobody was watching her? Anyhow it took some time and a lot of resolve from my side to disentangle myself from Marge's fierce embrace.

"But you are my friend!" I protested. "There was no need to be so silly!"

"You suspected something, didn't you?" I asked John.

He nodded unhappily. "Yes, I knew that my girl was up to something."

I shook my head, but how could I not forgive Marge? Gently I moved a step away. "It's all right now, just promise me not do such a foolish thing again and I think I may have a nice surprise for you!"

Marge's face lit up. "A surprise? I love surprises! But first let me show you my surprise for you!"

She handed me a flat parcel. My heart beat faster as I noticed the Tiffany logo – they operated a small shop on board ship. I opened the parcel immediately. It was a beautiful necklace, emeralds set in diamonds that sparkled in the light of the cabin, the kind of necklace you'd see in *Hello* magazine or at the Oscars. I

177

swallowed. It was beautiful beyond description, but how could I accept such a precious gift? And I was uncomfortable at the thought of being bought.

"Marge, I cannot accept this, it's too valuable. Let's still be friends – but I simply can't take it, although it's stunningly beautiful."

Marge was flabbergasted. "You don't like it? Would you prefer rubies?"

Suddenly John intervened with surprising authority. "Marge, listen and understand for once, Amanda is a bit different to your usual greedy bunch of friends, they'd take two of those if they could get them for free. Be happy that you've found a true friend who's not interested in precious gifts or your money."

First Marge wanted to object, but John's bold statement must have triggered a change of mind.

She gulped. "I see."

Then she took the parcel back and looked at it. "Amanda, I think I should be grateful to you. I'll keep the necklace for myself then, it'll be my 'Amanda' necklace and it'll remind me of you whenever I wear it." Quickly she took it out of the box and put it around her own neck. Looking in the mirror she uttered, "Are you sure Amanda, it's stunning. You can still change your mind! Now, what's your surprise?"

"I'm inviting you and John to come and visit me in Hamburg. Take some days off and I'll show you the city, we'll see a musical, have a boat trip and you can meet my best friend, Susan. She's quite something, you'll like her a lot!"

"That sounds fabulous! Amanda, what a wonderful idea!"

Marge looked up and discovered her face in the mirror. She shrieked with horror as she saw herself. "Why has nobody told me that I look ghastly, look at my mascara, I look like I've dressed for the Rocky Horror Picture Show!" she lamented, as she fled to the bathroom to restore her make-up.

We looked at each other. "Did you know about the letters?" I asked John.

"I suspected something, she was so excited. 'Fey', they'd call it in Scotland – but not scared at all. Marge has a vivid imagination. I think she's often bored, and then she tends to… invent things."

"You have my full sympathy," Daniel cut in, "but I have to leave now. There is plenty to be done. See you at dinner?"

"See you at dinner!" I answered. I hated to see Daniel leave, but what should I say?

Marge came out of her bathroom and insisted that we should spend the afternoon together. Suddenly I remembered the Zumba class and so that is where we spent a hilarious afternoon. I'm really not good at it. No matter what dance move the teacher told me, I'd forget it a minute later, but we had a great time, all thoughts of murder forgotten.

***

The atmosphere during dinner in the Westminster Grill was strange. Our table was almost complete, which in fact meant that two people were missing, one stored in the cool room, one somewhere in the depths of the Atlantic Ocean. And yet we all felt relieved that this terrifying saga had ended. Over the past few days I had felt as if I had landed right in a crime story, with a new victim being found with each day.

Neil and Daniel tried their best to keep the conversation going and I tried to put on a cheerful face, but I felt sad knowing that both of them would be leaving the boat the next day in New York. I'd miss them!

"I have to leave tomorrow by noon. I'll come to your cabin around nine in the morning, maybe you'll invite me for breakfast so that I can say good-bye?" Daniel suddenly whispered into my ear.

'Why not come tonight?' flashed through my mind, but hadn't I done everything to kill this relationship?

"Please do; any special requests?" I answered, and forced myself to smile.

"Just you – and a coffee," he smiled back.

Neil had seen Daniel whispering with me and like a jealous dog he glued himself to my side. There was no more opportunity for confidential talk.

We had a good-bye drink in the bar, but like a good girl I went to my Hollywood-style bed alone, relieved that the nightmare had ended, but sad to be losing my new friends tomorrow. Beautiful excursions in Canada and new fellow passengers would be waiting for me and I should be feeling very cheerful, but I wasn't.

Day 10 – New York

Daniel was on time. I would have expected nothing less. I had ordered a gigantic breakfast from Kenneth, and virtually half of the *Belgravia*'s breakfast buffet must have been on display in my cabin. Daniel settled in the sofa and I poured him a coffee. He chose a Danish pastry and ignored the fried eggs. He liked it sweet, apparently.

"You don't look very happy?" I stated rather than asked, as I handed him his coffee.

"We received a mail from the Chinese Embassy. Two of their attachés are demanding to visit the *Belgravia* in New York to see Richard Wu. I wonder what they're up to and how they found out that Richard Wu is under arrest on the ship? We talked with the department of the Foreign Secretary and they're demanding that we comply. The guy on the phone was wetting his pants, he was scared to death that we might upset US relations with China; it's complicated enough already."

I had planned this last morning to have been more romantic, but I could understand that Daniel was upset that this crucial information had leaked out. I pondered his statement: "Who's waiting on Richard Wu at the moment?"

Daniel frowned and started to list, "There's Ruxandra, a stewardess from Romania, Matt, the chief steward, a British guy who's been with Astra Lines for more than two decades and yes, Kenneth, who helps out from time to time…"

I groaned. "I can tell you that Kenneth is the weak link. He told me some days ago that Wu comes from the same city as his own ancestors, which makes them sort of cousins; he also received a fat tip from Wu."

Daniel looked at me with respect. "You're amazing! If ever you plan to apply for a new job, think about ringing me! Yes, that makes sense then."

"Daniel, can you please explain to me why everybody on this ship – including the captain – seems to listen to your command. Anything you want to tell me?"

Daniel cleared his throat. He seemed a little embarrassed. "Astra Lines is a public company, listed on the London stock exchange. The majority shareholder though is a company registered in the Bahamas. This company happens to belong to the Greenfield family trust – basically I am the representative of the family here on board…"

I swallowed hard. I had to digest this first. "And why was I placed at your august table then, did you need a normal average citizen at your table to meet some secret quota?"

Daniel laughed. "It was a mistake actually. The head waiter thought that you must have a link to the Lipton tea dynasty – which is total nonsense of course, as Lipton's tea is just a brand owned by a big corporation. But by the way, as you've saved us millions of US dollars, I have something for you, as a token of our gratitude." He handed me an envelope, not just a standard paper envelope, but a heavy, handcrafted paper adorned with the crest of the *Belgravia*.

"How did I save you millions?"

"The police wanted to stop disembarkation in New York to hunt down the murderer on the ship. It would have cost us a fortune in port charges, law suits from upset passengers, reimbursements of tickets, just to name the most tangible items, then don't forget all the bad publicity..."

I opened the envelope and gasped. It contained a voucher for trips for life on the *Belgravia*, all costs covered by Astra Lines. I couldn't believe my eyes.

"You don't like it?"

"Don't be silly – this is a dream come true! It's just too much!"

"You earned it, I repeat, you saved us millions! Look, there's a second sheet of paper!"

I took the second sheet out of the envelope. It contained a booking confirmation for the Queen's Suite for a September cruise in the Caribbean. I was speechless.

"Hmm, I expected at least a kiss of gratitude," came Daniel's comment and he moved close to claim his reward.

"Maybe I should come and live on the *Belgravia* then..." I answered dreamily, "and look for a rich husband. It seems that there's ample choice..."

"You dare!" Daniel threatened me and drew me closer. "First my kiss!"

I obliged, and oh my God, this man knew how to kiss. That's the positive side of a man having had a lot of practice...

He sighed. "I need to leave now..."

I swallowed hard. "Of course, Daniel. I understand and I wish you all the best. If ever you're passing through Hamburg, give me a ring."

I hated myself for saying this. Men can't stand women who ask them to ring. I know this from my avid consumption of romantic movies.

Daniel eyed the breakfast that had remained almost untouched. "On the other hand, nothing obliges me to leave *immediately*. Maybe I'll have another cup of coffee and some muesli."

I think he left three hours later. Discretion forbids me from saying more, but it was a delicious breakfast, probably the best I've ever had. Not that we ate much though...

Back at Home

My contact with the New York police had been short and surprisingly sweet, although I had feared the worst. In fact, not a lot of work had been left for the officers. As Daniel told me later, Richard Wu had been met by the Chinese delegation and suddenly appeared to be the proud owner of a diplomatic passport which guaranteed him free passage. A private jet was already waiting for him at JKF airport and he disappeared the same day back to Hong Kong.

Neil had embraced me hard before he disembarked from the *Belgravia* and I had to promise him that I'd visit him in England. He wouldn't accept any 'perhaps'.

Back at home, I had a lot to tell. My mother received a harmless and embellished version of my story. I had learnt to be diplomatic with her, as she still sees me as her little chick and tends to believe the worst. But Susan had relished my story; she especially liked the fact that my next cruise allows me to bring her along, as there's enough space in the Queen's Suite.

"Just imagine, Amanda, the eternal single, torn between two lovers. Does promiscuity run in your family?" she teased me. I threw three cushions at her to silence her. I didn't really know what to answer.

Susan also persuaded me to write down the story. There was a competition running in one of my favourite magazines, 'My Story', and the winner would receive a voucher for a three-star dinner.

Two weeks later I received their reply by email:

Dear Miss Lipton,

We appreciate greatly that you took the effort to participate in our 'My Story' competition. We regret though that your story cannot qualify as it contains too much fiction. Our magazine is known to publish true stories only. We've forwarded your story to our colleagues who may be looking for new authors for the 'romance of the week'.

Yours sincerely,

The Editorial Department

I gasped! Idiots… I deleted the email.

Two days later a much more interesting email arrived:

183

Dear Amanda,

I won't make it to Hamburg before September, but as I know that you'll be on the Belgravia by then, I booked the same cruise! See you soon!

Daniel

PS: pls reserve time for special breakfast

I was walking on clouds all that day!

***

One week later a new email popped up on my screen:

Dear Amanda,

I have a friend who works for Astra Lines. She found your name on the passenger list for a cruise in September. I cannot forget you. I took the liberty of booking the same cruise! I look forward to seeing you again soon!

Yours,

Neil Hopkins

Since then I've been wracking my brains – what should I do? I haven't a clue.

Maybe Susan will know?

What a mess…